Five Little Words

Five Little Words

Jackie Walsh

hera

First published in the United Kingdom in 2020 by Hera

This edition published in the United Kingdom in 2021 by

Hera Books
28b Cricketfield Road
London, E5 8NS
United Kingdom

A CIP catalogue record for this book is available from the British Library.

Print ISBN 978 1 80032 391 9
Ebook ISBN 978 1 912973 52 1

Look for more great books at www.herabooks.com

Printed and bound in Great Britain by Clays Ltd, Elcograf S.p.A.

Chapter One

I've never felt so happy. Pressing gently on the soft blanket below my hand, I smile. I cannot take my eyes off him. His tiny pink lips. His flickering eyelids. His marshmallow skin. How can something so small be the biggest thing in my life?

Conor briefly turns his attention from the road ahead to steal a glance at his new son.

'Is he okay?'

'Yes,' I say, leaning over to get a closer look while swallowing the jab of pain that shoots up through my body.

'You're okay. Aren't you, sweetie?' I whisper in his tiny ear. My heart leaps when his eyes open, little dark pools of innocence looking back at me. He yawns as I run my finger down the side of his face.

I've already imagined him at every stage of his life. His first steps. His first word. Running down the stairs to see what Santa left. His first day at school and me crying in the yard. Trying on football boots for his first game with Ballycall GAA Club. Then college, girls…or boys. I see his life fast-forwarding before me, right up to the day he leaves me, to stand on his own two feet.

'What a beautiful life you're going to have, little Shay,' I whisper, hoping, praying that he will but fully aware that not everything turns out the way you plan it. *Stop it Laura, don't go there, stay happy.*

Conor turns the car off the M3, down the narrow road that leads to the village I've called home for the past six months. The autumn sunlight leaps in and out of the car through the tall golden-leaved trees. I lift my hand to block the glare from my eyes. My other hand automatically moves to cover Shay's face. I've got this. I'm going to be a great mother.

'Almost here,' Conor says, snatching another glimpse of Shay before turning the bend. The church steeple piercing the sky is the first sign of life in this remote corner of the county. Then the road slopes down to where colour appears in the shape of shops, the school, the police station and the newly refurbished playground at the side of the church. I hope little Shay spends plenty of happy hours swinging from the monkey bars. After all, his daddy paid for them.

When we arrive at the village, the car twists its way down the narrow main street, past the shops and cafes before stopping at the traffic lights in the middle of the road. My attention is automatically pulled to the building on my right.

Hedigan's Pub has a red painted frontage, with black and gold lettering boasting the sale of premium brands. There's a board outside. *Today's Specials*, scribbled in chalk. Inhaling deeply, I picture her standing there placing the board into position, her hand eager to wave at familiar passers-by.

Everyone knew Vicky. I even got to meet her in the short time I've been here. All smiles as she busily wiped down the table before taking our order. I would have liked to have known her better. Maybe had a drink with her at the bar. But I've been pregnant since coming to live here so it was only ever 'a fizzy water for me, please'.

I hear a soft mumble: Shay, vying for my attention. He wiggles a little so I place my hand back on top of the blanket.

'We're nearly there, baby.' I kiss his face. Conor moves the car on down the road.

I'm hoping the arrival of this new little life will bring some joy to this devastated community. The news of Vicky's murder has suctioned the happiness out of the place, leaving everyone baffled, confused, sad, carrying on in disbelief that a young woman could lose her life so horrifically, in this, their perfect little village.

Chapter Two

Balloons, banners, ribbons; the whole house is covered in the stuff, blowing in the wind as the car crawls up the gravel driveway. That can only be the work of one person: Maggie. Conor's mother has been so excited about the idea of becoming a grandma. I can see her waving as she stands beneath the two big pillars that adorn the entrance of this monstrous house. Five bedrooms, each with their own en-suite. A living room the size of a football pitch and a kitchen so modern you'd need a degree in technology just to boil an egg.

Taking a deep breath, I smile out the car window as Conor pulls up. Maggie rushes towards the car and grabs the handle of the door, pulling it open and sticking her head in before I even have a chance to get out.

'Oh look at him,' she gleams. 'He's so beautiful... so tiny.' Her arm crosses over the baby's car seat and unlocks the belt.

'Come to Nana, little Shay.' Without asking, she lifts the car seat out and pushes her face into the tiny bundle, snuggling and kissing him.

What is she doing? I want to carry him into the house. I want to be the one to take him home. But no. Leaving me and Conor in her shadow, Maggie walks up the two granite steps and in through the front door.

'Welcome to your home, baby Shay.'

Conor looks over at me, shrugs and pulls an amused frown.

'Sorry,' he says.

He should be. I specifically asked him to tell his mother I wasn't coming home until tomorrow. Just one night of peace is all I wanted. One night to get myself and Shay settled before all hell broke loose. I want to challenge him, ask him why he couldn't do what I asked. But there's no point. This is not the moment to create a negative atmosphere. And I doubt Maggie would have listened anyway. She thinks I'm lucky to be here at all. She's made that quite clear, dropping subtle and not so subtle hints whenever she gets the opportunity, letting me know how so many women would love to be in my shoes. To have nabbed Conor, her son. The most eligible bachelor in the world, according to Maggie, with his good looks, his money, his future.

But I never saw him that way, which was one of the things Conor said he liked about me when we first met. I didn't know about his money or his company. He was just a guy I liked, who liked me. Then he became a guy I loved, who loved me. It was quite a shock when I discovered he came with his very own world.

Conor takes the suitcase and baby bag out from the boot of the car and follows me into the house. When he closes the door behind us, I notice some cards have been dropped through the letterbox. I slowly reach down to pick them up.

'How are you?' Maggie remembers to ask.

'I'm fine, just a bit...' but before I get a chance to moan about how tired I'm feeling, she's already telling Conor the list of people who called to congratulate her. *Congratulate her? What did she do?*

In the kitchen the festive décor continues: more balloons, more banners. Jesus, how much did that woman spend? It's not like the baby will even know.

'I'm going to take a selfie,' she says, placing the baby seat onto the sofa by the wall and sitting down beside it. Maggie pulls the phone from her bag and swipes the screen with her red fake nails. Her tentative finger doddles backwards and forwards before deciding on which button she should press. She's new to it all. Instagram, Facebook, a phone without a lead.

When she's happy with her snap, she holds the phone up to Conor.

'What do I do now?'

'What do you want to do?' he says, taking the latest, shiniest, smartest Samsung phone from her hand.

'I want to post it.'

Placing the cards on a nearby shelf, I leave the two of them to decide which social media site my newborn baby's face will be splattered all over and walk to the fridge to get some water. My mouth has dried up all of a sudden. I really should tell her: *No.* I don't want Shay's picture going all over the town. But again, not the right moment. And to be honest, I'm so tired I don't have the energy to show I care.

Conor looks over to where I'm standing and winks. Then, like the man I hope I married, he thanks his mam for being here when we arrived home and asks her if she needs a lift. Maggie looks from right to left, then at her bag, then at the baby.

'Oh sure... of course, I'll leave you to get settled.' Then she turns to me and says, 'Laura, get plenty of sleep and don't be afraid to call me if you need any advice.'

What does she mean by that? 'Thanks Maggie, but I think we have it covered.'

'We'll see,' she whispers, bending over to kiss Shay goodbye. 'Bye bye little Shay. I have to go. Daddy is throwing me out.'

'C'mon Ma,' Conor laughs, handing her bag to her.

—

The house is quiet now, just the three of us. Conor and I stare into the crib. I feel like my heart is never going to slow down, like it's beating to a rhythm it was always meant to. I cannot look away from him; his silky streaks of dark hair, his...

'Is that what I think it is?' Conor says, holding his nose.

'Time to try out the new changing unit.'

Both of us bend down to lift Shay, bumping our heads in the process.

'Time for you to rest, Laura, let Daddy do something.'

Lifting Shay like he might explode if he makes a wrong move, Conor holds him against his chest. I want to stay with him, share the moment, check Conor is doing it right.

Shay is about two years younger than Conor had hoped for, judging by the disposable nappies he bought during the week.

'For God's sake, Conor, we can't put these things on him. They're not for newborns, look!' I hold the nappy up. It could double as a sleeping bag for my little boy.

'I don't know, I just grabbed a packet. I'll go down to Spar and get... what have I to get?'

'Nappies for newborns. It will say it on the packet.'

Conor's eyes dart from the counter to the sofa to the coffee table. He can't find his keys. The poor guy is already struggling and it's only day one. Walking over, I put my hands on his face and make him look at me. His eyes are wide with fear.

'It's okay Conor. Relax. We have this.' Slowly I bring my lips to his, close my eyes and remind myself why I'm here. After a brief moment Conor pulls away, takes a deep breath and stares back at me.

'I'm sorry Laura. I... I—'

'Shuuush.' I kiss him again. This time he engages, sweeping his tongue around my mouth with vigour. He squeezes my body close to him. I want to scream with the pain but I don't. I bear it, letting him relax with me until eventually I have no choice but to pull away.

'I hope these stitches dissolve soon,' I say.

'Are you okay, Laura?'

'Yes, I just need to sit down. No – I just need to stand up. Actually, I think I'll take one of those salt baths the nurse recommended when you get back.' We both turn our attention to the crib, staring at our little miracle sleeping like... well, a baby. Conor puts his arm around me.

'Thank you Laura,' he says, looking at his watch. 'I'll run down and get the nappies now.'

–

Shay is awake, staring at me, kicking his bare legs while his tongue explores how far it can travel outside his mouth.

'Daddy won't be long,' I say, pulling the blanket up over his body. I turn around and notice the cards that were dropped in through the letterbox sitting on the shelf. Picking them up, I carefully settle myself on the nearby sofa.

I open the first one. There's a picture of a baby dangling in a towel from a stork's mouth. I open the card. *To Laura and Conor, Congratulations on the birth of your new baby! Ollie and Ciara.* Ah, the couple from the petrol station. Nice of them.

Then I open the second card. A blue teddy bear sits on the cover, his hands clapping, 'Congrats!' written in gold above his head. I open the card. *To Conor and Laura, Congrats, Margaret Cash.* That's the older lady who lives on her own in the next house about fifty metres down the road. 'Thanks Margaret,' I say out loud while opening the third one.

The pink envelope is addressed to me alone. Laura. The card inside has a picture of a tower of toy bricks with 'Congratulations on the birth of your new baby girl!' written above it. Ha. I open the card and read the words scripted in black letters.

> *Your husband is a murderer. Where was he the night Vicky was killed?*

Chapter Three

Your husband is a murderer. Where was he the night Vicky was killed? I read the words again, pulling myself off the sofa. A jab of pain lets me know this is real. This is not a dream; this card is in my hand and it's saying that Conor is a murderer. But who sent this? And why?

Maybe someone hates me. Someone jealous that this outsider, this city girl managed to nab their most eligible bachelor. There are a few candidates, especially Olive. But she wouldn't do this. Would she? No one could despise me enough to send a card like that.

But if the card wasn't sent to upset me, then someone out there thinks Conor did it. That my husband killed Vicky Murphy. But that's impossible. Conor was with me the night she was killed. All night. And while I haven't known him that long – only a little over a year – it was some year. Moving house, getting married, having Shay. We've done a lot together. I got to know Conor and the more I did, the deeper I fell in love with him. I think I would have noticed if he was capable of murder.

I read the card again and check the envelope to look for a clue. But there is none. My heart is thumping hard in my chest, and the thought occurs to me that it might just be a sick prank. One of the lads from the club. They're always playing the worst tricks on each other. But I don't think so. Not the day I come out of hospital with Conor's son. No, this is not a prank. This is not funny at all. This card was sent to upset me... or to warn me.

–

The sound of the key turning in the hall door disturbs the silence. *Quick, hide it.* I don't want Conor to see it. If he sees that card, what he has described as the best day of his life will be ruined. Pushing the card back into the envelope, I shove it between the other cards and place them on the counter under a magazine.

The stress of it all has me gasping for air when Conor bursts into the room swinging a shopping bag.

'Daddy to the rescue,' he says, rushing over to Shay and glancing into the crib before turning to look at me.

'Are you alright, Laura? You look like you've seen a ghost.' Conor walks over to me and puts his arms around me. His body feels warm. 'You're shaking, babe... are you okay?'

No, I'm not okay, but I can't say this. I can't let him know about that card. Whoever sent this is not going to ruin this moment...

'I'm... I'm okay, just a bit of pain.' I watch his face, looking for any sign of stress or worry. If he's hiding something behind that electric smile that hasn't left his face all day, he's doing a good job of it. 'I think I need to take some more painkillers.' *God, I wish I had some real drugs.* 'But first let's get this nappy on this little man.'

–

When Shay settles I find my bag and swallow two of the prescribed pills. 'Only if you need them,' the doctor said, 'because they will make you drowsy.' I need them and I hope they make me drowsy. Getting the vision of that card out of my head is what I want to do right now.

Conor calls down over the bannisters, completely unaware that someone is trying to sabotage our happiness. 'I'm running the bath for you, Laura.'

Putting the bag down to follow him upstairs, I take the container of pills out and put them in my pocket. I'm sure if the doctor knew what just happened, he'd tell me to fire away. 'As many as you need, Laura.'

The water is hot, stinging. I lower myself into the bath. It's one of those fancy ones where you can push buttons and the water massages you from different angles. Like a jacuzzi, but smaller. I won't be pushing any buttons today.

Holding my breath, I dunk my head. Now I'm totally submerged, hoping to relax, but my mind is trying to make sense of that card. I should have known this was all too good to be true. That it was only a matter of time before karma would find me.

Chapter Four

I don't remember going to bed. That extra pill certainly did the trick. Opening my eyes, I stare at the dark sky above my head. Conor had a skylight the width of the room installed above the bed. He loves to look at the sky at night and I have to admit, I find it very relaxing. Pain in the ass when the sun beats down on you first thing in the morning during the summer but Conor says he'll have an electric blind installed before summer comes around again.

Three stars above my head. That's all I can see. The moon is out of the picture. I wonder what they're called? Conor probably knows. He knows a lot about astronomy. He's forever talking about it. One of our first dates was spent in the company of Brian Cox, a physicist guy I pretended I'd heard of, when Conor suggested we go to the gig in the 3Arena. It was almost a year ago. A raging storm the previous day had threatened to cancel the event. Fallen trees and floods had extended Conor's journey to Dublin by almost an hour. Both of us had had to run across the cobblestone pathway of the Arena to get in before the show started. I had struggled in the high heeled shoes that Amanda, my sister, had loaned me for the night, but luckily we had got there just as the door was about to close.

Three hours looking at particles and stars and moons and black holes would have been torture if I hadn't been so amused by Conor's enthusiasm. I don't think he blinked once. The look on his face resembled that of a child entering the gates of Disneyworld. His attention was glued to the giant screen as Brian Cox filled his mind with possibility. Conor often mentioned how he would have loved to study astronomy if he hadn't inherited the family business when his father died.

I stretch my hand to feel his warmth beside me. He's not here. Lifting my head, I scan the room and see him sitting on the armchair by the window. Shay is in his arms sucking on a bottle. Gosh, I almost forgot, I have a baby now.

'Was he crying?' I say.

'Like a pack of hyenas. You were out cold.'

'I didn't hear a thing.'

Suddenly I feel vulnerable. Incapable. 'Gosh Conor, what if I never hear him crying in the night?'

'Don't worry, Laura. You will. Your body is just over-tired at the moment.' That and the overdose of painkillers which I'm not going to mention.

Conor is staring into Shay's eyes, rocking him gently. He looks as happy as it's possible to look, sitting there with his son in his arms. Watching my husband and baby in the dim light makes my heart swell. I must be the luckiest... *An image of the card crashes into my mind with heart-stopping clarity!*

It's like I'm seeing it for the first time. *Your husband is a murderer.* My heart quickens. I look across the room at Conor. His tossed hair, his gentle smile, his strong arms cradling his dream. Could he be a murderer? I close my eyes and take a deep breath. Why am I allowing myself to be scared by a frigging card? Conor was with me the night Vicky was killed. The night before Shay was born. He couldn't possibly be the killer. And he's too kind. Conor wouldn't hurt a fly. I've never even heard him speak badly of anyone. Or anyone speak badly of him. Mind you, he does employ half the village so they'd have to be pretty brave to criticise the local saint.

The only time I've ever seen Conor lose his cool was on a football pitch. It was a cold day. The frost was nibbling at us all. I was standing on the sideline wrapped in a jacket thick enough to visit the North Pole in, but it did nothing for my tortured toes. Hopping from foot to foot, I was praying for the ref to blow the whistle, when Conor went to ground. Seeing him jump to his feet and swing his hurl at the guy who landed him there surprised me and, apparently, the team manager, who took him off before he did any real damage. I was a bit taken aback. But that was the only occasion I saw him lose it – unlike his best friend Noel, whose temper seems to always be on patrol. I've only been at three of their matches and Noel was red-carded in all three of them.

'Go back to sleep, Laura, we're fine here.' Conor's whisper crosses the dark room. His voice is calming but still my mind struggles to relax. I have to stop. This is ridiculous. Someone is clearly trying to upset me for some reason and I can't let them. I'm going to be the perfect mother to Shay, the perfect wife to Conor, and no one is going to stop me. I'm going to rip that card up and get on with my life. Closing my eyes, I try to remove the card from my mind but it won't leave. Have I room for another secret? Maybe I should tell Conor. Or Amanda. That's what I'll do. I'll show my sister the card. Amanda will know what I should do.

Chapter Five

What the hell is that? Lifting my head off the pillow, I hear the sound of people's laughter travelling up from downstairs. I glance at the clock. It's after ten, almost eleven. Above the fading laughter, the unmistakable voice of Conor's mam offering something to someone dominates the proceedings. Dropping my head back into the comfort of the pillow, I inhale. *Don't get annoyed, Laura, it won't go on forever.* But I am annoyed, it's impossible not to be. What kind of a place is this? Has no one any boundaries?

I drag myself to the shower and change into a pretty shabby-looking tracksuit, reflective of how I feel – pretty shabby. I wanted to spend today alone with Conor and Shay but now the house is full of people who knows when we'll get a moment to ourselves?

Anxious to see little Shay, I hurry downstairs. Only four visitors have created all that havoc: Maggie, of course, her face still beaming from the excitement of her new grandson; Olive, her blond hair tied back showing her perfect bone structure. Brown eyes set in sallow skin allows her beauty to shine even without makeup. She hasn't removed her heavy jacket yet, so she mustn't be planning on staying long. I don't blame her. It must be awkward for her, standing in her ex's house as he dotes over his newborn child that he had with another woman.

The file in her hand tells me she's only here to give Conor something from the brewery, but Conor is busy laughing with Noel and Abbie, Conor's closest friends.

Abbie is lovely but there's something about Noel that doesn't sit well with me. I don't trust him. He's too confident, all *me me me*. He practically dismissed me when I first met him, looking at the bump, sneering, like he thought I had purposely got myself pregnant to hold on to Conor. I've never seen him show any empathy for anyone. It's like he lives in his own world, writing his own rules. But Conor seems to love the guy so I can't say anything.

Abbie is the first to notice me. She looks fabulous, as always, in a leafy green dress and expensive-looking boots. Apparently, her family are dripping in money and it looks good on her. Unlike me, standing here in a tracksuit. Feeling like I don't belong amongst the expensive furniture and top-of-the-range appliances that were chosen by someone else. I wonder whether Maggie had a hand in decorating this place. Or worse still, Olive.

Abbie's smile is just as impressive as her clothes, brightening her face. It's dampened with a hint of sympathy when she sees me enter the room. Her expression reinforces my self-doubt.

'There you are Laura,' she says, walking over to my side, taking my arm with both hands and pulling me over to the group. 'I hope you don't mind us calling in but Noel has to leave for Dublin and he insisted on seeing little Shay before he left.'

'No problem, thanks for calling.' The subtle smell of floral perfume hovers in the air as my eyes search out the magazine on the countertop with the cards hidden beneath it. It's still there and from what I can remember, I was so fraught with fear, it's still in the same position that

I left it. I move from Abbie's grasp in the direction of my baby. Maggie jumps up from where she's sitting, close to the crib.

'Now, you sit down, my dear. It's time for you to rest. I'll make you whatever you want.' She walks over to my side.

Maggie has arrived with a full face of makeup, which she moves close to mine, her eyes calculating my appearance. She's probably thinking, *she could have put on a bit of lippy*.

'What would you like?' she says.

I'd like you all to leave. 'Just a cup of tea, thanks.'

'Tea it is, so.' Maggie fills the kettle and stands waiting for it to boil. My heart is thumping hard in my chest, watching Maggie's every move as she hovers close to the magazine. I pray to God she doesn't lift it. If she sees the cards, she'll want to read them.

'The baby is great.' Noel's loud, deep voice echoes through the room, distracting me. He's standing with his hands on his hips, staring into the crib. 'Can't wait until he's out on the pitch kicking ball. Let's hope he's better than his father.' Everyone laughs.

'And his godfather.' Conor says.

Noel turns to look at Conor. 'What?'

'Yes, I was hoping you'd be godfather to Shay.'

Noel takes a few steps forward and hugs Conor. His eyes are wide with surprise. 'What?... I'd be honoured, Conor. Thanks.' The two men embrace, and I'm left gobsmacked.

What is Conor doing? I don't want Noel to be the godfather. To be forever tied to our family. I don't trust him and I don't want him teaching Shay to be violent on the pitch like he is. One time he broke a poor guy's leg.

I was there, it was no accident. He did it on purpose but of course not one of the fifteen hundred people who live here in Ballycall thought it was his fault.

Maggie's all smiles as she puts a cup of tea into my shaking hand. I'm doing my best not to cry here. I know I'm an outsider. But surely I should have a say in my own son's future.

Chapter Six

'But you said you were going to ask your cousin Aidan to be godfather.'

'I know but I changed my mind. I hardly ever see Aidan. Noel is always around. He's been my buddy since we were kids.'

The house has emptied out. Olive was first to go, promising to be of any help she could to me. Why does everyone presume I need help? Then Noel and Abbie left, leaving only Conor's mother to annoy me. Thankfully she had plans to meet a friend for lunch in the village, so we didn't need to throw her out this time.

'You should have told me, Conor. We should have discussed it.'

'I don't know why you're making such a big deal out of this, Laura. I never objected to you asking Amanda to be godmother.'

'I'm not making a big deal. I just wish you had discussed it with me first. I thought that's what we did.'

Conor walks over to where I'm standing by the crib and puts his arm around me.

'I know Laura, you're right, I should have discussed it with you first, but to be honest, I hadn't really thought it through myself. I just got carried away in the moment. There was Noel, delighted with our new arrival, talking about Shay playing football with us in the future. I haven't heard from Aidan in a long time. Not even a text to congratulate us. So I just reacted. Does it really bother you?'

What can I say? *Yes. I don't like the guy.* It's not like it would change anything except make things uncomfortable for Conor.

'It doesn't bother me at all. I'm sorry I reacted like I did, it's probably just the hormones.'

Shay smacks his lips together. He is so cute I could swallow him. Bending over to pick him up, I feel his heat against my face and take a deep breath to savour this little beauty.

'When did you last feed him?' I say.

'Mam fed him at about ten, so...' Conor looks at his watch. 'He'll be due between one and two maybe.'

I cringe when I hear him say his mother was feeding my baby. I'm losing control here. I'm going to have to get my act together.

'And did you change him?'

'Mam changed him straight after.'

No more extra pills, Laura.

The sound of feet shuffling past the window grabs my attention. I look out and see Pat walking by. Pat is an old friend of Conor's father and has been living on this land for as long as anyone can remember. His small abode is just inside the forest at the end of the garden. It seems wrong to call this vast expanse a garden. In the city a garden has an end. Usually quite an abrupt one. But here it just seems to go on and on and on.

Grabbing a blanket from the crib, I wrap it around Shay before opening the back door.

'Hi Pat,' I say, standing in the doorway. He stops and turns to look at me. 'Would you like to come in?' Pat walks closer to the house and glances in the window. To my surprise, when he sees Conor inside, he shakes his head slowly from side to side. Not wanting to go out into the biting air, I twist around so Pat can see the baby.

'This is Shay. It's short for Seamus,' I say, bringing a smile to Pat's face. Shay is named after Conor's father. Apparently he and Pat were the best of friends. Seamus allowed Pat to live in the small house on his land in return for odd jobs done about the place. It worked well for everyone until Seamus died. Pat was heartbroken; especially when Conor gutted the house and had it remodelled. Eventually Conor went to him, assured Pat nothing would change and that he was welcome to stay in the cottage for as long as he wanted. Over time, Pat settled back in and began doing odd jobs about the place like he had for Conor's father. He's not much of a talker but he's never refused an invitation into the house before.

With his head bent, Pat walks closer to me. Then, removing his cap, he stares at Shay, then he cries and walks away. There's nothing anyone can do or say because Pat is Pat.

–

Leaving for the office to drop the forms back that Olive needed signing, Conor asks if I'll be okay on my own. He had taken the week off work to be here with me but with Shay arriving early not everything had been in place. Apparently taking time off work is unheard of for Conor and something I'm going to have to work on. I'm not spending my life waiting for him to come home from the office. Or begging him to go on holidays.

During our short engagement it never came up, because I was always pregnant. Airports without alcohol just didn't appeal to me. But now I'm ready – well, I should be in a few weeks – and as soon as I think Shay can travel, or he's old enough for Amanda to babysit him, I'm going to suggest we take a break away.

With Conor out and Shay sleeping in the crib, the house feels eerily quiet. I'm eager to ring Amanda but she won't be home from work until after five and I don't like bothering her during her busy working day. Out in the hallway, I notice two more cards have arrived with the post. I open them straight away. Like ripping off a plaster. It's not that I'm expecting any more shocks, but I wasn't expecting the first one either.

Thankfully, they are just regular congratulations, no malice attached. But it does make me think I should check the handwriting on the malicious card. Maybe it will match up with one of these.

The magazine is still sitting on the counter where I left it. The knot in my stomach grows as I reach my hand out. I'm nervous, I don't want to read those words again, but I have to try and figure out who sent it. Lifting the magazine, I toss it to the side and grab the cards. Two cards. But there were three. Where is the other one? The one with the pink envelope. Grabbing the magazine, I shake it. Nothing. I shake it again. Nothing. Deep breath after deep breath – I try to calm the panic rushing through my body. I check the floor, the bin, the drawers, the presses, pulling and searching for the pink envelope, but I can't find it. It's gone. The card is gone.

Chapter Seven

What do I do now? Do I tell Conor about the card? Will he think I've gone mad? Will the hormones be brought into the dock? I'm certain I put it with the other cards underneath the magazine. Almost certain. Between pain and painkillers, I'm not sure if I can trust myself.

I didn't dream it. Did I? No. I saw the card. I remember the fear. I can see the letters. Where the hell did I put it? I look around at the mess I've created. Every kitchen press is open including the drawers, and some of the contents are strewn across the floor. I check Shay is still sleeping then hurry to tidy it up.

Everything is back in place, except my heart which is still close to my mouth, when Conor returns. My mind is completely confused now.

'Everything okay?' I hear his voice behind me.

'Yes, everything's fine.'

'Shay?'

'Asleep.'

'Grand, well I'm going to make both of us a nice lunch. Mam left some ham and salad stuff in the fridge.'

I keep my eyes firmly focused on the magazine I'm pretending to read. 'Lovely, I'm starving,' I say.

Conor places a plate of food in front of me on the breakfast bar. In the corner, Shay lies in his crib. Fast asleep. Dreaming sweet dreams, I hope. I wonder what he thinks of me? His mammy. Does he love me yet? Is he able to love yet? Or his daddy, does he prefer him? I know the day will come when Conor will be the centre of Shay's world. Football, fishing, going for a pint. But for now, it's all about Mammy. I must remember to enjoy it.

'Eat up, Laura, you're only picking at it. You need to build your strength up.'

Conor is right. I need to at least try and finish the food on my plate.

'It's lovely, Conor. I'm just not that hungry.'

'I thought you said you were starving.'

I did, didn't I? 'I was earlier, but my appetite seems to have disappeared. It must be the pills.' Hoping to change the subject, I swivel on the stool and put my arm on Conor's leg.

'Well, how are you feeling? Are you delighted with him?'

'I don't think I've ever been more content in my life. I'm with the woman I love and now we have Shay.'

Tears come to my eyes. I want to believe him. I want it to be true but something doesn't feel right. The card still haunts me. I have to stop thinking about it.

'And you?' he mumbles, stuffing a forkful of food in his mouth.

'I'm in heaven, Conor. I love you. I love Shay. We're all together. I love my life.'

Conor smiles. 'Good. Now eat some more.'

My thoughts are in a twist. Should I tell him about the card? Spoil his happiness? It's not often I see Conor worrying or stressing out about something and I don't want it to end.

The brewery takes all his time, and the fact that it's a family business means that everyone turns to him to solve problems. I've suggested to him that he might want to think about sharing the workload, employing a director or something, so he can relax a bit. He can certainly afford it.

Conor wasn't having any of it, saying he didn't trust anyone else to make the right decisions for the business. I sometimes wonder about that, why he has to feel in complete control of the place? It's just his job. Or is it? Half the village relies on the brewery doing well. That's a lot of pressure for one guy. Especially someone so young, who was thrown in the deep end when his father died. I only ever took a job to pay the bills so I don't understand the pressure he's under.

'What time is the nurse calling at?' he asks.

'What nurse?'

'The community nurse. The hospital said she'd call in to you this afternoon to check on you and Shay.'

'Oh yes. I don't know what day of the week it is anymore. I better take a shower... will you stay with Shay?'

Crikey. I don't remember the hospital saying that. Thank God Conor was paying attention. Those pills must be stronger than I thought. Now I'm beginning to doubt if I read those words in that card.

–

Two hours pass. I think I've changed Shay's nappy about five times just to make sure it isn't dirty when she arrives. What sort of a mother would she take me for? I hope she thinks I'm doing a good job and that Shay is safe with me. The last thing I want is for her to be checking up on me all the time. One wrong move in front of her and that's what could happen.

Conor is in his office off the hallway when the doorbell rings. There's a bit of muttering before they both walk into the kitchen.

Nurse Elaine immediately walks over to me and takes my hand, placing her other hand on top of it and introducing herself. She has a nice smile. I'm immediately relaxed.

'Well, you look good,' she says. 'How is Mammy doing?'

'Mammy's great,' I say. 'Though she'll be a lot better when these stitches dissolve.'

Elaine laughs. 'I know. They really are painful but you'll notice an improvement as each day goes by.'

Moving over to the baby, Elaine dotes on him for a bit before removing his baby-grow and checking he's still in one piece. 'Did he arrive on time or did he keep his mammy waiting?'

'He was early actually, by almost two weeks.'

'Well he's definitely not suffering from it.' I smile at her words. I'd been worried my rushing around, refusing to relax had brought on the early labour.

'You're doing a great job, Laura,' she says, to my relief. 'Keep up the good work.' Happy with my A-plus, I dress Shay and put him back in the crib.

Conor is sitting on the sofa. I wish he'd go back to his office and leave me on my own with the nurse now. I don't want him listening to every word. He doesn't need to know the ins and outs of everything my body is going through. What to do with the leaking boobs. How to make it less painful to go to the toilet. This is nothing to do with him, so I casually suggest he go back to the office if he has things to do.

'I can take it from here.' I say.

Conor takes the hint and leaves.

When all the regular stuff is covered by the nurse, she picks up her folder and stands.

'Is there anything else you wanted to ask me?'

'Er...'

'Anything at all, Laura?'

'Well, there is something.'

Elaine sits back down. 'Go ahead.'

I don't know whether to say what I want to. If she thinks I'm going mad she'll be knocking down that door every day. But I need to know. I have to ask her.

'The drugs they use...'

'The drugs they use where?' she says, shifting forward in her chair.

'When someone is giving birth to their baby, the painkillers, the gas... all that stuff.'

'What about it?'

I take a deep breath before looking her in the eye.

'Can they make you hallucinate?'

Elaine moves her back into the chair and straightens her neck. 'Can they make you hallucinate?'

'Yes, like say... a day later.'

Her eyes have changed expression. Elaine does think I'm mad.

'Are you having hallucinations, Laura?'

Looking away from her gaze, I consider what to say next. I'm sorry I opened my mouth, now that I've seen her expression. I'd better play this down. I don't want her thinking I'm going mad, or have postnatal depression or something. Christ, what if she thinks I'm unstable? That Shay isn't safe in my care?

'No... I don't think so. I just need to know if the drugs can do that,' I say, trying to sound nonchalant.

Shaking her head, Elaine sighs. 'Well I've never heard of that happening and no one's ever asked me that before.' Her hand is now on my knee. 'People forget things alright but that's the exhaustion. Seeing things—' She stops short. 'Laura, I'll check it out for you, but I'm almost certain the answer will be no. I can't imagine we'd be giving mothers drugs that would make them hallucinate. Do you know what drugs you were given?'

'No, but...' I point at the file leaning against her bag. 'Won't it be written in there somewhere?'

'Actually, I don't have your correct file yet. The internet is very poor in the clinic and it didn't arrive in time.' She nods at the folder. 'That's just a few notes I've taken... When your details arrive, I'll update them and check out what drugs you were given. Meanwhile, if you think you're having hallucinations, Laura, call the doctor. Don't suffer in silence. Us women are great at that, thinking we can handle everything on our own. Don't do that to yourself, get help.'

Shit. Now I've opened a can of worms. She'll probably put it in the file that I was hallucinating. I'd better fix this.

'It's no big deal, Elaine. I was just wondering because I lost something that I thought I had and I guess the tiredness just made me a bit paranoid. Forget about it.'

Shay whimpers. Picking him up, I cradle him close to me and walk Elaine to the door. Conor comes out of the office to say goodbye.

'I'll be back in a few days but if you need me in the meantime, just call,' she says, giving me a secret wink so Conor can't see. If that's supposed to make me feel better about asking her the question, it doesn't. In fact, it makes me anxious. What have I started? What if she goes poking around and... what if they take Shay from me?

Chapter Eight

There is only one star tonight. One bright star shining down on me as I lie staring at the sky and all its questions. Apparently my father is up there. I don't remember him. I was very young when he died. Mam showed us some photos of him in a dark overcoat crossing the bridge on O'Connell Street. He had a lovely smile and dark curly hair. Mam said that's where I got my dark curly hair and green eyes from. Amanda's hair is fair, just like mam's.

I remember my mam having a fit when Amanda wanted highlights in her hair for her confirmation day. Amanda insisted she was old enough but mam didn't give in. She was strong like that. She had to be, raising the two of us on her own. It's not like she had a sister of her own to help. Mam was an only child. She told us that when dad died, his family were great for the first few years, always calling to the house, making sure she was okay, that we were okay. But over the years that fizzled out until we only saw them at Christmas. Mam never complained about it. She said they had their own lives and worries to contend with.

—

The room is warm. By my side, Conor sleeps with his legs out over the duvet. He doesn't snore. Not even after a few pints in the club – which he only ever goes for after a match. I've only known him a little over a year and so far he's perfect. Just perfect. If he knew how imperfect I was would I be lying here now?

Amanda was in a restaurant with some clients when I called her earlier so I didn't tell her about the card. That conversation is going to need her full concentration. I asked her to ring me tomorrow when she had time to talk.

The clock at my bedside says it's two fifteen. Shay will wake soon and this time I'll be ready. I'll take him to the armchair, cuddle him close and feed him before he wakes his daddy. Conor deserves a decent sleep. He's done almost everything so far: the cooking, the shopping, the midnight feed, the nappy changes – which I now feel safe leaving him to do on his own. He's also kept my spirits high, smiling and laughing, constantly talking about Shay and how lucky he is to have us both.

There is a lot of fear floating on the surface of my thoughts tonight. Have I misled this man? Should I have told him? Yes, and yes. But I was scared of how he'd react. Afraid he would leave me and then I'd be stuck in that stupid apartment, with a new tenant in the spare room every year, going nowhere with a broken heart.

I loved him when we met. I still love him and, as Amanda pointed out, I deserved a break. A new start. Some happiness for a change.

The smallest gurgle ripples from the corner of the room. Shay is stirring. Pulling my feet from under the duvet, I stretch my arms in the air, then walk quietly over to the cot.

'Hello, baby,' I whisper. He's staring up at me, wriggling below the soft white blanket that one of Maggie's friends knitted for us. I'm very grateful for all the gifts that we've been given. The surprise baby shower that Amanda arranged brought more than enough clothes, blankets and bottles to keep us going. I was amazed by everyone's kindness. Not so much for the stuff, more that they had come to the party. For a while, I felt accepted into their circle.

The party went on for hours, everyone playing silly games and everyone except me drinking prosecco. I didn't drink of course, though I would have loved a glass before everyone arrived to calm my nerves. There were almost thirty people here. I'd never met some of them before but they knew Conor. Amanda had contacted Olive to invite everyone she thought might like to come. Amanda said Olive was very obliging and seemed happy to help. Which makes me wonder about her motives. Why was she so helpful? It should have been painful for Olive, considering she probably presumed she'd be the one with the bump. After dating Conor for five years she had to have felt hard done by when he dumped her to go out with me. And yet, she still works for him. His right hand apparently when it comes to the business. Going into the office and seeing him everyday must have been hard after the breakup. But she did it. Still does it. I hope she hasn't been biding her time waiting for her opportunity to exact revenge. Could Olive have sent the card? When I first heard Conor's ex worked so close to him, I wasn't happy about it but Conor assured me what they had wasn't love. He realized that when he met me. Olive is more like a sister to him now. I wonder if she feels the same way?

If Maggie is to be believed, Olive wasn't the only one who would have liked to marry Conor. As far as Maggie's concerned the whole village was interested in him. And there they were. All gathered in my house to check out the winner. I'm sure some of them thought I got myself pregnant to trap Conor.

I place the bottle into the warmer and lift Shay into my arms. He smells like hope.

When he's had enough, I change him and place him back in the crib, where he immediately falls back asleep. He's such a good baby.

Back in the bed, I pull the duvet tight around my neck and close my eyes. It takes a while but eventually I fall asleep, only to be abruptly woken to the sound of Conor's phone beeping. Lying still, I listen to him rummaging at my side.

'Is everything okay?' I say in a quiet voice.

'Yes, it's just the alarm down at the brewery. You go back asleep, I won't be long.'

Conor pulls on a tracksuit and leaves the room. I stare up at the lonesome star, wondering why the hell he doesn't get the brewery alarm fixed. That's not the first time it's gone off in the middle of the night and Conor is always the one who has to leave his bed and go and sort it out.

The sound of Conor's car echoes in the silence. It took a while for me to get used to the quiet. The bliss of isolation. In the city, cars passed my window all night long and at the weekend, drunk fools joined them. That's one thing I don't miss. But I do miss the convenience of everything. The shops. The cinema. The gym. Everything was within walking distance, including my job. Now I have to make sure I don't need anything after eight p.m. or I'll have to drive to the next town which is almost fifteen minutes each way.

I also miss the fact that you could be anonymous in the city. Living peacefully amongst the big crowds with no one knowing who you were. Everyone in this village knows everyone else's business. They make it look like they're all one big happy family who would do anything for one another. But there are secrets here. Lurking behind the smiles and expensive clothes. Vicky Murphy's death proves that. Stabbed with her own knife and left to bleed to death on the floor of her apartment while the perfect little village slept.

And now, someone wants to bring that to my doorstep. To destroy my happiness. And the only person I can talk to about it is Amanda. She'll help me decide what to do. Amanda has been with me through all my ups and downs, stood by me when no one else believed me. What will she make of this? More trouble. There are times I think it searches me out. No matter what I do, something bad has to happen to spoil it. To bring me down and keep me in my place.

Chapter Nine

I thought I'd be all glamourous and shiny when Amanda arrived: makeup covering my pale face, my hair blow-dried, fully dressed for the day and a Jo Malone scent leaving a trail as I walked down the hall. But no, not to be. Instead, I'm still in my nightclothes. My hair is hanging limply over my pale face. The only smell in the air is baby puke. Amanda called first thing this morning to say she had the morning off work so she'd pop down for a couple of hours to see her little nephew.

Shay has been crying since he woke up at six a.m. and no matter what I do, he won't stop howling unless I'm rocking him in my arms. I knew it was all too good to be true. Babies are supposed to cry. They're supposed to make everything you thought you were going to get done that day a distant dream. Conor had to run to the bank first thing so he couldn't even mind him to let me have a shower. Thank God it's only Amanda calling.

Her little two-tone Mini comes up the driveway and I can already feel myself relax. Moving to the hall door, I open it and wave. Amanda pulls up outside the house. She's a good bit smaller than me and skinny as a broom handle. Her smile reaches from ear to ear as she steps out of the car and runs up the steps to me.

'You look like crap,' she says, hugging me, careful not to squeeze Shay in the process.

'And you smell even worse.'

'Thanks. You look great.'

She laughs, moving her attention to Shay.

'Hi sweetheart... oh Laura, he is so beautiful.'

'I know, he's the best... aren't you Shay?' I say, smiling down at him.

Amanda closes the door as we both walk down the hallway.

'Is Conor here?'

'No, he had to go out. I hope he'll be back soon, I feel like I've been in these clothes for a week. I need to take a shower.'

Amanda puts her arms out. 'Here, I'll take him.'

'I'm not sure he'll...' but when I place him in Amanda's arms he doesn't object, no screaming to get back into my arms. He looks comfortable and happy. *Go Laura, Go.* Rushing out of the room, I glance back to make sure it wasn't a trick he was playing on me, but he still looks content in Aunty Amanda's arms.

'I'll be quick.' I call out.

'Take your time.'

—

The hot steam soothes my tired body. With my eyes closed, I lift my face into the gushing water and relax. I'm happy Amanda is easy with Shay. She's great with Conor too. Always laughing and sharing jokes. They both get on like a house on fire.

Amanda was so happy for me when I first met Conor. She liked him, thought he was perfect for me. Of course when she saw the big house and realised I was dating gold, she was even happier. 'No one deserves it more,' she'd said, trying to get me to move on and enjoy what I had, instead of always waiting for the balloon to burst.

I feel so much better now. It's amazing what a shower can do. I ease myself into a pair of jeans and pick a blueprint shirt from the wardrobe. My hair is tied back, and I dab a little bit of makeup on my pale face. Seeing Amanda groomed to perfection reminds me of what Conor is looking at every day in work. I better keep up.

When I walk into the kitchen, I find Amanda sitting at the counter, flicking through a magazine, my heart skips a beat.

'Where is he?' I say.

'Relax, Mammy. He's in the crib fast asleep.'

I hurry to the crib and place my hand on his chest to feel his tiny lungs expand. My shoulders slump with relief on feeling the movement. From the other side of the room, Amanda watches me.

'Are you alright, Laura?'

'Yes, sorry, just panicked a bit.'

Sliding off the high stool, she walks over, looking into the crib before turning her attention to me.

'Everything is going to be okay, you know,' Amanda says, her beautiful blue eyes focused on mine. 'You need to let go of the past, Laura. Things will be fine.' She holds my stare for a moment longer before her concerned face brightens with a smile. 'C'mon, let's have a coffee, tell me everything.'

When I've finished with my petty complaints about unwanted callers and nappies that don't fit, I apologise for my negativity and ask her to bring a bit of excitement to my day with some of her own news.

The card sits at the front of my mind waiting for the right moment. I don't want to jump in with the drama straight away because I know things will change as soon as I do.

Amanda sits opposite me. Her face full of excitement as she tells me about her latest flings, the twenty-four-hour party she was at last week and the guy in her office who won two hundred thousand euro in the Lotto but is still first into the office every day.

When she starts to tell me about someone else from her office, I interrupt her.

'Amanda,' I say, putting my arm out and placing my hand on hers like I'm looking for a pause button, 'I have to tell you something.'

Immediately she moves forward, closer to me. She knows this is not good.

'You need to promise not to tell anyone else.'

She nods.

'I got a card in the letterbox.'

Silence. Amanda's eyes aren't blinking.

'Fuck.' It's Conor. I can hear his keys opening the front door.

'Sshh... I can't say anything in front of Conor, I'll tell you later.'

—

Another hour passes. Coffee, feeding the baby, coffee, changing baby. Conor still hasn't left my side and I can tell Amanda is eager to hear my news before she has to leave; she keeps looking at me as if to say, *Get rid of him.*

Eventually, when Conor sits on the sofa looking like he's never going to leave the room, Amanda asks me if we could go for a walk. I look over at Conor.

'Fire away, I'm not going anywhere.'

Out in the garden, I feel a cold chill cloak my body so I tuck my hands tightly into the pockets of my jacket. I tell Amanda about the card as we make our way towards the forest at the far end. Amanda is as shocked as I was. Even though she has makeup on I can see she's turned a different shade of pale. She hasn't said anything yet. I hope she's trying to digest the news and come up with a resolution. Eventually she speaks. Asking all the obvious questions: when, where, am I sure I couldn't have imagined it? But I've been there, hoped that, and kept on coming up with the same answer. *Laura, you held that card in your hands. You read those words. Your husband is a murderer. This is not in your imagination. You did not hallucinate.*

On reaching the edge of the forest, Amanda continues to walk in through the thickening terrain. Her high-heeled shoes crush the dry golden leaves below her feet. For as long as I've known her, I've never seen Amanda in flats. 'When you're an inch short of five feet tall you learn to deal with the pain,' she used to say. Until a few years ago when she said, 'I think I've finally done it. My feet are now numb.' We laughed that night. We laughed for the first time in a long time.

'I don't think you should tell him yet,' she says, her head turning towards me. My cautious footwork has me straggling in her wake but I quicken my step to catch up with her.

'Why?'

'You need to find out more. Are there any suspects yet? I know it's only been a few days but I bet there's plenty of local gossip. Get down to the shops or something – the butcher's maybe? Everyone talks in the butcher's in these places, or better again, the hairdressers? Go get a blow-dry. Find out what the local take is on this murder.'

I'm listening intently. Amanda has a point. I know nothing about what happened; the news broke the same day as my waters, so I never got to hear much of the gruesome detail, let alone the gossip. I brace myself, taking a deep breath before I ask the question.

'Do you think it could be true?' I say.

'What?' Amanda stops abruptly and turns to look at me, the earlier excitement on her face nowhere to be seen. 'Do you?'

'No, God no, I'm just asking... I – I'm scared, Amanda. Someone is trying to hurt me. What if someone knows?'

'Look at me.' Her hands grab hold of my face. 'No one knows anything, okay? This is a prank, one that you'll figure out when you get a bit more information.'

Tears are trickling down my face. It feels good to cry. To be with someone I trust. I know I can tell Amanda anything and she will always try to help me.

'You need to find out what you can and keep me posted. Together we will figure it out.'

'And you're certain I shouldn't tell Conor?'

Amanda stalls for a moment, looking away from me towards the forest. 'No, not yet. You will have to tell him at some point but not now.' Moving her gaze to the sky, she inhales a deep breath before looking back at me. 'Hopefully you'll be able to tell him with a full explanation... who sent the card and why.'

Amanda's right. There's nothing to be gained by upsetting Conor yet. Things are lovely at the minute and I'm not going to let the crazy person who sent the card ruin it.

I hear the crunching of dry leaves. It can't be us; we're standing still.

'Someone's coming,' Amanda whispers, adding to the covert atmosphere we've created. My heart speeds up for a brief moment before I see him. Pat shuffles past us, his hat tilted on his head. His eyes shift sideways to look at us, but he doesn't say anything. I nod a hello.

'So that's the famous Pat?' Amanda says.

'Yep, that's him. The old man who came with the house.'

We laugh before making our way back towards the house. Conor is standing at the window looking out at us. He turns away when I notice him. My tears have dried up. I feel a lot better now that Amanda knows about the card and is going to help me figure it out.

When we walk back into the kitchen, Conor is sitting with Shay in his arms. He smiles when we step in the door. 'I hope you ladies had a nice chat?' he says, winking over at me.

I walk with Amanda out to the car. I'm about to close the car door when she says, 'I told Mam. She didn't say anything, but she knows about Shay.'

'Do you think she might ring me?'

Amanda puts her hand in the air to cut the conversation. 'Not going there, Laura. I just want you to know she knows.'

I wave Amanda down the driveway and out onto the road until her car disappears around the bend. So, Mam knows she has a grandson. I wonder will she call me? I'd love to call her, just to hear her voice, but I tried so many times in the early days. I don't think I could take another silent response. The piercing click of the phone going dead.

Chapter Ten

I'm taking Amanda's advice: I'm going to mingle with the natives and see what I can find out.

Conor is concerned that I'm planning to drive so soon after the birth what with the stitches and all, but I tell a little lie; I tell him that the nurse said I was to start back driving as soon as is possible, and that I feel much better. I wouldn't take the chance if I didn't.

I'm slightly nervous driving out through the gates. It seems weird to be behind the wheel, travelling on my own again. By the time I reach the village, I'm back into the swing of it.

There's a small car park by the playground where a couple of cars are parked, but it's mostly empty. I check my lipstick in the mirror before venturing out on to the main street.

The first time I took these steps, the village gave me the feeling of being on holiday. Everything was strange, different, exciting. Living here was going to be wonderful. I would get to know everybody and everybody would get to know me. Little did I know what was in store.

Three ladies are sitting in the coffee shop when I look through the window. This would be a good start; I'm sure they have plenty of opinions on what happened to poor Vicky, and maybe even let slip someone's name who wasn't happy about my marriage to Conor.

I recognise one of the ladies from the Spar store down the street. She glances up but doesn't acknowledge me.

Maybe if I sit at a table next to them, take out my phone and just eavesdrop, I'll overhear something of interest, or they might ask me to join them. With determination in my blood, I head for the door. There are two tall people entering in front of me. They push open the door and walk to the counter. They don't belong here. I can tell by their stern faces and suited clothing. When I glance through the window again, I see the three women looking ominously at each other, nudging one another when they see who is walking in. They must be the detectives.

My courage evaporates, replaced by a sickening feeling. That poor girl. They're here for one reason only: to find out who killed Vicky Murphy. They're not the regular police. The village only has the one detective, Fintan Ryan, a friend of Conor's. He's been to the house once or twice, nice guy, married with two kids. I wonder what Fintan Ryan would think if he knew about the card I received.

Having decided against going into the coffee shop while the detectives are in there, I walk on down the road and arrive at the main Spar store. It's the closest thing to city life in this place. The shop is modern, open two years, according to Conor. He said it replaced Murphy's grocery store which had served the community for over sixty years. Grabbing a basket, I decide to saunter around. Hopefully I'll bump into someone I know.

Six tomatoes and a head of lettuce in, I see Ciara... I can't remember her surname, and decide I have bait for my fish.

'Ciara!' I call out, waving as I walk over to where she's standing reading the ingredients on the back of a packet of sauce mix. 'Thank you so much for the card. Conor and I really appreciate it.'

'You're welcome. Congratulations. How's the baby doing?' She puts the packet back on the shelf.

'He's great, really good: sleeps, eats, does what babies do.' I think about his continuous crying for hours this morning but I'm not going to rat him out on his first tantrum.

'That's great and you look wonderful yourself.' Ciara casts her eye up and down my body as if inspecting it.

'Oh, bit of a way to go.' I say, holding my belly.

'No, you look great.'

I'm mindful that I'm looking for information. The compliments are very welcome but they're not getting me anywhere. In the distance I see the older lady who lives in the house further down the road from us. She doesn't see me.

'I just saw two detectives going into the coffee shop, have you heard anything yet?' I hear my words and realise I did that with the grace of a rhino. I need to be more discreet, slip it into the conversation or I'll just sound nosy. Thankfully Ciara is nosy too. She shuffles closer to me.

'Not much, they haven't got a suspect yet, but I did hear there was blood everywhere. No sign of sexual assault, thank God.' Ciara blesses herself when she mentions God. 'And nothing was taken from the pub. Detective Ryan said she was lying there for hours before she was found, poor thing.'

I'm listening intently, my mouth half open, when Ciara looks at her watch. 'Got to go, the mother-in-law,' she says, flashing her eyes upwards before moving on towards the checkout. I continue down the aisle. When I get to the butcher's counter, I decide to buy some sausages and rashers. Maggie will go on about the fat content, but I think I deserve a treat. Behind the rows of meat, Mick the butcher stands with his hands resting on the counter.

'Can't make your mind up, hah? Don't know whether ye want the cow or the pig, hah?'

I smile back at him. 'I'll take the pig.'

'What'll it be, so?'

—

When I have everything in the bag, I leave the shop. I stand outside for a minute and look up the street at the setting. A row of small businesses, each with their own unique fronting, line each side of the road. How could someone have committed such a terrible crime here? And why? If there was no sign of sexual assault and nothing was taken, it wasn't a burglary. Someone must have been trying to shut her up. But why? What did Vicky Murphy know?

In the city, murders happen so often people are used to them. They're shocked for a minute before turning on Netflix. But it's different here. Everyone knew Vicky, she was one of their own. It's like the village itself was targeted. The death of Vicky will be remembered here for years to come. She was well liked. Other than that, and the fact that she was a barmaid, I don't know much more about her.

Happy to have some news for Amanda, I stroll back to the car. Amanda's reaction had puzzled me a bit. I didn't expect her to be so concerned, so adamant I pursue the culprit behind Conor's back. I hope she doesn't think Conor is the murderer. Or that I'm in danger. Whichever it is, I'm glad to have her by my side.

I pass by Georgina's Hair Salon. I've never actually had my hair done here before. Up until a few weeks before

Shay arrived, I had made the trip to Dublin to The Hair Shop in the arcade where I always got my hair done. I'll have to stop that. I need to start trusting and supporting the locals more if I want to fit in. I could buy the odd piece to wear in Harriet's Closet. Allow Bernie the beautician to remove my excess hair. But first, I'll make an appointment in Georgina's. Something I can easily undo if needs be.

Pushing on the gleaming pink handle, I enter the premises. A woman in her fifties beckons me over to where she is sitting behind a large glass table. It's pretty chic in here. The spotless mirror on the wall opposite tells me I'm doing the right thing. My hair is a mess.

'Laura, isn't it?'

'Yes… yes…' I'm a bit taken aback that she knows who I am but I had probably been pointed out to everyone and anyone when I first arrived. *There she is… his new girlfriend… her name is Laura.*

'I'd like to make an appointment to have my hair blow-dried. Sorry, I don't know your name.'

'Georgina. I'm the owner of this establishment.' Her exaggerated smile is accompanied by a nod of the head.

'Hi Georgina, pleased to meet you.' I put my hand out to shake hers but she's pulling out a book from under the counter and hasn't seen it.

'So you decided to give us a shot.'

I'm slightly confused by this comment – is she pleased or being sarcastic? I don't know what to say, so I just nod. Lifting her face from the book she asks me when I was thinking of having it done. She tells me she has an appointment at ten thirty tomorrow morning. I take it, hoping that, come ten thirty in the morning, Shay won't be screaming for his mammy.

Thanking her, I head for the door only to hear her call after me.

'And don't worry love, we're fully qualified.'

Why did she say that? Making out I think I'm some big shot from the city who wouldn't be bothered with their little salon. The cheek of her! I've a good mind not to show up in the morning. But that would only give her more reason to dislike me. No, I'll go, build bridges. If people around here think the city girl believes she's too good for the place, I need to let them see that's not the case. In fact, it's quite the opposite. The truth is, I feel lucky to be here at all, to be getting a second chance.

Chapter Eleven

Later that night when Conor is in his office off the hallway, I decide to ring Amanda and fill her in on what I've discovered so far. I'm surprised at how relaxed I've become since dragging Amanda on board.

She answers the phone after two rings. 'Well, what did you find out?'

'I met Ciara, one of the girls who was at the baby shower, and she told me there was no sexual crime and no burglary. That wasn't in the paper.'

'Did she mention anything about a suspect?'

'She said they hadn't got one yet, and she got her information from the detective so it's probably true.' Amanda remains quiet on the other end of the phone. 'I don't think she'd have been telling me all that if she thought Conor had something to do with it. Do you?' Amanda doesn't answer me. Her silence worries me. 'Amanda, do you think Conor could have done this?'

'No... No... I was just thinking. You need to find out more.'

'Well I did make an appointment in the hair salon for tomorrow morning so I might find out more then.'

'Good. I bet the woman is thrilled to be getting you as a client. Mrs Caldwell.'

I laugh at this idea, but don't tell her what really happened. I don't want Amanda to have any excuse to dislike the people here. This is where I live now. These are Conor's people.

'Maybe,' I say.

'Anyway, see how you get on and ring me. I'll get back down to you as soon as I can. You can show me the card then.'

'But I don't have it.'

'What do you mean, you don't have it? Where is it?'

'It's gone.'

'Gone where?'

'I don't know. I put it with some other cards but it's disappeared. It's gone.'

'Laura...'

'Amanda, I know what you're thinking. Did I imagine it or dream it? I can assure you I did not. That card was in my hand. Someone took it. It's gone.'

There's silence at the far end of the phone. Then Amanda speaks.

'Okay, I want you to do something for me... I want you to write a list of anyone who you think might have sent that card. Can you do that?'

Jesus, I feel like I'm in the middle of some big investigation now. Amanda is determined I find out who sent the card. She's still trying to protect her big sister.

'I'm not sure, Amanda. Maybe I should just forget about it. After all, I know it could not have been Conor, he was with me the night Vicky was killed. He came to bed with me that night... maybe I should let it lie. If it was someone trying to upset me, that might be the end of it.'

The sound of her dragging in a deep breath echoes down the line. 'Laura, you have to find out who sent it, someone has it in for you... or Conor, or both. You can't ignore this. What if something else happens? What if something happens to Shay?'

My heart stops; buzzing swirls around my head.

'Why did you say that, Amanda? Nothing is going to happen to Shay.' My panicked voice shouts down the line.

'I'm sorry, I shouldn't have said that, Laura. I didn't mean to upset you, I wasn't thinking.'

Holding my hand over my thumping heart, I try to slow down the fear that has erupted inside me. My mouth dries up. I listen to her asking me to forgive her. When I finally find the ability to speak, I tell her I have to go, I'll ring her tomorrow.

–

There are no stars in the sky tonight. A big window of darkness hangs above my head just like my soul. The fright I got when Amanda mentioned something happening to Shay suctioned all the excitement and energy out of me. She knows she should never have said that. Not to me, not after what happened.

Turning away from the vastness, I watch the crib. Little Shay is dreaming sweet dreams. *I will do everything to protect you, Shay. Mammy will always be here for you.* I toss and turn a little more before allowing Amanda's words to take hold. What if someone does have it in for me? What if someone has found out what I did? Switching on the bedside light, I grab the notebook and pen from the drawer and flick through the pages until I find a blank one. My hand trembles. I begin my list.

Chapter Twelve

Olive is top of my list. The disgruntled ex. Revenge for taking her man. She also could have taken the card back when she called that morning before anyone got to see the evidence. But then, why is she being so nice to me? Abbie is also on my list. She wasn't at all happy I'd broken up the happy foursome who did everything together. Apparently Conor and Olive, and Noel and Abbie, were the best of friends until I came along and gatecrashed their party. Abbie was also in the house the morning the card disappeared. Maggie was there too but there's no way she did it. Not his mother.

The only other possibility on my list is a disgruntled employee: given the number of people working at the brewery, it's possible Conor may have pissed off one of them. And Pat? I can't really see Pat sending the card, but he wouldn't come into the house the other day when he saw Conor inside. For some unknown reason Pat didn't want to meet him, which was odd. I've also written *someone from my past* on the list. I hope Amanda doesn't give out to me when she sees it there because I'm supposed to be letting go of my past. But it's not letting go of me.

–

The village is quieter than usual. I get a parking spot right outside Georgina's hair salon. Shay was on his best behaviour this morning, making it easier for me to leave him. I'd feel bad leaving if he was crying. Conor had looked comfortable holding the little bundle as he waved me off.

'Take your time,' he had said. 'We're fine here.'

I had smiled at them both, blowing kisses before driving away, Amanda's words still hovering on the perimeter of my nerves. *What if something happened to Shay?*

Georgina is behind the reception desk when I step inside. Her attitude a little less sarcastic than yesterday. Maybe she was just joking.

'Good morning Laura. How's the baby?'

'He's doing just fine. Conor is with him.'

An older woman is sitting at the first station. A young girl – who I now know is fully qualified – is putting rollers in her hair. Beside her, a middle-aged lady is trimming the end of a long black veil of dark wet hair.

'Can I take your coat?' Georgina says, leading me to the washbasin at the back of the salon.

'This is a lovely place you have,' I say, trying my best to come over as an absolute darling. Hairdressers have a lot of clout with their clients. Especially in a place like this. Whatever she says about me when I'm gone is liable to stick.

'Thank you, we like it.' She babbles on about how she remodelled it the previous year and some other stuff. I nod, appearing interested until my attention is dragged to the young woman with the long black hair at the second station. She's staring at me in the mirror and it's freaking me out a bit.

'Chloe.' Georgina calls through a door beside the wash-basins and out walks Chloe, a girl about sixteen years of age with a shy demeanour. She stands behind the basin with a towel in her hand. I take that as my cue to sit down. Closing my eyes, I let the hot water caress my head. I haven't been pampered in a long time, I'm going to enjoy this.

My head is wrapped in a towel. In front of me, in the mirror, I see the face of a woman who looks tired: black shadows below my eyes, dry skin, signs of ageing presenting as fine lines on my forehead. I remind myself I've just had a baby. I'm bound to look tired. But I'm also aware of the worry lodged in my mind. Stress and skin are not friends.

'Hi, my name is Rachel.' The young stylist has finished with the girl who found me very interesting, and is now standing over me. She asks me how I like my hair blow-dried and plugs in a hairdryer. The older woman to my left is reading a magazine. How am I going to get talking to anyone?

Ten minutes later, Georgina walks over to Rachel, telling her there's a call for her. Georgina immediately explains she would not have interrupted Rachel's work only her mother is very sick in hospital. I tell her it's not a problem, that I'm enjoying my time here, and I smile. The lady on my left turns her head from the magazine she's reading.

'You're Conor's wife, pleased to meet you. I'm Iris.' She holds out her hand and I take it. 'My husband works with Conor, worked with his father too.'

'Oh.' I say, not quite knowing what to say next.

'Yes,' she continues, 'forty-eight years, he'll be retiring soon.'

'That will be nice for you.'

'We'll see.' She giggles.

Now is my chance to bring up the subject. 'Did you know Vicky?'

Iris swings her seat to face me, her expression turned to one of both sadness and interest.

'I don't know who could do a thing like that, a young harmless woman, doing her best in life. Everyone loved Vicky, you know. Did you ever meet her?'

'I did, just a few times.'

Behind me, Georgina arrives to apologise that Rachel hasn't returned yet and I comment on how I'm in no rush, happy to be getting a break from the house. Iris looks up to direct her next question at Georgina.

'We were just talking about Vicky's murder. Do they have anyone for it yet?'

Resting her hand on the back of my seat, Georgina says, 'Not that I've heard.'

'It must have been an outsider passing through,' I say.

Georgina huffs before saying. 'I wouldn't bet on it.'

In the mirror I see Georgina's face, excited at the chance to gossip. I will not disappoint her.

'You don't believe that, then?'

'Not for one minute.'

'Why?'

'She was in here only days before it happened, getting her highlights done. Vicky liked to get her highlights done every other month.'

Iris has her mouth open, her eyes glued to Georgina's lips. 'Did she say something?' she says to Georgina.

'She didn't have to. I knew something was up; there was something edgy about her, something different. I asked her was she okay and she just nodded a yes.'

'Sure that could have been anything,' Iris says.

'Of course it could,' Georgina says. 'But now she's dead.'

Listening intently, I decide to join in. 'So you think she might have been in trouble?'

'Don't think it, I *know* it: something was going on.'

In the mirror I notice Rachel walking back to us. Apologising, she lifts the dryer in her hand and switches it on just as Georgina says, 'I'd be willing to bet it was no outsider. Whoever killed Vicky knew her.' Walking away, Georgina raises her voice so I can hear over the noise. 'Probably some big shot who thinks he can get away with murder.'

My heart stops. Was she directing that comment at me?

—

Outside the door, I get into my car. With my new shiny hair and racing heart I take my phone from my pocket.

Amanda answers after one ring. Immediately she starts apologising for saying what she said the previous night about something happening to Shay. I tell her not to worry about it and fill her in on what Georgina said, and how I felt she was directing the big shot comment at me.

Amanda doesn't say anything at first, which makes me nervous. What is she thinking? Is she thinking that Conor is definitely a local? And a big shot? Am *I* thinking that?

'Did you make the list?' Her voice interrupts the silence.

'Yes.'

'Okay, ring me tonight and we'll go through it.'

'Amanda,' I don't want her to go. To leave me here on my own with these thoughts building up in my head. These crazy thoughts.

'What?'

'Do you think…?'

'Do I think what, Laura? Come on, I'm in a hurry here.'

'Ah it doesn't matter, we'll talk later.'

I hang up the phone and stare at the drops of rain landing on the windscreen in front of me. Taking breath after breath, I urge myself to relax, willing the darkness in my mind away. Conor didn't kill Vicky. Conor didn't kill Vicky. He was with me. He couldn't have got up in the middle of the night without me noticing. He isn't capable of murder. Georgina did not direct her comment at me. I have to stop ruining things for myself. I need to allow myself to be happy. I'm going to be happy.

Chapter Thirteen

Back at home, Conor stands up from his cozy corner on the sofa when I walk into the room.

'Well look at you, beautiful.'

'Thank you,' I say, puffing my hair with my hand. 'Is it alright?'

He's beside me now, looking down into my eyes. I like that Conor is taller than me, it makes me feel protected for some reason. Safe. Well it used to. Now, I'm not so sure.

'Yes Laura, it's lovely. But sure, you're always beautiful to me.'

I let his comment soothe me then wonder does he really mean it. Olive is so much prettier than me and Abbie, she could pass for a model. When I look in the mirror all I see is plain old Laura. Nothing special about my green eyes or brown hair. I'll never win awards for my bone structure, and the freckles dotted across my nose have always annoyed me. Conor loves them. Says they're shaped like a constellation. Little Dipper. Well at least he didn't say, Big Dipper.

'How was Shay?' The TV mumbles in the background. 'Not a bother.'

After removing my coat, I walk over to the crib to check on my world. Shay's head is tilted sideways, his little arms stretched up either side of his head. Already I think I see differences in him, he's bigger for one, his nose not so pointy. Or maybe I'm just getting used to it. The tuft of dark hair on top of his head sticks up. I place the palm of my hand on top to flatten it, then kiss him gently, careful not to wake him up. Conor updates me on what, when and how he took his bottle, changed his nappy, got him to sleep, then offers to make me a coffee.

'What time are you heading out to the match?'

'Oh, I didn't know if I should go or not.'

Conor is standing still with the kettle in his hand, a look of anticipation crossing his face. *Is she really going to let me go?*

'Why wouldn't you go? I'll be fine here,' I say, turning my attention back to the baby. 'Myself and Shay will have a grand afternoon together, won't we?'

'Well, if you don't mind?'

I don't mind; I want him to go. I want to have another look around the house. It's possible I put the card someplace else, especially with how tired I was feeling and the painkillers. I might have even put it in the bookshelf where I hid Conor's birthday card last month. I don't think so. I'm certain I put it under the magazine but it's worth a try.

Conor looks at his watch, his big expensive birthday present from his dad. I want to say for his twenty-first, but apparently he was given a new car for that achievement. He points his two fingers at me like shotguns.

'You're sure about this? Because I don't mind missing it, it's only a friendly game.'

'Go out and have some fun, Conor.'

'Okay.' He leaves the kitchen, takes the stairs two at a time and whistles his way to the bedroom. That doesn't sound like a man who's just killed someone. And anyway,

58

he'd have to have a motive. Which, given that I never heard him mention Vicky Murphy's name once before her death, is highly unlikely.

A short time later he's back down, showered, shaved and dressed like a handsome devil.

'Are you going for a pint after the game?' I say, feeling guilty for having harboured some doubts about him earlier.

'Is that not pushing my luck?' Conor raises his eyebrows and smiles at me.

'No Conor, go, I can ring you if I need you. I'm going to relax on the sofa and get lost in Netflix.'

'Well, if it's okay with you, I'll go in for the one, catch up with the lads.' He pulls his jacket on and checks there's money in his wallet. As if.

'Just one favour,' I say.

Conor lifts his head, eyes fixed, like I'm about to make him pay.

'Make sure your mother doesn't know you've gone out or she'll call here to check up on me.'

He laughs, holding his finger over his closed lips as he mumbles, 'Not a word.'

—

Conor's only been gone ten minutes when Shay decides to exercise his lungs again. I'm rocking him from side to side, holding him up, holding him down, into the sunlight, out of the sunlight. When is he going to stop? I check his nappy, nothing. Try him with a bottle, he just spits it out. God, what does he want? Is he missing his daddy?

Not one of the four million soft toys he was given are of any interest to him. He just wants to scream. I'll never get to search for the card at this rate.

I put Shay back in the crib, where he continues to cry. Patting his head, I tell him I'll be back in a minute, we're going for a walk.

It takes a bit of pulling and tugging but eventually I get the buggy open. The doors are so wide in this house I could get a bus through them. The kitchen itself is huge; the actual cooking area only takes up a quarter of the room. There's also a dining area, two sofas, two armchairs, a TV and now a baby area. The utility room is off to the left with its own toilet and shower. If there was a bed in here there'd be no need to leave.

'Mammy's coming, and look what she has for you! Woooo,' I swerve the buggy over to the crib and put it into a lying down position.

Putting two blankets into it, I lift Shay out of the crib and gently place him on top of the blankets. He quietens immediately. The silence is bliss.

Without a word, I slowly begin to move the buggy around the room. Still nothing. I look up at the ceiling and mouth, 'Thank you.' Then, after pushing the buggy twice around the expansive kitchen, I drive it out to the hallway, lean over the handle and whisper to my little boy. 'Mammy's going to bring Shay on an adventure. We're going to find some treasure.' He's still awake but I can see his eyes are flickering closed.

The front room is colder than the rest of the house. A mesh of greys, purples and greens. Expensive furniture sitting on classic rugs. If I'd been living here when all the decorating was going on, I might have done things differently. But I'm not complaining. Not at all. It's a castle. I'm like a princess who has met her prince and will now live happily ever after in the back-ass of nowhere.

The bookshelves are straight in front of me. All the classics in alphabetical order. I doubt Conor ever read any of these books. The only book I've seen in his hand is a cheque book. Maybe I'll read them. Lie on the sofa amongst the greys and purples and greens, Shay resting in my arms, as I turn the pages of someone else's life.

Shay appears to be asleep now. Slowly, I move my hands from the handlebar and step backwards, holding my breath. After about thirty seconds, I believe my luck and walk over to the bookshelf. I need to find that card. The thought of someone having taken it scares me. Makes me feel even more vulnerable.

–

Well, there is definitely nothing obvious to see. No pink envelope sticking out from anywhere. Could I have stuck it inside one of the books?

One, two, three, I flick and flick and flick, remembering to replace every book where I found it. Not that Conor would notice but someone else might. His mother, for instance. She seems to have a photographic memory of where everything was before I came into the house. When I rearranged the kitchen presses she noticed straight away.

I'm on the second row and feeling like this is a waste of time when Shay starts crying again. He's probably hungry now. Placing the book that I'm holding on to the floor, I rush over to my little boy, brush my fingers over his face to let him know I'm here, then grab the buggy and push.

I'm about to push him out the door when I glance back and notice I left the book on the floor.

'One minute, baby.'

Over I go, lift the book. *Wuthering Heights*. I'm about to place it back on the shelf when something falls to the ground. A photograph. Slowly, I bend down – I still get the odd jab of pain so I have to be careful. There's a face looking back at me. A girl. My heart thumps in my chest. Lifting the photo, I hold it closer to my face. The cries from the buggy fade into the background. The room darkens. Why is there a photo of Vicky Murphy hidden in that book?

Chapter Fourteen

My hand shakes. I turn the photograph over and see her details printed on the back. *Vicky Murphy, D.O.B 30/04/1991. Address, Apt.1 Hedigan's Pub, Ballycall.* Her phone number is on it too. It looks like a headshot taken by a professional photographer. Vicky is posing with a serious look on her face. Her blue eyes stare from a narrow pale face. Lips tightly shut above a pointy chin. Her red hair is cut into a bob. It's shorter than in the photograph doing the rounds now. Vicky looks so innocent. So unlikely to have come to such an end.

'Jesus, Conor. What are you doing with this?'

Shay cries his way back into my attention. I quickly shove the photo in my pocket, replace the book and push the buggy back into the kitchen.

'Don't jump to conclusions, Laura,' I tell myself, holding Shay who sucks on the bottle. Shay looks content now, arms hanging by his side, every piece of attention dedicated to getting the formula into his belly. There are no worries in Shay's head, no paranoia and fear distracting him. God, I wish I could be like that. Unable to worry, unable to imagine things, things that are so far-fetched. I think I might be losing my mind. Could Conor be involved in this murder? Or is there a simple explanation for that photo being here? Shay looks up at me, lips still wrapped around the bottle. He's staring, like he's sussing me out.

'Hey little boy, I'm your mama.' *A lunatic maybe, but definitely your mama.*

Through the window, I see a mesh of clouds hanging above the town. The game will be well underway by now.

I turn on the television but the photo of Vicky Murphy still crowds my mind. I wonder when it was taken? How long was left of her doomed life? What the hell was Conor doing with it? Did he have some sort of dealings with her? Something to do with the brewery? If so why didn't he mention it when she was killed. Unless he can't tell me. Is he hiding something? The big shot. Was he having an affair with Vicky? *No. Don't go there Laura. He's never given you any reason to suspect that.*

It doesn't look good. I bet if I told Detective Fintan Ryan about the card and this photo, he'd begin to look at Conor as a suspect. But he was here with me. Sleeping in the bed beside me. How could I forget? My waters broke at six the following morning. Conor jumped out of the bed in a panic, grabbing keys and bags and phones and almost forgetting me. We laughed. It was the last laugh I had that day.

I spend the next few hours switching through the channels convincing myself nothing is going on then convincing myself something is going on. Conor is hiding something from me. But he doesn't even lock his phone. So why has he a photo of Vicky Murphy hidden in a book.? I consider calling Amanda to tell her what I've found. But I'm afraid she will tell me to wait, not alert Conor to my discovery until I find out some more. And I don't want to do that. I want to confront him today as soon as he comes in the door. Whatever happened, I want to know about it.

Outside the window, Pat walks past the house. His head is bent as always, his step slow. He wears a cap no matter what the weather. His feet are shuffling along in heavy boots, a brown suit jacket over a hairy jumper and worn baggy jeans. He has a face full of worry, even though he can't have much to worry about. No family to provide for, no mortgage to meet. No one to tell him what he should or should not be doing.

I watch him disappear down the side of the house, probably on his way to Hedigan's Pub. It's the only time he leaves the land, except for Sunday Mass when he has his weekly wash. He has a different set of clothes for that occasion: suit, shirt and tie. His shoes are always polished to a high shine and he holds his head a little higher as he strolls through the village. When Mass is over, he visits Seamus's grave. Then on to Hedigan's for two pints before lunch. By two in the afternoon, he's back in his regular clothes.

'Shay,' I say in a soft tone, holding the bottle so he can see it's on its way. 'Look what Mammy has.' Putting the bottle under my arm, I lift him out of the crib and take him to the sofa. I notice it's getting darker, so I check the time by pressing the TV remote which is lying on the sofa beside me. Six thirty p.m. Where is Conor? The game would have ended over two or three hours ago.

Within the space of five minutes my question is answered by the clicking of the front door lock. Straightening my body in the chair, I brace myself for what I have to do.

The smell of beer arrives in the kitchen before he does.

'Hope you don't mind. I went into the clubhouse just for the one but the lads all bought me a drink to congratulate me.' He's looking down at the little bundle.

'No, I don't mind, I'm glad, did you enjoy yourself?'

Conor walks over and opens the fridge door.

'Yes, it was a good crack. Are we ordering a takeaway?' he says, grabbing a slice of cheese and shoving it in his mouth. I wish I was hungry, but my stomach is twisted with stress. I still have the photo in my back pocket.

'If you want.'

There is never any disagreement about what takeaway to order because there's no choice. The only place that delivers is the Chinese takeaway beside Hedigan's Pub. There is a fish and chip shop further down near Georgina's place but they don't deliver.

'Can we wait for a while? I'm not that hungry yet.'

'Sure, but not too long, I'm starving.'

Shay is back in the crib, fed and changed. Conor is following the soccer results on the TV. I'm building up courage.

Maybe I should wait until he's sober – cornering him when he's not in his full capacity might be a bit unfair. Not to mention that it might influence his reaction. Or maybe it's the right time. The bolt on his box of secrets will be loose.

'Conor.'

'Yes.'

He's not watching me. His eyes are still firmly focused on the results coming up on the screen. My hand is on the photo in my pocket. *Take it out, Laura.* Vicky Murphy is now on view.

'Why do you have a picture of Vicky Murphy, Conor?'

'What?' He takes one last glance at the screen before looking at me. 'What?'

I'm standing right in front of him now, holding my discovery up to his face.

'This photograph, what are you doing with it in our house?' *Our house*; it's the first time I've called it that. It feels weird but also empowering.

'Where did you get that?' he says, standing and taking it out of my hand. I watch him closely as he stares at the photo, a look of sadness on his face. 'God, I feel so guilty now.'

My heart is in my mouth. Why does he feel guilty?

'What?'

'Yes, she gave it to me a few months ago, I was supposed to give it to this guy I knew in Dublin.'

'What are you talking about, Conor?'

'Vicky, she was looking to do some freelance work for a guy she knew I knew. She gave it to me to pass it on but I didn't. I was a bit fed up at the time with people asking me to do them favours. The whole town thinks I've a magic wand.'

Conor shakes his head as he looks at the photo before handing it back to me. He sits down on the sofa and lifts the remote.

'But… why was it hidden in a book?'

'Was it?' he says, jumping in the seat when a football result appears on the TV screen. Conor punches the air. 'Go on ya good thing.'

'Yes Conor, it was hidden in a book.'

'Well I guess I must have put it there out of the way… Was there a CV with it? It was attached to a CV I think. Laura, I'm going to have to order soon, I'm starving.'

Not knowing what to think, I turn my back to Conor and walk to the kitchen presses. Conor is not at all bothered that I found the photo. He didn't flinch at all. He has a perfectly reasonable explanation as to what it was doing in the book. So why am I doubting him? Pulling open the drawer, I shove Vicky Murphy's photo inside and take out the menu.

Chapter Fifteen

'What kind of work was Vicky looking for?'

The grease from the spring roll drips down my chin, so I pull a serviette from the bunch in the bag and wipe it. Conor lifts his head from the plate. He doesn't normally shovel food in at that rate. He really must have been starving.

'Journalism,' he mumbles through his overflowing mouth before lowering his head to the plate again.

'I didn't know she was a journalist.'

Hurrying his swallow, he takes a slug of water from the glass by his side then looks at me. 'Yeah, she was in college up in Dublin.'

'Really... and did she commute?'

'No, as far as I know she stayed in Dublin during the week.' Conor puts his fork down and looks me straight in the eye. 'Laura, I don't know much about her, she just gave me that photo in the bar one night and asked if I could put a word in for her with a guy I know from the *Herald.*'

I get the feeling he doesn't want to talk about Vicky anymore. I don't blame him. She asked him to do something, he didn't do it and now she's dead. I'd better change the subject.

'Would you like to sleep in a spare room tonight Conor, so Shay won't disturb you? I'll do the feed.'

Conor stretches his back out and yawns.

'I don't think he has much chance of disturbing me tonight, not with all that food in me on top of the pints.'

Smiling, I reach over and grab one of his chips. I never order them, just rob his.

'Hey, I thought you said you weren't hungry,' he says.

–

I was wrong when I said Conor didn't snore after a few pints. He's like a lion choking on the carcass of his prey in the bed beside me. Shay doesn't seem to mind. There isn't a murmur from his corner of the room but I'm completely awake, staring at the sky. Twisting and turning, I eventually accept I'm not getting any sleep tonight. The next time Conor drinks too much he can sleep elsewhere.

My toes wriggle into the comfort of the plush white carpet when I get out of the bed. Over at the crib, I check Shay is okay before leaving the room.

On the landing, silence surrounds me. I make my way down the sweeping staircase and walk into the kitchen. There is an extra hum in the air now, buzzing from the fridge, the dishwasher, the bottle cooler. But it's still eerie and empty.

Sometimes I miss the noise of the city keeping me company at night. Those long nights, sitting by the window, staring out at the world ticking by, wondering would I ever sleep again. There were times when I never went to bed at all. I sat and stared, waiting for the sun to rise. Waiting for the streets to fill with bustling commuters, noise, smells. Life. Here we go again.

A noise from out back disturbs me, sending my nerves into overdrive. Footsteps. I can hear someone walking slowly outside the window. Creeping over, I peep out the window and see the unmistakable shape of Pat shuffling below the moonlight. He disappears into the trees. It's four fifteen a.m. according to the oven clock. He really is a weirdo. What is he doing out at this hour? Maybe he got a lock-in at Hedigan's, but that's unlikely, with Vicky's funeral tomorrow. I expect they would have closed on time tonight. They'll be extra busy tomorrow. At first, I wasn't planning on attending the funeral but when Amanda heard about it, she said I had to go. I had to find out what I could about Vicky and mingle with the rumours. She even offered to come here and sit with Shay for me. I wasn't buying into it until she mentioned the fact that my absence could be frowned upon by the locals. So, I agreed to go to the church part of the service only. I don't want to leave Shay any longer.

Conor once told me Pat doesn't have a body clock. He sleeps and wakes whenever he does. Conor often found him doing chores in the middle of the night. I can't say it to Conor but I wish he wasn't living in the forest at the end of our garden. Knowing he could arrive at the door or look in the window at any time is unsettling. It takes away from our privacy. Maybe Conor could get rid of him, set him up in one of those little apartments above the shops. He could say it was for his own good, that he'd be closer to everything as he got older, including the pub.

'Laura, are you there?' Conor's voice echoes down the stairs. Rushing to the hallway, I look up and see his sleepy head hanging over the bannisters.

'What are you doing up?' he says. 'Shay is awake.'

I rush up the stairs. 'I couldn't sleep so I got up. Has he been crying long?'

'Don't think so.' Conor's head is hovering over the crib, his hand gently resting on Shay's belly. 'Mammy's coming, baby, we'll feed you now,' he whispers, through the smell of stale beer and curry.

Holding Shay in my arms, his manic sucking breaking the silence, I watch Conor fall back asleep. There is no sign of the choking lion this time. It's strange, I've only just discovered he snores. I hope I'm not in for any more surprises.

Chapter Sixteen

'I know... I have it.' Amanda is holding Shay in her arms, rocking him from side to side, trying to stop him screaming. I've written everything down for her. When to feed him, when to change him, to check on him every ten minutes while he sleeps. I've shown her where all his clothes are, just in case, and left a basket of toys – which he has no interest in yet – beside the crib.

'You're only going to be gone for two hours, Laura. I'll be fine. Shay will be fine,' she says, picking something from the shoulder of my black dress. Amanda stills for a moment, looks into my eyes before turning her gaze away. It's as if she's about to comment on how the dress looks on me but stops herself. Does she feel it too? Is she remembering the last time I wore this dress?

'Do you think he knows we're leaving him?' I say, rubbing my finger across his forehead.

Conor laughs. 'Yes, Laura, he knows we're leaving him.'

Amanda joins in the laughter, continuing to rock Shay, more dramatically now, sweeping him up in the air and back down again. I don't want her to do that but if I say something she might get offended. She does it again.

'He'll throw up on you, Amanda.'

'Ugh.' Amanda stops rocking and sits on the sofa. Shay is beginning to quieten but I really am nervous leaving him with neither Conor nor myself here. Maggie said she'd skip the funeral to mind Shay when she heard I was going but I had already arranged for Amanda to mind Shay. Maggie wasn't too impressed, said it was very early to leave him with a sitter.

'I'm his grandmother, there's a difference,' she said.

'And Amanda is his aunty.' That was the end of it. I'm so glad it was Conor who answered that call.

The truth is, I don't have to go. I barely knew Vicky. Skipping her funeral would have been my choice. I'm sorry I let Amanda convince me to go because now I'm walking out of my house and leaving my baby behind. If I could I'd run back in, I would, but they'll all think I'm going mad.

Deep breaths, count; that's what I learned during those first months, afterwards, when the fear and anxiety was at its worst. Deep breaths. It didn't help then and it's not helping now. Noticing my discomfort, Conor turns to look at me. Putting his hand on my leg and squeezing it, he says, 'We have to do it sometime, Laura, at least we're not going to be far away.'

I smile at him. 'I know, I'll be fine, sorry for being such a wuss.'

'You're just being a mammy.' He turns the engine on, and the car crunches down the gravelled driveway. My head is tilted, looking back, eyes on the house. Amanda is standing in the doorway holding Shay's tiny hand up, mimicking a wave. Tears are gathering in my eyes, so I take a tissue and dab the corners, careful not to smudge my mascara.

I had to go through the whole ordeal this morning; prepping, putting on my best exterior. The whole town will be here and I'm the new wife of their hero. All eyes will be on me. I know it. All eyes, including those of the person who sent that card through my letterbox.

When we arrive at the village, the traffic is at a standstill. People have come from everywhere. Vicky Murphy has served a lot of pints and it looks like all the recipients have come to say goodbye.

'I haven't seen the village this busy since the senior footballers were in a play-off for the championship final. I think we're just going to have to ditch the car here and walk.' Conor pulls over to the right and stops the car.

'Are you leaving it here?'

'No choice.'

Looking down at my shiny Louboutins, one of the many surprises Conor showered me with during my pregnancy, I realise I did not come prepared for this. The church aisle was the only exercise I thought I'd be getting today. Now I have to take these heels down the broken paths and cobblestone steps of Ballycall village. I hope I'm not too overdressed. Flashing my expensive clothes may not be the best way to start friendships. But I am the wife of the town hero. It's expected of me. Even though I feel like a fake.

Opening the car door, I step out, pleading with God to hold out on any punishment he thinks I deserve.

The street is full of dark suits matching the grey October day. I walk with as much confidence as I can feign amongst the crowd of mourners quietly chatting as they head up the steep incline of the church grounds. In front of me, an old man links arms with a younger man. Conor is like the mayor, nodding and shaking hands. There are embraces, handshakes, kisses being dished out all over the place.

On the far side of the church grounds, Olive stands. A few dark jackets to her left, Georgina is holding court in a bright yellow coat.

Olive has caught my eye but before I have a chance to wave, she quickly looks away without acknowledging me. Another time that might ring alarm bells, but Olive was a friend of Vicky's. She must be heartbroken to be standing here in the cold air, waiting on Vicky's coffin to arrive.

Noel and Abbie arrive behind us, Abbie in a long blue pleated skirt and a light grey coat which looks a million dollars on her. It probably was a million dollars. Apparently, Abbie is loaded, heiress to a small fortune. Noel was lucky to get her to move down to this small village when she was used to living amongst the rich and famous in the wealthiest and most respected part of Dublin. She must really love him.

'So sad,' Abbie says, pushing herself closer to me. I nod. I feel sad but I only met the girl once or twice, so I'm not filled with the same grief that most people here are struggling with. I'm a bit nervous, though. Nervous at the thought that someone watching me, someone who will talk in a friendly voice to me during the next couple of hours, is the same person who put that card through my letterbox.

Chapter Seventeen

When the hearse arrives carrying the coffin, a dark silence sweeps over the churchyard. This is no ordinary funeral. This woman was killed.

Heads are lowered. The car pulls to a halt outside the big wooden doors of this tiny church. There's a second car, one with the family. I hadn't really thought to ask much about Vicky's family. For some reason I thought she was on her own here.

A tall lady steps out of the second car; that must be her mam. Her coat collar is pulled up around her neck, hiding her from the gawking crowd. Dark glasses and a black beret-style hat complete her camouflage.

An older man is holding her arm. The woman walks, head bent, towards the coffin which is being lifted out of the first car. This is when I break down, seeing the sadness in real life. The broken souls, lying bare for everyone to see. The older man looks like he could be the woman's father, Vicky's granddad. I don't want to think about the grief they must be going through, burying their baby, sending her on ahead to wait for them. And not because of an accident, or an illness. Because of someone else, someone who quite possibly could put their hand on their shoulder today, comment on how wonderful their baby was and say how sorry they are for their loss.

A few younger people get out from the back of the car, brothers, cousins maybe. I'm sure I'll find out once the service starts. I was so caught up with having my own baby I didn't pay much attention to the details been spoken around Vicky's murder and the family left behind.

The cortège slowly enters the church. A lone piper plays Vicky up the aisle. Her mother's step buckles once or twice. My heart is aching for her. What she is going through, burying a child, should never happen. Is she thinking this was not the way she imagined Vicky making this journey? She should be in a white dress, her gallant hero glancing back in his bow tie at the top of the altar. Not this. Not a wooden coffin.

Noel and Abbie manage to shuffle into the pew beside Conor and me. People stand in every space they can find. The churchyard must be full with the overflow. Olive is in the row in front of me, head bent, a tissue dabbing her eyes. I've never had a best friend die. It must be really sad for her.

When the service gets underway, I think of little Shay and what he's doing now. Is he asleep? Drinking his bottle? I hope to God Amanda isn't swinging him again. What if he fell? What if he hit his head on that low beam over the island? Panic is rising inside me, but I must control it. Taking Conor's hand, I close my eyes and attempt to pull myself together.

The service is long, just like I expected it to be. The priest talks about the tragedy but also about the wonderful person Vicky Murphy was to so many people. He talks about her intelligence, her beauty, her kindness, every-thing that no one probably mentioned when she was alive.

To my right, I can just about make out Georgina snif-fling into a tissue. She doesn't believe the killer was an outsider, she believes it was a local. In the seat behind her Maggie sits tall, head in the air, eyes concentrating below the peak of a navy hat. Maggie has outfits for everything – a glamourous woman, with expensive tastes. She catches me looking at her before turning her stare back to the altar.

The priest asks everyone to take a moment's silence and the church sounds like it has emptied out; not a thing can be heard, not even a cough. Then there is a ringing sound, a mobile… someone's mobile phone is ringing, it's close by. Whose could it be? No one dares check. The silence is broken for a second time by the priest asking everyone to be seated.

'Switch off your bloody phone,' Conor whispers.

'What? That wasn't me, was it?'

It was. Shit, the ringing came from my bag. Discreetly, I slip my hand in and silence it. I hope no one saw me. Maggie is glancing with a disapproving frown, but she couldn't possibly know for certain it was mine; it could have been Conor's, or anyone's sitting nearby. I don't have a personalised ring tone. If she asks, I'm going to tell her it was Conor's.

Then I feel a bolt of fear. Who had called? It had to have been Amanda; something dreadful has happened or she wouldn't have rung me. My heart almost stops. I reach into the bag and take out the phone. I stifle a sigh and take a deep breath. The number is unknown to me, not Amanda's.

'Put that away.' Conor's whisper has an edge of anger to it. I shove the phone into my pocket and whisper back that I thought something might be up with Shay.

'Switch it off.'

He turns his head towards the altar, and I'm left sitting here feeling like a twat. Does he not understand? I thought it was about Shay, his son. Would he rather I didn't care? That I ignored the call, rather than embarrass him in front of his army of worshippers? Maybe Conor should be on the altar.

Turning away from him, I glance at Abbie who's sitting beside me. There's a smile hiding below her expression and she winks at me. Thankfully someone supports me.

We're reaching the end of the service. Thank God. I realise I shouldn't be here. The church is not the place to come when leaving a baby with a sitter for the first time. Distraction is what's needed. Not a place where all you can do is think.

The priest invites everyone to shake hands, make peace, and we do, Conor and I. He squeezes my hand, a soft smile brightening his worried face. I'm forgiven.

Then he shakes Abbie's hand and I shake Noel's hand and those of the woman in front and the man behind.

I've just about shaken as many hands as possible, when Olive turns around. Holding out her hand to Conor she shakes it, then mine, then Abbie's but when Noel stretches his hand out, she blanks him, purposely. Olive turns back around. Noel pulls his hand back quickly but not before Abbie and I stare at the empty response. I think my display of reckless indifference with my phone will take second place to Olive's blatant refusal to shake Noel's hand. What was that about? Am I the only one who saw that? Why would Olive not shake Noel's hand?

My mind goes into overdrive. What does Olive know? Has something happened? How will I find out? I could ask Abbie if there's any bad history between them, and why she thinks Olive would blank Noel. It was pretty clear

Noel was willing to let bygones be bygones; if there is animosity between them it seems to be one-sided. But what if this gesture does not belong to the past? What if it has something to do with Vicky?

Not wanting to make another holy show of myself, for Conor's sake as well as my own, I get in the queue and accept the communion. Passing by the bereaved family, my heart sinks, seeing their red eyes, sunken faces and heads leaning on one another. The priest mentioned Vicky's mother, her grandfather and two cousins. There was no mention of a father or siblings so she may have been an only child. Her mother is a single mam who, according to the priest, never worked, spending all her days caring for Vicky until the girl went out into the big world only for this unbelievable crime to befall her.

So where had Vicky got the money to stay in Dublin during the week? A few nights as a bartender wouldn't have even covered the college fees.

In the distance, I see Pat dressed in his Sunday best. He's leaning against the wall halfway down the church. He holds his cap with both hands in front of his chest. His eyes are cast to the floor.

I walk back to my seat where I kneel down and pray that Shay isn't missing me.

Chapter Eighteen

It has taken forever to get out into the fresh air. The crowd crawled along to the tune of 'Nearer, My God, to Thee'. I thought I'd never get to ring Amanda.

'He's fine, asleep, drank all his bottle, happy,' she says.

My body relaxes and I tell Amanda I'll be home soon.

'Did you find anything out?'

'No, nothing much, though there was one weird moment when Olive refused to shake hands with Conor's friend Noel.'

'Really? I wonder what's going on there. See what you can find out. It could be important.'

The graveyard is attached to the church grounds and even though Vicky was born in the next village, where her mother and grandfather still live, her mother decided to bury her here in Ballycall Cemetery. I wonder why that is?

The grave is dug. The coffin sits on planks of wood ready to be lowered into the earth. Vicky Murphy is going home. Tears are welling up and I have to look away. This is so wrong. She had her whole life ahead of her.

Slipping towards the back of the crowd, I leave Conor's side. I cannot watch this. Abbie is also standing at the back of the crowd, so I move over to her.

'I hate this bit,' I whisper.

'Me too. It's so sad, such a waste of life.'

A lone piper plays some tune I don't recognise and the coffin is lowered. I can't see it, but I can hear the volume of sorrow rising. Abbie holds my arm as we both lower our heads.

—

The sky is darkened by threatening clouds. The first drop of rain lands on my cheek. The service is over. Everyone is making their way to Hedigan's Pub, to drink and chat and — as the priest put it — *to celebrate Vicky's life*. Conor is standing a few yards away from me, deep in conversation with a few other people. His hands are in his pockets, his head lowered. He's kicking the stones below his feet. When he feels the raindrops, he grabs the arms of the two men by his side and says his goodbyes.

'Are you coming?' he says, approaching me. 'It's going to lash.'

'Coming where? Are we not going home?'

'There he is. I'll see you down there,' Abbie says, walking off to where Noel is standing talking to someone. Conor takes my hand and we both follow the crowd out of the graveyard.

'We have to go in for a few minutes, Laura. Show our respects.'

'I don't. You go. I want to get back to Shay.'

'Ten minutes, a quick cuppa and then we'll head home. Amanda said he's grand, didn't she?'

'Yes, but...'

Before I know it, I'm standing in Hedigan's, squashed between a pillar and an old man sitting on a stool, drinking whiskey. Conor is in a queue for tea. I'm not drinking alcohol at this hour of the day, not with Shay to care for.

'Your coat is lovely.' The old man looks up at me, raising his glass. I guess he wants me to reply.

'Thank you.'

'Did you know Vicky?'

'Not well. I'm Conor's wife, he knew her well.'

'Conor…?'

'Conor Caldwell.'

'Oh, that fella.' He tuts before turning his back to me.

And there was I thinking I'd married God. Turns out, not everyone thinks so.

Conor arrives back balancing a cup of tea on a saucer in one hand and a pint of Guinness in the other. I'm not going to question his choice of beverage; if he wants to stay here all day he can. I'm going home after I drink my tea.

'There's sandwiches up there but I couldn't get near them.'

'I'm fine, I'll have something when I get home.'

I want to ask him who the old man on the stool is but Olive has arrived beside us and is talking shop, which makes me feel like the outsider that I am, standing here, looking pretty in my posh coat and high heels. I imagine some of these people think of me as a trophy wife. The girl from the big city. But I'm just trying to fit in a bit more.

I listen as Conor and Olive discuss some important issue about the brewery that just can't wait. I wish I under-stand what they are saying so I can join in, even nod in agreement, but I can't. I haven't a clue about the business except that it exists. From now on, I'm going to ask Conor more about what goes on there.

Abbie and Noel are walking over. What will Olive do now? Noel is carrying a pint; Abbie has what looks like a gin and tonic. A part of me would love to get stuck into a session. It's been so long since I actually sat and laughed with a group of people. Today would have been the ideal situation to get to know more of the locals, let them get to know me. Leaving so soon is going to make me look like I don't want to be here. I know what they'll say, headed by Georgina no doubt, 'That city girl, thinks she's too good for our company.' How wrong can people be? The truth is, I crave their company. I want to belong here. To make a life here with Conor and Shay. I want people to like me, to talk to me. Not to judge me. I want the opposite to what I left behind.

'What a crowd,' Abbie says, shoving her small body in between two tall men who are standing beside us. On hearing her voice, Olive's head jerks to the side. Conor is still talking but Olive isn't listening. Abbie pushes in beside her.

'How are you, Olive? I'm so sorry, I know she was a good friend of yours.' If Abbie noticed what I noticed in the church she's choosing to ignore it. Olive nods her head, but her eyes are peeled to what's going on behind Abbie. She must be looking to see if Noel is coming up behind her. Conor starts to chat again, this time about Vicky, but Olive looks nervous all of a sudden. Noel has come into view.

'I'll see you later,' she says to Conor, stepping closer to me before saying, 'I hope you don't think I'm being rude but I want to catch Vicky's mum before she leaves. Seemingly she's not staying long.'

'Not at all, go, we can catch up again,' I say, delighted she thought I deserved an apology. I'm only seeing snippets of this girl but the more I see, the less I think she could have sent that card. I'm not sure if that's a bad thing or a good thing because if she didn't send it, who did?

Chapter Nineteen

An hour later, I eventually turn the key in the door. I would have loved to stay in the pub with Conor but Shay comes first, and I only left one bottle prepared for Amanda to give him. I suppose I could have told her what to do but I didn't suggest that to Conor.

'Well?' Amanda says, opening the kitchen door when I step into the house. 'How did you get on?'

Yanking the shoes from my feet before unbuttoning my coat, I head straight for Shay. His little pink face looks so peaceful as he sleeps in his crib.

'Fine.'

'And how were the villagers? Did they come for you with torches of fire?'

Amanda is sipping coffee at the island, eager to know what went on.

'Lovely. Everyone was really nice to me. I would have liked to stay.'

'Go back then, I'm in no rush home.'

'Thanks, Amanda but I'm glad to be home with Shay.'

'Well he's as good as gold, that little fella. I'll babysit anytime, especially with that big TV, it's like a cinema in here.' Amanda steps forward to have a look at the television. 'You really landed on your feet here.'

'I know I did Amanda, but it doesn't always feel that way.'

'What do you mean?'

I don't want to tell Amanda that I'm worried Olive is not the person who sent the card. I was hoping it was some sort of revenge act for me having stolen her man, but I've changed my mind. If I do tell Amanda how I feel, if I say it out loud, I'll have to admit that something worse is going on.

'Nothing, it doesn't matter.'

'Is it the card, Laura?'

'Yes, I can't stop worrying about it.'

Amanda puts her cup down and walks over to where I'm sitting on the sofa.

'Don't let it bother you, you know it's not the truth: Conor was with you the night Vicky was killed. It's someone being bad, Laura. It's someone trying to upset you.'

Her hand on my shoulder makes me feel vulnerable. Tears fill my eyes.

'But why? What did I do?'

'Nothing.'

'What if they all hate me?'

'They don't all hate you, don't be so dramatic, Laura. It was one card.'

Eventually, I wipe my eyes, pull myself together and watch Shay sleeping in the crib. The mere sight of him relaxes me. Amanda makes herself a sandwich, offering to make me one too but I tell her I ate in the pub. I don't like lying to her but I'm not in the humour for a lecture on how I need to eat to keep my strength up. So I make tea and we chat some more. Between the eulogy and the talk in the pub, I've learned a lot about Vicky, and Amanda is eager for me to tell her.

The pub was just a part-time job for Vicky Murphy, who had grown up in the next village. The only child of Erin, she had been quite the tomboy in her day. Stories of her getting into fights on behalf of her male cousins were legendary in the town. When she finished school she wanted to leave her village but her mother didn't want her going to Dublin so young. They agreed she could move to the next town for a year or two before moving on.

Ten years later and Vicky was still here. She had discovered a love for journalism, inspired by a young man she had been dating for a few years. He had moved to London, leaving Vicky with the bug. Eager to get into the business, Vicky regularly submitted pieces to papers and magazines and had had a few pieces accepted by the *Journal*. Inspired by her success, she had decided to go to college in Dublin. That's where Vicky's life was at when the plug was pulled.

'Investigative journalism?' Amanda says, after washing her sandwiches down with a mug of tea.

'So they say.'

'Hmm, interesting.'

'So she lived in Dublin during the week?'

'Yes, three or four nights apparently.'

'That would cost a bit... I wonder where the money came from?'

A little whimper escapes from the crib. Shay is wakening.

'Shit, I have to make a bottle.'

'Done.' Amanda walks to the fridge and takes out two bottles which she had made while I was at the funeral.

'Oh, how did you know what to do?' I say, eager to find out if she did it right.

'You have it all down here.' She holds up the instructions I'd written down for Conor.

'Did you use the right scoop?'

'There was only one in the tin. For God's sake, Laura, it's not brain surgery.'

'Sorry, I'm just so nervous all the time.'

Amanda walks over to me shaking the bottle.

'That's perfectly understandable,' she says. 'Especially after...' *Don't say it, Amanda. Don't say it.*

'Anyway, you're doing great, you're going to be the best mammy ever.'

'Do you think so?'

'Yes, I know so... Now, back to Vicky.'

Amanda is intrigued by the fact that Vicky Murphy was hoping to be an investigative journalist. She thinks that means she was investigating something that someone didn't want her to. Did she discover something and was killed because of it? Maybe she discovered something about the brewery? Or something bad about a prominent member of the village? Something that put her in danger.

I wonder if that's what the cops are thinking? I suppose it's possible, but it's also possible she was just in the wrong place at the wrong time. Met a psycho. Someone passing through. She may have tried to fight off an intruder. From the sounds of it, Vicky Murphy was a brave woman who wasn't afraid of sticking up for herself. There were lots of stories about how strong she was for a small woman – one guy relayed how she had turfed two big men who were fighting out of the bar one night, single-handedly. Did that same bravery lead her into danger? Amanda is convinced she was investigating something that got her killed. She says I'm not to worry, and to stop thinking it has something to do with Conor. But how can I stop worrying? If it was nothing to do with him, why was I sent that card?

–

The door opens and in walks Conor.

'Has Amanda gone?'

'Yes, you just missed her... I thought you'd stay longer.'

'Nope, I'd enough yesterday to do me a lifetime, how is my little man doing?'

'Great, not a bother.'

Conor walks over to the crib.

'Are the cops saying anything at all about Vicky?' I ask, sprawled out on the sofa. I've already changed into my pyjamas and was just about to flick through the channels when Conor arrived home.

'No, I don't think they have a lead yet. But they will get the bastard. They have to, they can't leave the village in fear of who could be next.'

'What?' I jump into a sitting position. 'Do they think it could be a serial killer?'

Conor can tell he's frightened the life out of me.

'No, not a serial killer, Laura. I'm just saying people will be nervous. Aren't you nervous?'

'Not until now. Fuck's sake.'

Pulling myself off the sofa, I walk to the window and look out at the vast space at the back of my house that a serial killer would find quite easy to navigate.

'Sit down, Laura, it wasn't a serial killer, it was probably someone Vicky knew. It usually is in these cases.'

Conor is right. I've seen enough on the TV to back up that particular scenario. It's usually someone close to the victim. Which, according to my estimate, could be anyone in this village; they're all close here, too close, if you ask me. I watch him unzip his jacket. A cold shiver runs down my body. Maybe the killer is someone I know too. I shake the thought from my head and walk over to the crib. Now that we're talking, I think I'll probe him a bit more.

'Have you any suspects in mind?'

He takes the remote from the sofa and sits down before saying, 'No, I don't, in fact I'm finding it hard to believe it could be anyone from the village.'

'You know most people who live here, don't you?'

'Yes, and not one person comes to mind.'

'Do they all like you?'

'Well, that's a funny question.' He presses the remote and waits for the TV to light up. 'I don't know the answer to that, and I don't really care, Laura.'

He pats the cushion on the sofa for me to sit down. I check that Shay is still asleep – dark tufts of hair, eyes closed, his little head sticking out from the top of the blanket. The nurse said it isn't necessary to cover him all the time if the room is warm, but I like to make sure he's snug and safe, wrapped up tightly, where nothing can harm him.

I am hoping Conor might elaborate, mention one or two enemies of his, someone who may have sent the card, but he's not giving anything away.

'There was an old man,' I say. 'He started talking to me in the pub but when he realised I was your wife he turned away.'

'Runner.' Conor laughs. 'Don't mind him, he's a nut job.'

'Why do you call him Runner?'

'I don't know, it's what my father always called him. They had a falling out and he hasn't spoken to me since.'

'Is there anyone else?'

Conor turns his attention from the TV and looks at me.

'Why all the questions, Laura?'

Now's my chance; I have to tell him about the card. He could put my mind at rest. Maybe even tell me who he thinks sent it. This is it, I'm going in.

'Conor...'

I'm interrupted by the doorbell. Conor jumps out of the seat to answer the door. I'm left with my mouth open in mid-sentence. The moment is gone, and when I see who bursts into the kitchen, four gins to the wind, I realise it won't be coming back tonight.

Chapter Twenty

'I hope you don't mind us popping in like this, but Helen just had to see the baby.'

Maggie sounds even louder with drink on her. By her side is a woman of the same age, dripping in jewellery and covered in face powder. The scent of perfume invades the room. Did she spill the whole bottle over herself?

'Laura, this is Helen; Helen, Laura.'

I shake her hand and suddenly I become conscious that I'm wearing pyjamas and it's only about five o'clock in the evening.

'I was just telling Helen how good a father Conor is.' She turns her head around to look at Helen. 'He gets up in the middle of the night to feed and change the baby.'

It takes a little more effort than usual for Maggie to walk in a straight line, but she manages it and heads to the crib.

'That never happened in my day,' she huffs.

Knowing this will not go down well with the new mammy, Conor interrupts.

'Laura is the real hero here. She has everything under control. I don't know what I'd do without her.' He pulls me close to him and hugs me. Resting my head on his shoulder, I inhale his scent. That's one for me.

The baby has woken – hardly surprising with two old dears breathing gin down his neck. Shuffling in between them, I lift Shay and rock him over my shoulder. Helen has run out of words to describe how lovely he is. Of course he's the image of his father and Maggie is standing so proudly, it's as if she dreamed him into existence.

'Would you like a coffee, Helen?' Conor asks.

I stare at him but he doesn't see me. The last thing I want is these two women hanging around when I should be relaxing in my husband's arms with Shay resting on my chest.

'I'm sure they'd like to get home. It's been a long day.' I say.

'Actually,' Maggie giggles, 'if you don't mind Conor, we'd love a G and T.'

'Sure.'

The room has suddenly become a prison cell. How am I going to handle listening to these two yapping on? Maybe I'll say I've a headache, that I have to lie down. Conor can entertain them.

After placing two glasses on the counter, Conor leaves to get the gin from the drinks cabinet in the front room. Maggie and Helen have removed their coats and are making themselves comfortable on the two chairs each side of the TV. I'm sitting facing them, Shay asleep in my arms. I'm hoping to make my exit as soon as Conor reappears.

Helen leans towards me, whispering in a low voice. 'Did you hear what they're saying about Vicky?'

My fake headache has suddenly disappeared. Shaking my head in reply, I wonder what I am going to hear. Did they find her killer? Had Vicky something to hide?

'Well,' Helen looks behind her as if making sure no one is listening in. How drunk is the woman? There's no one else here. 'Apparently, she wasn't quite as single as everyone thought—'

Maggie interrupts. 'What Helen is trying to say is that rumour has it, Vicky Murphy was having a secret relationship with someone who is already married.'

'An affair.' Helen nods.

The judgmental silence is interrupted by Conor walking into the room, holding the gin in his hand.

'We have it', he says, lifting the bottle to show the ladies.

'What do you think of that?' Maggie says, looking my way.

With my mouth open, my eyes jump from Helen to Maggie and back again.

'Well…' I really don't have anything to say but they're staring at me waiting for a disapproving response.

In the background, I hear the sound of gin gurgling over ice.

'What do you think of what?' Conor says, taking the glasses in his hand and walking towards the two women. Now their attention is on him.

'Vicky Murphy. Apparently she was having an affair,' Maggie says, reaching out to collect her prize. Conor hands the other glass to Helen.

'Are we really going to go there?' Conor says, walking away from his mother. Lifting another glass, he looks over at me. Gin and tonic is not on my list of things to do tonight – not in this company anyhow – so I shake my head.

'Well… that's the song of the whispers,' Maggie says, the glass about to meet her lips.

'And we all know how that tune goes,' Conor says.

'What do you mean by that?' Maggie is annoyed by his response.

'You know full well what I mean, let the girl rest in peace.'

Shuffling forward in her seat, Maggie turns her head and looks at Conor, her face older-looking without the smile. I'm bracing myself for a whole new experience. Maggie and Conor are going to disagree. This should be fun. They have never been anything but civil, over-the-top compliant with one another if you ask me. The prospect of some friction between them makes the whole intrusion tolerable. I'm almost sorry I don't have a drink in my hand.

'That was a completely different situation.' Maggie says, a slight slur creeping into her delivery.

Conor ignores her. I've seen him like this before when people have tried to engage him in an argument. He's calm, won't be drawn into battle. But Maggie won't give up.

'Your father wasn't killed, he had an accident.'

Still nothing from Conor. Eventually Maggie returns to her comfortable position to continue her discussion with Helen and myself, but a tiny whimper disturbs her plans. All heads turn to Shay who's now crying in my arms.

'I'll change him,' Conor says, the anxious expression leaving his face as he takes Shay from me and walks out of the room. The sound of Pat passing by the window steals our attention.

'Are you okay with him living back there?' Maggie says, her eyes staring at me above the near-empty glass. Shrugging my shoulders, I give her a half-hearted smile. I'm not comfortable enough to share my inner thoughts with this woman… yet. I hope in the future we can become close, that I can treat her like she's my mother, not just Conor's. I want to be able to share my concerns, plan big days for Shay with her, go shopping, share recipes. Things that I would love to do with my own mam but can't. Maybe being close to Maggie would help fill that void.

'I hated Pat living there,' she says, looking over at Helen. 'But Seamus wouldn't get rid of him.' Maggie drains the drops from the glass. 'That's why I left this house when Seamus died. Best thing I ever did. I'm delighted to have my own little space – no interruptions, no Pat walking into the kitchen whenever he likes.'

The drink has dissolved Maggie's filters. I've never heard her talk like this. Conor told me his mother moved out of the house when his father died because she wanted a smaller place, that the old house was too big for her. He didn't mention her dislike for Pat.

I need to turn the conversation back to Vicky. If she was having an affair, surely that changes things. A marriage at risk, the possibility of losing everything, the scandal. Whoever it is, he has to be a suspect. Such matters might not raise an eyebrow in the city but in a village like this… gold dust.

'I wonder who Vicky was having the affair with?' I say.

Both women look at me, their bodies drained of the energy they arrived with. Helen shakes her head.

'No one knows. Or at least no one is saying.'

Someone has to know. The wife, maybe? A friend of Vicky's? Someone knows. Will they tell the police? Have they told the police already? My mind flashes to the scene in the church when Olive refused Noel's hand. Was Noel the one Vicky was having the affair with? Olive is definitely angry with him over something. And from what I can gather, Olive was Vicky's closest friend, so if anyone knows, she does.

'I couldn't put my finger on it,' Maggie says, her words slower, her voice lower, 'but I always knew there was something about that girl, something I didn't trust.'

Helen nods in agreement.

'I thought you liked her?' I said, thinking of all the tears shed, the condolences offered; Maggie dabbing her eyes with her cotton handkerchief when the coffin passed her by.

Taking a deep breath, Maggie straightens herself in the chair and ponders before saying, 'It's not that I didn't like her… I didn't really know her that well, never spoke to her outside of the few times I was in the pub.'

Helen is still nodding when Conor arrives in the room, rattling his keys.

'Is Shay alright?' I say.

'Fast asleep.' Conor winks at me. 'Okay ladies, time to hit the road.'

–

Shay is still asleep when I walk into the bedroom. The big cosy bed calls out from the centre of the room, with its duck-feather duvet and puffed up pillows all wrapped in soft silky satin. The idea of watching TV no longer appeals to me so I take my book from the bedside locker and lie on top of the duvet waiting for Conor to return from dropping his mam home.

A part of me feels smug. Maggie was drunk, she tried to start an argument with Conor. She slurred her words and almost tripped down the stone steps outside the front door. She will probably feel very uncomfortable the next time she sees me. But the truth is, now I like her more. She's not perfect either.

Chapter Twenty-One

'I didn't notice anything.'

'Well, it was pretty obvious.'

Conor is denying seeing Olive purposely avoid shaking Noel's hand. I asked him as soon as he came up to the bedroom. I don't want to come straight out and suggest that maybe Noel was the person Vicky was having the affair with. Conor can be very defensive when someone he cares about is being bad-mouthed. It's something I really like about him; he's loyal to the end. He even defends Pat anytime Maggie slags him off.

'Do you know of any reason she might be angry with him?' I ask.

'No,' Conor says.

With one arm against the wall, Conor leans over the crib, staring at his son. He just can't seem to get enough of him. The room is getting darker so I switch on the bedside light. I want to get a clearer picture. Seeing how happy he is with Shay fills me with pride. It also makes me feel safe. We're a real family now, solid… I hope.

'They always got on well as far as I could tell,' he says.

Olive is Conor's right hand when it comes to the business. She's been his personal assistant since he took over from his dad. It must have been very difficult for Olive when they split up, going into the office every day, facing the man of her dreams who had handed her dream to another woman. I doubt it was a picnic for Conor either, even though he was the one who broke up the relationship. When we first started dating, I didn't know he already had a girlfriend. He kept that one quiet. Only coming clean when we started getting serious. The kind of serious you get when you find out you're pregnant.

Moving away from the crib, Conor slides onto the bed beside me and kisses my cheek. His arm reaches behind my back, pulling me closer to him. The woody scent of his aftershave kills the smell of Sudocrem in the air. Conor puts his lips on mine, caresses my tongue, pulls me tighter. If he's thinking what I think he's thinking, he can think again.

'Conor.' I pull back slightly and look into his dark green eyes. 'I'm sorry.' I don't want to disappoint him, I want to make love to him, to hold him, to be one again with him, but it's too soon.

Conor smiles. 'I just want to hold you, Laura. I love you.' Snuggling into his embrace, I think about how lucky I am. The Caldwell family, all huddled together in the one room. How could I have doubted this man? He would never lie to me. But something shifts in my head. A fear determined to keep me on edge. Conor kept me a secret from Olive for a few weeks, lived one life here with her, another with me in Dublin. I don't want my mind to go there, the murder, the card but… if he's capable of that, what else could he be keeping secret?

Chapter Twenty-Two

Something is bothering me, chipping away even further at my serenity. But I'm not sure what it is. It's something I heard earlier, something Maggie said.

Placing Shay into the crib, I walk to the window and pull back the curtain. I can see a glow through the trees in the distance. Pat must be up. Probably spent the evening sleeping off the drink and now finds he's wide awake. I wonder what it was Maggie didn't like about the man. I know walking in and out of the house without knocking would do it for me, but people are different down here. It's not unusual for someone to help themselves to their neighbour's hospitality.

There are times I can't believe I'm here, shrouded in someone else's family. I still feel like an intruder, but as times goes on, it's getting easier. I must listen to what Amanda says. I deserve it, it's my time now. The past is exactly that and there is no reason to go and visit it.

Amanda has always been my best friend. Sisters don't always get on like we do. We share everything, including secrets. She stood by me when I needed her most. I'm not sure I'd have kept going if she hadn't been by my side.

I remember the day we packed up my belongings for the big escape to the country. I cried the whole time, fearful that Amanda would be lonely without me. Knowing I was going to miss her company. Her laughing.

The nights we'd sit up talking until there was literally nothing left to say.

She sat beside me in court. The second worst day of my life. I remember how Amanda hugged me when the judge spoke. The relief, evident on her face and in the tears we shed.

Leaving Amanda was hard but her happiness for my new situation eased the burden. And anyway, I'm used to hard.

I drop the curtain and get back into bed. The heat from Conor's body is so comforting, cloaking me with safety and— that's it. I remember now. Maggie. That's what's been bothering me. She said she never spoke to Vicky except for the few times she was in the pub. I remember her exaggerating the word 'few.' But I had seen her with Vicky, the day I braved the terrible weather and walked to the village.

-

Three weeks had passed since I'd set up home here and I was still waiting for the delivery of the new car Conor bought me as a present on my wedding day. I had bought him a pair of cufflinks!

The rain had eased off by the time I reached the village. With very few people to be seen, I remember thinking, God, how am I going to survive here? What will I do all day?

Conor encouraged me to leave work as soon as I moved here, and I hadn't put up a fight. The thought of commuting to Dublin every day hadn't appeal to me. I had been planning to leave as soon as the baby arrived anyway, so a few months earlier wouldn't make a difference. It would give me a chance to settle in. To get to know everyone.

It had taken no more than five minutes to walk the length of the village, by which time I'd arrived at the church. Praying wasn't something I'd ever subscribed to but I soon realised if I was going to survive here, I'd have to get myself some new hobbies.

The church grounds had been empty, eerie, not a sound to be heard but the splashing of my feet in a rather large puddle that had gathered by the entrance gate. Having braved the moat, I had continued towards the church door and had been about to enter when I saw two people huddled by a marble Virgin Mary in the graveyard to my left. Maggie was one of them. What was she doing in the graveyard in this brutal weather talking to Vicky, the barmaid from Hedigan's? I had recognized Vicky from being in the bar with Conor a few days earlier. She'd gone out of her way to introduce herself to me. But why had Maggie handed her something which Vicky had quickly shoved in her pocket? It had all looked pretty suspicious to me, cloak and dagger stuff. Why the graveyard? Surely they both could have met somewhere more convenient in this weather. It wasn't like Maggie visited Seamus's grave every day.

Conor had told me all about her routine. Every Sunday straight after Mass, she and Conor would go to the grave and Maggie would change the flowers. 'Do you have to go?' I remember asking him once, hoping to go up to Dublin for the day. But Conor had explained that Maggie hated going to the graveyard on her own.

Well, not that day, because Vicky had left and Maggie had been standing in the graveyard by herself.

I had thought about going over to her but realised she might not have wanted me to see what just happened, so I had continued into the church expecting her to arrive in behind me any minute. She hadn't. Apparently Maggie had everything under control. She didn't need God's help.

Then I had forgotten about it. With all that had happened since, the clandestine meeting had never come back into my thoughts – until now. Until I heard Maggie say she didn't really know Vicky. She only met her the few times she was in the pub. Maggie is lying. But why?

Chapter Twenty-Three

I didn't sleep much last night. I'm regretting not showing Conor the card and now I don't have it. I have questioned whether I could have put it somewhere else. I was in such shock. But I know I didn't. I can still see myself covering it up with the magazine. Someone else took it.

The longer I drag this out, the worse it will be. Conor will kill me when he finds out I've been keeping this secret. But I still don't have any idea why I received the card at all – whether someone actually thinks Conor did kill Vicky, or whether someone just wanted to piss me off, burst my dream. I wanted to have a clearer idea of what I was dealing with before I told him about it. But here I am, days later, and still with no clue as to who sent it.

Conor has taken Shay downstairs. I'm dragging myself out of bed and into the shower when a thought suddenly bursts into my head. What if Conor found the card himself and disposed of it? Would he not ask me about it? Unless he thought I hadn't seen it. I closed the envelope. He would never have known I had read it. But surely he'd say something if he found it. Unless he didn't want me to read it. In case I believed it. In case it's true. I shouldn't have listened to Amanda. I should have said something to him straight away. Now I'm totally confused and I don't know what to do. With the hot water running down my body, I decide the best thing to do is to try and forget about it once and for all. It's ruining everything.

I dress myself and put on some makeup. I am Mrs Laura Caldwell and I should look like Mrs Laura Caldwell.

The smell of toast leads me to the kitchen where Conor is standing by the island with a glass of orange juice in his hand.

'Are you going into work today?' I say, noticing he's wearing a suit. I thought he had a few more days off.

'Just for a meeting, I'll be back after it.' But I know he won't. Once he passes through the doors of the Caldwell Brewery he becomes a slave to himself. I'll be lucky if he's home for dinner tonight.

The briefcase is open on the countertop. Conor is checking the contents when the doorbell rings.

'Who could that be?' I say, walking to the hallway. I'm hoping it's not Conor's mother coming to help the poor daughter-in-law survive her first day without the hubby. When I get closer to the door, I see a large dark shape. It's definitely not Maggie. The glass distorts the image but I can see it's a man, a big man in a dark suit. I'm nervous turning the latch.

'Hello, Laura,' he says. 'Is Conor here?'

'Yes, come in.' I stand back to let him enter. Detective Fintan Ryan has been here a couple of times before but not usually this early in the morning.

'Is everything okay?' I ask, leading him into the kitchen. But I don't know if he hears me; he doesn't answer.

'Fintan,' Conor says in a loud cheery voice when we enter the kitchen. 'To what do I owe this honour?'

He steps out from behind the island and walks towards Fintan with his hand out. The men all seem to do that here, shake each other's hands every time they meet like they haven't seen one another in years. Fintan ignores Conor's hand.

'Can I have a word, Conor?' he says, looking over to where I'm standing. 'In private.'

'Sure, sure. Laura, will you take Shay upstairs with you?'

There's a lot of silence between the words. Something is up. Conor and Fintan are good friends and would usually have plenty to say to one another. I wonder what is so important that I can't hear it. If something was up with Maggie, I'm sure Fintan would just blurt it out in front of me. It must have something to do with Vicky Murphy.

My hands shake when I lift Shay out of the crib. What is going on? I'm about to walk away when I notice the baby monitor flashing on the shelf beside the crib. With one swoop of my finger I reverse the setting and leave the room. Closing the door behind me, I leave the two men behind and rush to the bedroom with Shay in my arms.

Chapter Twenty-Four

There's a tiny dark birthmark below Shay's ear. Conor thinks it's shaped like a star but it looks more like a blob to me. I brush my finger across it watching his eyes sparkle, looking up at me.

'Hello baby,' I say, sitting down on the bedroom chair holding Shay close to me. The monitor is right beside me.

'Mammy is being bold,' I whisper, increasing the volume button on the monitor. Conor's is the first voice I hear.

'Jesus, Fintan, what are you saying?'

'Someone has said something to alert them; they asked me if I knew anything about it. I said I didn't, but Conor, this is my job; I'm supposed to be retiring next year.'

Silence.

'Who told them? For Christ's sake, who knows?'

'I don't know. They didn't tell me... I just thought I'd come here as soon as I heard.'

More silence.

'So, you told them nothing?'

'Of course not, I acted dumb. I said I didn't believe it was true, that you wouldn't do something like that but—'

'Okay, okay.' Conor's voice is going up and down, like he's pacing the room.

My heart is beating so hard Shay must think I'm patting him. What are they talking about? What the fuck did Conor do and why is Fintan covering for him?

The words shout at me from inside my head. 'Conor is a murderer.' My head is tilted so close to the monitor that I almost slip off the chair. Pulling myself back into a safe position, I hold Shay across my chest, rocking him from side to side. The light on the monitor flashes into the red.

'Fuck!' Conor shouts, banging something while he does it. I jerk in the chair, clinging with fear to my little baby boy. I have never heard Conor express his anger before.

A tear lands on Shay's nose. I dab it with my finger.

'Mammy is sorry, little baby.' I cry more, rubbing Shay's warm soft skin with my hand. 'Mammy is very sorry.'

–

They've obviously left the kitchen now because I can only hear fading murmurs. They must be in the hallway. I hear the bang of the front door.

I put Shay onto the bed and look in the mirror. Grabbing a face wipe, I attempt to disguise the fact that I've been crying. The monitor is still on. Conor is coming up the stairs. Glancing over to make sure Shay is safe, I rush to switch it off. If Conor found out I was listening in, I don't know what would happen next. Am I afraid of him now? Back at the mirror I'm dabbing cream on my face when he walks into the room.

'Is he alright like that?' Conor says, noticing Shay lying on our bed.

'Yes, he can't roll yet.' I check on my little baby, then look back in the mirror where I can see Conor's face. It's a lot redder than it was earlier but his voice is giving nothing away. Conor sits on the bed and rests his hand on Shay's belly.

'See ya later, kid.' Conor kisses his son on the head before walking to my side, taking my face in his hands.

'Were you crying?'

'No, I rubbed cream in my eyes by mistake. What did Fintan want?'

'Nothing much, just a question he had, that's all. Will you be okay on your own today?'

I nod, thinking how the 'one meeting and I'll be straight home' has suddenly expanded into a day.

'Well, ring if you need anything.' Kissing me on the lips, Conor walks to the door. He turns back for one last glimpse at his precious baby.

'I'll keep in touch... Bye, Shay.'

I press my shaking hands down on the top of the dressing table and take deep breaths. In the mirror I can see Shay moving his legs, in out, in out. His lips are pouting, fingers moving. I should be swooning over him, playing with him, encouraging his every movement, but my body is frozen to the spot.

Conor was able to walk in here and act like nothing happened, like Fintan had never been here, had never given him the bad news that made him shout in anger. My body feels empty inside, the life vacuumed out of it. I should have known this was all too good to be true.

Chapter Twenty-Five

The day has been endless. Instead of enjoying every minute I had on my own with Shay, I worried. I thought I'd be excited about welcoming my husband home from his first day back in work. But I have spent most of the day crying, coming up with some outlandish scenarios as to what is going on.

Changing Shay's nappy was a chore, feeding him an even bigger one. I have to get it together. Conor will be home soon and I don't want him to realise I suspect something.

I asked him what Fintan wanted and he lied. Maybe he's trying to protect me. He knows I've been up and down since having the baby. It's possible he'll tell me all in his own time when he sorts things out.

I thought about ringing Amanda and telling her what happened but I changed my mind. Amanda would probably tell me to take Shay and run. She wouldn't understand: I love Conor. I know he didn't kill Vicky because he was with me the whole night. And more importantly, I know he didn't do it because he doesn't seem to have a bad bone in his body. I'd have noticed if he was a bit of a psycho. Wouldn't I? I hope I haven't made a big mistake... again.

The key turning in the door makes me jump with fear instead of happiness, reminding me that I know nothing.

I fake a smile and wait for my husband to walk through the door. Shay is bouncing on my knee, fed and changed. He looks as happy as every baby should, his little pink cheeks glowing below his inquisitive eyes as he stares into the space in front of him. I wonder what he sees, what he thinks. He hasn't noticed his daddy enter the room, but I have.

The jacket of Conor's suit sways open, his tie is loosened. Dropping his briefcase onto the countertop, he says, 'Well, how was Shay?'

'Great,' I say, keeping my eyes on the baby.

'And you?' he says, walking over and kissing me on the head before going to the fridge.

'Grand, no one called, quiet day… I made dinner.'

'Lovely, I'm starving. Is it ready? Or have I time for a shower?' Conor walks back over to me and takes Shay in his arms. 'God, I wish I could stay here with you all day,' he says.

'How did it go?'

'Work? Same as usual.'

'So the place didn't collapse in your absence.' I smile, trying my best to act normal while moving past him on my way to the pot on the stove. The only thing I could bring myself to cook was a stew, just throwing it all in the pot and letting it be.

'No, it didn't,' he says, his eyes fixed on his son. 'Maybe I will be able to spend more time with you, little man.'

If you're not in jail, I'm thinking. 'Go have a shower, I'll heat the stew.'

'Stew, great.'

Conor puts Shay down and leaves the room. How can he be so cool after what happened this morning? Maybe

I read it all wrong. Maybe it's not as bad as it sounded – after all, I did miss the beginning of the conversation.

There's no point kidding myself. I know what I heard. Conor is putting up a front. Something has happened, but how do I find out without admitting to him that I was listening in? And why is he so good at pretending? Has he done a lot of it?

'Maybe you should just live with him for a while first,' my colleague, Rose, had said when I told her I was leaving to get married having known Conor for only four months. Of course I thought she was jealous to say such a negative thing. But now I wonder if she was right. How much do I really know about this guy?

He had proposed as soon as I told him I was pregnant, which some people would admire in a man. I was so nervous at the time. I'd convinced myself he was going to dump me when he found out, but his face had filled with joy. Conor had been over the moon with happiness. He had treated me like some sort of a princess, making sure I had everything I needed, anything I wanted. He had already renovated his mansion the previous year so it was ready and waiting for our life to begin. Why wait? We were so in love. Are so in love.

And yet, here I am, pushing the truth away. But I can't ignore it any longer. Not now, not when I know for sure he's hiding something. Conor could have left the house that night while I was sleeping.

–

The stew smells nicer than it tastes but Conor is shovelling it into his mouth like he's just come back from the war.

'Did you have any lunch?'

'No, I had to go somewhere, running and racing all day. This is delicious,' he says, scooping up more.

Cooking was the one thing I was proud of when we first met. It's not that I'm particularly great but apparently Olive never had much of a flair in the kitchen so she was an easy act to follow.

The first time I had asked Conor to come to my apartment for dinner, I had been nervous. I knew I could make a mean spaghetti bolognaise but that wouldn't impress anyone, so I had dug deep and managed to perfect a beef wellington with potato gratin and some steamed veg. It was all the rage at the time.

Amanda and her then partner, whose name I can't remember – there were so many of them – had joined us. Everything went to plan. Conor had thought I should be a contestant on *Masterchef*, and ever since it's been my thing. I'm the expert when it comes to cooking. Anytime Conor mentions my culinary prowess in other people's company, my ego is freshly watered. I almost feel like I deserve to be with him.

'What are we going to do now?' Conor says, leading me to think he's about to reveal what he and Detective Fintan Ryan were discussing.

'About what?' I push my plate to the side, lean forward and wait eagerly.

'Well, now that Shay is here, I'm back to work. This is the new normal, Laura.'

'Oh.' Lowering my head, I rest my back into the chair.

'Why? What did you think I was talking about?'

Now is my chance. I have his undivided attention, I'll ask him. 'Is everything okay, Conor?'

Conor stops eating and looks up at me. 'Yes… why?'

'I thought you were a bit off after speaking to Fintan this morning... did he bring bad news or something?'

Conor will be disappointed in his acting skills but I have to pretend I noticed something odd about him. I can't tell him the truth.

'No, everything is fine.' He drops the spoon, full at last. 'Will I check if there are any good movies on?' he says, changing the subject and heading over to the sofa. He lifts the remote control and switches on the TV. So that's that then. He's not going to share.

—

The night drags on: three episodes of some Harlan Coban series, Conor checking his phone every ten minutes and two harrowing screaming sessions from Shay. When I asked Conor why he kept looking at his phone he said he was waiting to hear from some guy whose beer order had gone wrong. I didn't believe him. He looks far too worried for that to be the problem.

At twelve o'clock, I give Shay his last feed and take him up to the bedroom. The sky is pitch black. Lying there, waiting for Conor to come up to bed, night terrors begin to creep into my thoughts. It's like a switch going on, telling me it's time to exaggerate all my fears now. So I do. Conor killed Vicky. Is it possible? Did he leave in the middle of the night while I was sleeping? Fintan is definitely covering up something for him. But murder? And why? Was Conor having an affair with Vicky? Did she threaten to tell? I can't see Conor murdering Vicky to save his reputation. But what if it wasn't his reputation that needed saving? Who else would he be willing to kill for?

Chapter Twenty-Six

It's been a year and four months since I first met Conor. I'd been coughing all night. Amanda heard me in the room next door and ordered me to pick up a cough bottle on my way to work. I considered skipping work, ringing in sick but I knew I shouldn't, I was lucky enough to have been offered the job. If it wasn't for Amanda, I wouldn't have; she hassled her boss on a regular basis to give me a chance. God knows what else she had to do for him.

Pete Gunner, the boss, was a nice enough guy but he still lived with the schoolyard attitude that boys were the best. He looked surprised when he discovered women could do the job, patting them on the back or continuously looking at them while shaking his head in admiration. His out-of-date attitude towards women was sharply at odds with his cutting-edge approach to business. He ran one of the few motivational businesses in Ireland at the time.

Imanage offered companies new ways to do their business, updating them on approach, technology and marketing. Pete also developed some of the first team-building exercises for staff. At first I didn't understand any of it. Imanage didn't sell anything except ideas – mostly other people's ideas. But it worked. Pete's workforce was growing as big as his bank balance, which was when

Amanda got a job there. Followed soon after by her struggling big sister.

If Pete was expecting the same bubbly enthusiasm Amanda was able to fake, he must have been slightly disappointed when I walked through the door.

No surprise I wasn't awarded one of the motivational roles. My contribution was more traditional: sit at the reception desk, answer the phone, direct the visitors to their allotted areas. But on this day, the day of the cough, I was asked to sit in on one of the motivational talks. Apparently the flu that I was bravely fighting had swum through the whole building taking down some weaker targets, and now they were short an assistant in the green room. It wasn't a green room like they have for people going on TV. All the rooms at Imanage were identified by colour instead of numbers. 'Forward-thinking,' according to Pete. Easier for the clients to remember, and there were other reasons too. Something to do with belonging and feeling like a team. Pete Gunner seemed to have taken the school playground very serious.

My role was not going to change anyone's life. I was to sit in the room, hand out literature when directed and try and look interested. I didn't have to believe any of it, but by the time I left the first session I was so fired up I was already planning to run for president.

It didn't last long. By the end of the day I didn't have the enthusiasm to vote for president, never mind run for it. Hearing the same thing over and over loses its effect. But as luck would have it, I was assigned the same role the following day, a day that was to change my life forever.

In the spirit of my temporary promotion, I made an extra special effort when getting dressed for work. It was something I'd learned in the session the day before: to dress as I want to be treated. So, the navy suit that went so easily unnoticed behind the reception desk, was replaced by a light tweed skirt with a leather belt, a tight white polo neck and short black leather jacket. All courtesy of Amanda.

I have to admit, I did feel a lot more confident pushing open the rotating doors and walking towards the green room in heels that would normally be kept for hen parties.

I arrived early, part of the new improved Laura, and so had the guy sitting alone in the room. His tightly-fitted grey suit clung to his toned body. His dark hair, lightly gelled, cut short above his square-shaped face. He was clean-shaven, smelt of effort, and when he caught my eye, I immediately blushed. He stood up when I walked in. I presumed he thought I was the lecturer.

'Sorry if I'm a bit early, I can never predict the traffic,' he said.

With my new-found confidence I waved him back into his seat.

'You can never be early, only late.' Something else I'd heard the day before.

I could see him smirking, his smile reached from ear to ear displaying a perfect set of teeth. He was probably wondering how much more of this shit he was going to be subjected to as the day progressed.

'Are you here for the course too?' he said.

Disappointed that he didn't think my words of wisdom rendered me already qualified, I said, 'No, facilitating.'

'Oh.' This seemed to cheer him. He leaned back in his chair and crossed his legs.

'Well, not facilitating as such, I'm assisting.'

'Well aren't we the lucky group?' he said.

I smiled at him – maybe I shouldn't have, but compliments and I had become such distant friends I was delighted to get reacquainted.

'Did your boss send you?' I said.

'Well, I kinda wanted to come.'

I wanted to say, *are you mad? You volunteered for this?* But I didn't – I didn't think Pete would appreciate his staff undermining his years of hard bullshit.

'Oh, why is that?' I smiled at him.

The guy laughed, stood up from his chair and walked over to the water station just as I got there. He poured some water from one of the jugs and offered it to me. I took it. Then he poured himself one.

'Just want to stay on top, find out what's new; you don't always know what the latest trends are when you're living outside the capital.'

I took one look at his suit. 'Oh, I'd say you're doing okay.' Then I walked away with my glass of water.

It was the best motivational class ever. I was motivated by greed, lust and possibly even love. Once or twice I caught him glancing my way, and anytime I had to hand him some literature he kept the paper longer in his grip before taking it from me than he had to, smiling up at me, flirting.

When the end of the session arrived I could sense him standing behind me. By now I knew his name was Conor because everyone had introduced themselves and their line of business. The guy worked in a brewery. At first I thought it was one of those new craft breweries popping up all over the place but no, Callbrew was an old, famous brand. The guy of my dreams could even get free booze.

I didn't expect any further contact from him, assuming that he already had a beautiful girlfriend – or many of them – and that his interest in me was just a distraction from the boredom of the classroom. But nothing could stop me dreaming.

The following day, I was reassigned to my proper station back at reception, the sick people returned and I was back where I belonged. Answering the phone. I'd kicked off the shoes below my desk and was resigned to wearing the navy suit when I answered the call. It was him; I recognised the lilt in his voice. Was he ringing to book another session? Or to complain about the last one, maybe? No. He was asking if he could speak to me, Laura, the girl from the green room.

Chapter Twenty-Seven

The sun is beaming into the room when I hear Shay's cry. It feels like twelve o'clock in Spain but it's ten o'clock in Ballycall.

With Shay rocking on my shoulder, I walk to the landing window at the front of the house and look out at the day. Everything is so peaceful. Green, clean and without any human blight.

I yearn for human blight. Which is why I decided myself and Shay were going to get dressed and visit our friendly village. Being stuck in the house has made me lose my mind. I'm beginning to think unbelievable things. I lay in bed last night believing Conor could be a murderer, or be involved some way in what happened to Vicky. Which is ludicrous. I need to clear my head, distract myself and panic less. If there is something I should be concerned about, Conor will tell me. I'm sure. That's what I want to believe. But how can I when he didn't tell me what the detective wanted?

'Mammy is going mad cooped up in this house, Shay.' Searching through his wardrobe of tiny clothes, most of which will have to be donated before he even gets a chance to wear them, I find a snowy, grey, all-in-one padded romper suit.

'This will be lovely on you. Perfect for our little adventure.' I pull the tag off and try to remember who brought it to the baby shower but I can't. There was so much stuff. So many people. So much wrapping paper.

'C'mon Shay, let's get going.'

I haven't driven with Shay in the car yet. I need to shake all the doubts out of my head and concentrate. At some point I'm going to want to bring him to the city – take him to Imanage and show him off to my ex-colleagues. I don't care if they're interested or not, they can pretend.

Amanda said they were asking for me. They wanted to know how I was getting on living so far away from all the big lights. She painted a pretty picture for them: my fabulous house, my wonderful husband, my friendly neighbours and of course, the most beautiful baby in the world. Local murders were not mentioned.

I never thought anyone could be jealous of me. It was Amanda people envied. She was prettier, bubblier, attracted any amount of friends. I just stood by her side and benefited. Sometimes I wonder what my life would have been like if I hadn't got Amanda to run it for me. Would I be here now? I doubt it. Or maybe I would. Maybe I would have excelled if I hadn't looked for her approval all the time.

With Shay safely in the car seat, I buckle up, press the ignition button and leave to find some form of life.

–

The village is a little busier today, the sun a welcome change from the recent wet days. In front of me an old man walks with an old woman across the street. They link arms, both warmed by grey coats, her with a red hat, him with a black one. I slow the car to a stop to let them by. Neither looks up as they drag their feet, and each other, across the road.

That could be me and Conor someday; holding each other up, having faced life's challenges. Doing the shuffle of survival. A part of me wants to ask them how they managed it. How did they learn to trust one another? How do I learn to trust Conor?

I find a parking space close to the coffee shop and unload Shay.

'I'll get better at this,' I tell myself, having finally secured the seat into the buggy. The path is worn, broken in places. Shay is being bopped around left, right and centre. I think he likes it though. His eyes are open wide, taking everything and nothing in. Thankfully, he's not objecting.

–

Shay is objecting. I've only just sat down with a frothy cup of coffee when I hear him. For a new baby he sure can cry loudly. Rocking the buggy won't do it. I'll have to take him out.

'Do you need a hand there, Laura?' Helen is standing behind me, her hand reaching out to hold the buggy in place while I lift Shay into my arms.

'Thanks Helen, I didn't see you.' I look around to see if Maggie is with her. I hope not. It's not that I don't like Maggie. I do. But I feel like I have to watch my p's and q's when she's around. I have to be careful not to say the wrong thing or ask the wrong question or I'll be subjected to the exclusive mother-in-law stare that she has perfected specifically for me. Helen sees me scan the room.

'Don't worry.' She smiles. 'I'm on my own. Do you mind if I sit here?' Helen points to the chair opposite mine, hanging her bag on the back of it before I have time to answer.

'The usual.' She nods up at the counter.

The bottle is still warm when I take it out of the bag and shake it. Shay's eyes widen, his tongue making an appearance. Like father, like son. The girl with the long dark hair who was in the hairdresser's the other day is placing Helen's order on the table. A pot of tea and a slice of apple pie.

'Would you like one?' Helen says, pulling the plate closer to her. 'Derbhla makes them herself... Don't you, Derbhla?'

Helen looks up at the girl who nods. I'm not in the mood for apple pie but I am trying to make friends here, and if it means eating Derbhla's homemade apple pie, well, so be it.

'Well if you made it yourself,' I say, smiling up at the girl who has nothing to say.

With Shay sleeping in the buggy, I finally get to drink my coffee. It's cold but I'm not going to complain. The last thing I want is to appear fussy. Not with the 'city girl' tag dangling around my neck.

Helen is picking the last few crumbs from the plate. We've already discussed the weather and the beautiful apple pie that should only ever be made with fresh apples, none of that processed stewed stuff. She even managed to apologise for arriving at the house unexpectedly the night of the funeral. Maggie had insisted. I told her it wasn't a bother and that she was welcome anytime.

We are getting on marvellously. Maybe I should take this opportunity to find out more.

'Have you been friends with Maggie long?' I say, putting my hand out to tighten the blanket over my little boy.

'Oh, all our lives, Laura. We both grew up here.'

'You must have been a big help to her when Seamus passed away.'

'Indeed, indeed. A terrible time it was for Maggie, such a horrible thing to happen.' Helen is draining the last of the tea out of the little flower-printed teapot.

'What happened exactly?'

'Well, I'm sure Conor told you.'

'He told me he died in an accident, I just presumed it was a car crash.'

'No no no. It wasn't a car crash. There was an accident in the factory.'

My cup is now empty, but I lift it to my lips anyway to keep her talking.

'He got locked into one of the vats and drowned.'

'What?'

I think my sudden jerk of disbelief has shocked Helen into retreating. She's sorry she said anything now.

'Sure, it was a long time ago. Accidents happen.' She turns her head to call for the bill. 'I better get going, Georgina is expecting me shortly,' she says.

Helen takes her bag and walks to the counter. Before leaving, she tells me she's paid for mine too. Nodding a thank you, I tell her I hope to see her again soon – then pity myself for meaning it. What has my life come to? Where are all the young people?

With Shay fast asleep in the buggy, I decide to make a move. I can understand why Conor never elaborated on his father's accident. What a horrible thing to have to recount. Poor Conor.

The other night he told his mother not to gossip about Vicky's murder. He made some comment about knowing how that felt. Rumours. There must have been rumours going around after his father's accident. But what were they?

Derbhla pulls the door open, making it easier for me to push the buggy out. With nowhere to be, I decide to indulge in the fresh air, take a walk to the church grounds, stroll around the graveyard. Maybe bump into some old ghosts.

Chapter Twenty-Eight

It's only one o'clock in the afternoon, how am I going to fill this day? Two laps of the graveyard is enough for anyone. I left the house hoping to make contact with the living, not the dead.

There was an abundance of flowers on Vicky's grave. I wonder what her headstone will say? That she went too early? That's what it says on Seamus's headstone. I can't help thinking about something so horrific happening. Conor is going to have to talk to me about it. He should want to talk to me about it. Maybe he has blocked it from his mind. Recalling the details might be too hard for him.

The day I asked him how his father died, I was sitting in the passenger seat of the fanciest car I'd ever been in. I can't remember how his father came up in conversation, but when I asked him what killed him, I expected him to say a heart attack or cancer.

With his eyes firmly on the road ahead, he told me he had died in an accident. Conor didn't elaborate and I didn't ask. I presumed it was too upsetting for him to rehash and he hasn't spoken about it since. The poor guy, I wonder was he there at the time? The most I ever heard him speak about his father was at our wedding when his loving words brought a tear to Maggie's eye.

With the highlights of the village completed, I get back into the car. Where to now?

I decide to call in at Conor's office. See exactly what goes on over there. It might help unravel the mystery surrounding the detective's visit. Or, I could find out more about the accident involving Conor's dad. But I must be discreet. I don't want Conor thinking I suspect anything is amiss.

Conor will be thrilled to see little Shay. He can show him the chair he'll probably be sitting on in twenty-five years. Or maybe not. Conor says he doesn't want any of his kids to feel like they have to take over the business. He wants them to make their own choices. Have the life they chose. Unlike himself. Bottling beer is a far cry from discovering stars.

It's a noble position for Conor to take, but we'll see if he still feels that way when one of his own progeny decide they don't want to play for Ballycall GAA Club and choose to play for an opposition team.

The road is narrow, lined with ditches and bramble. How the big trucks come in and out of the factory, I'll never know. I'm finding it hard enough in my car, and it's a big car.

Safer for the baby, Conor had said when I told him I'd rather have a small one. I was picturing myself parking in the busy city, nipping up and down to Dublin whenever I got the chance. But I had settled for what Conor wanted, because at the time, I thought he was nervous of cars because of his father.

The entrance to the brewery is closed and I don't know the code, so I'm forced to press a big intercom button on a pillar. A voice crackles from the speaker and says something I don't understand before a man appears, wearing a high-vis vest. I open the window, checking behind to see that Shay is still asleep.

'Can I help you, ma'am?' A middle-aged man with an evident love of calories, lowers his head to look in the window at me. A chin, darkened with stubble, ageing skin and green eyes full of life. He glances into the back of the vehicle before settling his stare on me. I imagine he was quite handsome in his day.

'I'm Laura, Conor's wife.'

'Laura,' he says, looking into the back seat again. 'So this must be little Shay.' His northern accent sounds as strong as the day he left school. No sign of the country lilt slipping into it. I wonder how long he's been working here.

'Isn't he a grand wee thing,' he says, 'much like his grandfather.' That answers my question. He knew Seamus.

'And how are you getting on here in the wilds?' He turns his attention back to me. 'I hope Conor is looking after you well.'

'He is.' I smile, eager to move on. 'Is he here… Arthur?' His name is stitched onto his jacket.

'He is indeed… hold on now.'

Arthur moves towards the hut and presses a button, releasing the barrier for me to drive through. I find a spot to park the car and prepare to unload.

Shay observes from the car seat that's hanging on my left arm. I walk towards the entrance door. The building is old, with grey dash, weather-worn walls and lots of small steel-framed windows. Conor says he'd love to knock it down and start again. He has a habit of doing that. I hope he doesn't apply the same principle to our marriage.

My right shoulder is strained from the weight of Shay's bag. Nappies, wipes, bottles, a change of clothes, creams, tissues. A lot of 'just in case' stuff. My own necessities have been reduced to a purse and one lipstick. But it doesn't bother me. I'm happy to be the perfect mother.

Unable to push the heavy door open, I drop the bag onto the ground and heave it, holding it open with my foot while I reach down to pick the bag up. I must look as graceful as an Olympic discus thrower attempting ballet.

Eventually my persistence pays off and I'm inside. The sweet grainy smell that permeates the air outside is a lot stronger in here. There are days the smell reaches right across to the village. Smell pollution. But no one complains, all happy to pocket the money this place brings to them through one channel or another.

Despite the building having a run-down look to the exterior, the inside is quite modern: a row of offices with heavy wooden doors; glass windows, coloured walls. There are signs too. Slogans. *Callbrew: the best beer for the best cheer.* And a display of awards, little stone plaques announcing how good the beer is year after year.

I'm dragging the heir to the throne down the corridor towards Conor's office, when I hear a female voice call me. It's Olive. She's sticking her head out from one of the office doors. She must have seen me pass by.

'Olive. Hi.'

Olive is wearing a tight leather skirt to the knee with a silver-grey silky shirt tucked inside. Her hair is tied back and her face is brightened with a big smile and very little make-up. I'm sorry now I didn't put more effort into what I was wearing.

'How lovely to see you,' she says, leaving the room and walking towards me. 'And Shay, how is the little lad?'

'He's great, eager to see his daddy at work.'

Olive bends down and brushes Shay's face with her finger.

'Hello, Shay.'

A gentle waft of unfamiliar perfume hits my nose. A pleasant, though brief reprieve from the smell of industry.

'Are you going to see your daddy?' she says.

'Yes, we were passing by, so just decided to pop in.'

'Well I'm sure he'll be delighted, won't he, Shay?'

Olive takes a step backwards and turns her attention from Shay to me.

'Will you drop into my office when you're finished with Conor? Deirdre would love to see the baby.'

'Of course I will,' I say, delighted with the opportunity to talk to women my own age.

Deirdre is Olive's assistant. Between them, they do almost everything in admin according to Conor, even the accounts. Apparently the guy who's supposed to do the accounts is away with the fairies and spends most of his time doing crosswords or Googling other possibilities for his life. Conor says he can't replace him because he's the son of one of Seamus's best friends. A man who helped him set up the business all those years ago. Just like Pat did. Conor seems to owe a lot of people on his dad's behalf.

—

Conor is on the phone when I open the door. I can see a smile warming his face. He is happy to see us. He ends his call, stands up from his desk and walks around to where I'm relieved to be unloading Shay onto a nearby chair.

The sun beams in from a nearby window catching Shay's eyes, so I turn the chair around. The comfort of Conor's kiss landing on my head relaxes me.

'Well, this is a nice surprise,' he says.

'I was bored, had to get out of the house.'

'You must be feeling back to normal so.'

'Almost.'

Conor removes his jacket before lifting his son out of the seat.

'Hey little man. How are you?'

His whole body oozes with happiness when he sits at his desk. Shay is wiggling in his arms. There are no signs of stress on Conor's face. No frown on his forehead. No pale skin or jittery moves. In fact Conor looks happier than I've ever seen him. Certainly not folding under the weight of whatever news Detective Fintan Ryan gave him. But he could be acting for my benefit. Again.

Olive knocks on the door before sticking her head in.

'Would you like a cup of tea? Coffee?'

She's so nice to me. Maybe she's the one I should be trying to get information from.

'I don't have time,' Conor says. 'I've got that meeting in ten minutes... but Laura might.'

Conor stands, cooing at his son as he walks over to put Shay back in the car seat. Feeling slightly awkward, like a fish out of water amongst these two former lovers, I look to Conor for guidance. Should I have coffee with his ex?

'Go on,' he says, winking at me. 'You're in no rush, are you?'

Nodding my head, I accept Olive's offer. 'Tea would be lovely.'

Olive leaves the room. Conor is putting on his jacket to follow.

He kisses me on the forehead. 'I'm glad you called in today.'

I wonder if he would say that if he knew I was here searching for information. Hoping to find some clue as to what is going on with him. What was the detective afraid of? Why was that card sent to me?

With Shay's car seat on my arm, I walk towards the door.

It must feel strange for Conor, having to walk day after day through the building where his father died in such a horrible accident. Maybe he'll open up to me if I walk beside him.

'I'd love you to take me around the brewery someday to see the giant vats and all the beer flowing through the pipes,' I say.

Conor rushes in front of me to open the door.

'Sure, we'll do that someday,' he says.

Walking out the door I feel my nerves growing. I didn't expect to be having tea with my husband's ex today. But I'm prepared to go wherever the search takes me. I might get some useful information about Vicky Murphy, or, if I can pluck up the courage, drop Noel's name into the conversation. Maybe she'll allude to why she wouldn't shake his hand at Vicky's funeral.

Chapter Twenty-Nine

'Ah, you get used to it, don't even notice it after a while,' Deirdre says, in a much gruffer voice and certainly with a heartier attitude than Olive's. I didn't know how to break the ice when they'd stopped swooning over the baby, so I asked how they lived with the constant smell.

'When I started here it was worse,' she continues.

Olive is pouring hot water into three mugs.

'There was no dividing wall between the offices and the factory... the noise was pretty bad too... biscuit?' She takes a packet from a drawer and places it on the table.

Shay is nodding off in the car seat on the floor beside me. His little eyes begging him to close them. I've already had apple pie that I didn't want today and now I find myself lifting a chocolate digestive from the plate in front of me. My plan to get back into a size ten for the christening is not going well. This had better be worth it.

Olive is mainly quiet, contributing just a word here and there or a laugh. She's allowing Deirdre to conduct the conversation. When I get the chance, I bring up the subject of all the presents Shay received, and the cards. Deirdre nods like a car toy, Olive listens and smiles. 'But there was one card...' I say, my gaze focused on Olive. 'Whoever sent it forgot to put their name on it... I'm afraid I won't be able to thank them.' I say this hoping it might stir a telltale sign in Olive. A red face, a freeze, something that might signal she knows what I'm talking about. But there's nothing, just a shrug of the shoulders as she lifts her cup to her lips.

'Don't worry about that, Laura,' Deirdre says. 'We'll tell you as soon as they start complaining that you never thanked them. That sort of talk travels quick around here.' She laughs, stands up and walks over towards the kettle. Olive grins. 'You can bet on that,' she says. I thought about mentioning what was written in the card. And I might have if I was alone with Olive, but I fear Deirdre may be lead singer in the local gossip choir so I say nothing. After all, Olive might just be a good actress.

'As I said, Laura, I think you're going to have to wait until someone gives out about you,' Deirdre says as she walks back to her chair. I take this as my signal to leave.

'Thanks for the tea and biscuits,' I say, standing and noticing the photographs on the wall behind me. 'Oh, who are all these?' I say moving closer to the wall.

'Oh, that's the Caldwell brewery family album,' Deirdre says.

And that's exactly what it looks like. There are snaps from the Caldwell brewery family fair, the Caldwell brewery Christmas party, the Caldwell brewery summer fair. It looks like everyone in the village gets invited. Pride of place at the centre of the shot is Conor, holding a trophy in the air with one arm. My stomach turns when I see his other arm wrapped around Olive. *Brewery of the year 2015* engraved on a gold tag at the bottom. Behind the happy couple, hundreds of workers all with their hands in the air cheering. My eyes concentrate on Conor's. He's glancing down at Olive, smiling. The same smile he gives to me now. I feel myself deflating on the spot. I knew they were a couple but seeing them in action has upset me. I swallow hard, knowing I should say something. But what? This is so awkward.

'Caldwell brewery must do great work for the community,' I say, turning away from the photo and stepping towards Shay. I realize now how much of an outsider I am. Shay is my only link in this heavy chain.

'Yes, they certainly keep the village alive,' Deirdre says. I'm tucking the blanket tightly around my baby boy. 'There's over three hundred employed here,' Deirdre continues. 'All happy.'

'That's great to hear. Was it always that way? Has no one ever had a problem working here?' Olive turns. 'What do you mean?' I'm after backing myself into a corner. Olive doesn't like my question. 'Oh, I was just wondering if there's ever any trouble with all those people employed. There must be some issues now and then.'

'Not really,' Deirdre says. 'We're fairly lucky that way. Of course, there was that incident last month when...'

'No,' Olive interrupts her. 'No trouble. As Deirdre says, we're very lucky.' Olive stands and lifts Shay's bag. 'Here, I'll help you with that,' she says, making sure I leave. Deirdre is wide-eyed behind her desk, looking at Olive.

With Shay on my arm, I hurry out of the building. I can't believe Olive interrupted Deirdre like that. It was so obvious she wanted to shut her up. But why? What was Olive trying to keep from me? Maybe she just wanted me to feel that it was none of my business. I might have taken the man, but the brewery was hers. I'll have to ask Conor about it. Is there a disgruntled employee on the loose? I need to know. They could have sent the card.

Chapter Thirty

Noel walks into the kitchen, a grey suit clinging to his muscled body. He has a lot going for him in the looks department. Brown hair with a reddish glow, always gelled back off his face, showing off his sculpted cheekbones and flawless skin to perfection. His smile displays a set of perfect teeth. His brown eyes are always alert, nervous, like he's waiting for something to happen.

Conor was only in the door twenty minutes before Noel arrived. Thankfully, I had already confronted him about the disgruntled employee. I didn't want that sitting in my box of worries for the night. It turns out, it wasn't so much an incident as a disagreement, something to do with the accounts.

Mark Dunne, a nephew of one of Caldwell's employees, had been put on placement at the brewery. He had been studying accountancy and needed a few month's work. Conor didn't go into much detail except to say it didn't work out, and after two weeks he had had to let him go. The uncle hadn't been happy about it. I wonder what Amanda will think of this. Conor brushed it off as no big deal but Conor doesn't know about the card. If Noel hadn't walked into the house, I might have told him.

'I need a word,' Noel says, leaning over the crib to where Shay sleeps peacefully. If that's my cue to leave, I don't register it.

'What's up, bro?' Conor says, taking a large file out of his briefcase and placing it on the table. He comes home with paperwork every night and drops it on the table. Then places it back in the briefcase the next morning not having looked at it. Whatever his plan is when he leaves the office, it disappears when he arrives home to his family. Unless of course, it's something he doesn't want to leave on the premises when he's not there.

'It's about the christening. The godfather thing.' Noel lifts his face from the crib as he speaks. 'It turns out I've to go away for a while, three months, maybe more.'

'Where are you going?'

'Oman, of all places. The company are setting up a new system and I've to supervise the installation.'

Emptying the dishwasher, I listen intently but say nothing. If Noel can't be Shay's godfather, I won't lose any sleep over it.

'When are you off?'

'The end of next week sometime.'

'Jesus, Noel, they didn't give you much notice, did they?'

'They did mention it a while back. Abbie wanted me to go but I said no at the time but now I'm thinking it's a nice bonus. A great opportunity. We might like to get one of these for ourselves.' He rests his hand gently on Shay's head. 'And when that happens the idea of working away from home will probably be less attractive.'

Abbie must be thrilled about getting Noel to move to Oman. She's been at him for a long time to make the move. It's her father's business and she wants Noel to rise to the top of it. Going to Oman will help.

Wanting a child has been top of Abbie's list since she and Noel married three years ago. She told me about it when we disclosed our wonderful news to them. Apparently Noel wasn't ready. I'm surprised Abbie didn't put up a fight sooner to get her way. She was brought up getting whatever she wanted whenever she wanted. Noel is always dropping her wealthy upbringing into the conversation, commenting on how spoilt she is. Well now he's going to Oman, just like Abbie wants. I wonder what changed his mind all of a sudden?

The dishwasher is empty now. Taking my time, I allocate the cutlery to its designated slots, considering how convenient this all is – if Noel is the married man Vicky was having the affair with, this sudden exit is perfectly timed.

'And you'll be back when?' Conor says.

'That's the thing, I don't know. These things have a habit of dragging out and I don't want to mess with your plans for the christening. Abbie said I should tell you straight away.'

I knew it was unlikely that Noel had remembered the christening.

Conor is rubbing his hands in his hair, trying to activate his thought process. With no knives left to sort, I move out from behind the island.

'Well thanks for letting us know, Noel, and don't worry about it,' I say. 'Hopefully Shay will have a little brother or sister sometime in the future. You can be godfather then.'

Noel looks at me like he's only just noticed I'm in the room. 'Laura, I'm sorry about this. I really was looking forward to becoming Shay's godfather.'

'And you still can be.' Conor says.

What? No, he can't. 'How? He won't be here, Conor.' My voice sounds harsher than I intended but Conor needs to know I'm not having a proxy godfather at my son's christening. Conor continues the conversation like I'm not in the room.

'When did you say you had to leave?'

'Next week sometime – the end of the week, I think. The flights are not confirmed yet.'

'So you're here this Sunday?'

'Yes but—'

'Look, leave it with me. All is not lost.'

I'm speechless. Is Conor really suggesting what I think he's suggesting? With his hand now resting on Noel's shoulder, he says, 'I really do want you to be godfather to Shay, Noel.'

Noel is nodding and smiling like he's just been awarded a gold star from his teacher. I'm left with my mouth open, unable to utter a word. Is Conor suggesting we christen Shay on Sunday? He'll only be two weeks old. And we've nothing organised! Has he lost all sense of reason?

The two lads continue their conversation out to the door.

The priest. The church. The food. The invitations. The decorations. The christening robe. My size ten outfit.

I'm lining up all the reasons to abandon this idea before it takes hold, so I can list them to Conor as soon as he walks back in here. Surely if he doesn't want to ask his cousin, he could ask one of his many friends from the football club? I want time to organise the christening. I've been looking forward to it.

Hovering over the crib, I rub my finger across Shay's cheek and attempt to swallow the sadness that descends on me. It comes quite often now.

'Well… what do you think?' Conor walks back into the room like he's swallowed fourteen cans of Red Bull on his journey.

'I think it's a terrible idea.'

'Why? What's the problem?'

'Well, the priest for a start, you have to give him notice.'

I want to cry and to tell Conor this is a mad idea and it's not going to happen, but his excitement appears to be shooting off the charts. Removing his jacket, he throws it over the back of the chair where it slips to the ground. I'm almost expecting him to roll up his sleeves. He doesn't. He takes up his phone and opens it.

'I'm sure Father Cormac can't wait to splash water on a baby's head again. There hasn't been a christening around here in a long time. It's not like the city, Laura. We don't have to queue up.'

'But I want to organise it properly. I want to invite the right people.'

Eventually Conor pays attention to my objection. He puts the phone down and walks over to me. Running his hands through my hair, he looks into my eyes.

'We can do this, Laura. Together we can do anything we put our minds to.'

I don't want to. But the words don't leave my lips. Conor is going ahead with this whether I want it or not. He's not used to anyone telling him what he can and cannot do. I'm in his house, in his village. This is Conor's world. I'm just a visitor.

Chapter Thirty-One

On a clear bright day, I can see the top of the bridge that crosses the river Call in the distance. I'm looking at it now, the angled steel sculpture piercing the beautiful view like some goad at nature. *Look what I can do.*

Before the bridge was built, it took an hour to get to Dublin in a car. Now it takes forty minutes.

'That's nearly four hours a week,' said my husband, the mathematician. 'Think of what someone could do with that extra time.'

I wanted to say '*build bridges*' but it was early on in the relationship. It was at a time when I thought my safest response to everything he said was a nod, a yes, or a smile.

It was early on in my pregnancy too. I was happy, at last. This was my chance for a normal life. To take back what I'd lost. Marrying Conor would be the best thing I could do. He proposed as soon as he heard I was pregnant. And now that we were committed to one another, Conor wanted me to meet his mother. Nervous wasn't the word. Mothers and I hadn't gone well up to now. I spent most of the journey to Ballycall worrying about what would happen if she didn't like me. I tried to prod Conor for some information.

'What's she like?' I had asked him when he called to finalise the details of when he'd pick me up. I had no car at the time, I didn't need one. Imanage was a ten-minute walk from my apartment. No bridge required.

Conor had answered like any other man. 'Smaller than me. Dark hair. I think she has blue eyes.'

But that's not what I had meant. I wanted to know if I was likely to be licked by a kitten or mauled by a lion.

As it happened, Maggie was somewhere in the middle. A litten. Very nice at first. She congratulated me on the baby and assured me I'd have everything I needed. She admired my clothes and reminisced about her own pregnancy, showing me photos of Conor as a baby as I twiddled with the dessert. My stomach was full to capacity having just finished off his mammy's version of Sunday lunch — a huge plate covered with beef, gravy, roasters and veg. Some people never forget the famine.

Everything was going well. Conor was relaxed and I had managed to relax too. It was only when she asked me about my own mother that I saw a shift in her attitude.

'I don't talk to my mother,' I said.

The room fell silent. Maggie stared at me like I'd just insulted her cooking, before getting up from the table and taking some empty plates to the sink. Conor had quickly changed the subject.

Nod. Yes. Smile. I should have said she was dead.

—

After bathing and dressing Shay, I lie him down in the crib. The nurse is due to call at eleven so we both have to look shiny and happy. No complaints. No questions. In and out with her and hopefully that will be the end of it.

After showering, I dress in my finest 'coping well with motherhood' clothes. A pair of black jeans and a freshly ironed pink shirt. Happy with my costume, I practice my smile in the mirror. *Laura, you look the part.*

Out on the landing the sound of gravel crunching gets my attention. Is that a car? I rush to the window at the front of the house and pray the nurse isn't here already, I haven't had a cup of coffee yet.

A car approaches but it's not the nurse. My heart stops. Everything blurs, but I can still make out the police vehicle moving up the driveway.

'Fuck.' I rush into the bedroom, scrabbling for the phone with trembling hands.

'Conor. Quick.' I can barely breathe.

'What is it? What's wrong, Laura?' His voice is panicked.

'Come home, quick.' My words are barely audible between gasping breaths.

'Is Shay okay? Did something happen to Shay?'

'The police are here.'

With the phone still in my hand, I return to the window and see one of the two investigators assigned from Dublin to the Vicky Murphy case getting out of the car with Detective Fintan Ryan. Where are they going? Why are they walking past the door?

Pat. They must be walking down the side of the house to Pat's place. Back in the bedroom I wait for them to appear on the pathway leading to the forest. My heart is thumping, my phone gripped tightly in my hand. Where are they?

Then I see them, walking away from our house and down towards the forest. I close my eyes and urge my body to relax. They're not here for Conor. Not this time anyway. They're here for Pat. Does Pat know something? Did Pat kill Vicky?

Conor's phone is engaged when I call it, so I send him a text message telling him the cops are looking for Pat. No need to come home. Taking deep breaths, I flop down onto the bed and close my eyes. No sooner has my body relaxed, when the doorbell rings.

The nurse walks in, all smiles. She doesn't comment on the police vehicle parked beside her Nissan.

'I'm a bit early, Laura. I hope I haven't come at a bad time.'

'No, it's fine.' Shay is in my arms. I'm flustered and unprepared. My face is probably white, or green from the shock. For a brief moment I thought the cops were here to arrest Conor, especially after overhearing the conversation he had with Fintan the other day. My nerves are still rattled. The last thing I need now is this nurse asking me questions.

'Okay,' she says. 'Where would you like me to go?'

'Oh, we'll go in here.'

I direct her into the front room. I don't want the cops in my view, to be reminded of the card, the photo, Vicky's coffin coming up the aisle.

'Are you okay?' she says, gently placing her hand on my shoulder. The sudden caring gesture ignites my vulnerability and I start to cry. Full-on crying, like a baby... like Shay.

'Here, let me hold the baby. You sit down,' she says, taking Shay from my grip.

'I'm sorry, I just got a fright earlier and I feel a bit...'

'That's okay. Do you want to talk about it?'

Do I want to talk about it? That for a brief moment this morning I thought the cops were here to arrest my husband? That my whole life flashed in front of me? That every doubt I ever had had become a reality, a quick

147

preview of my very own hell? Do I want to talk about it?

'No.'

'Well if you change your mind, Laura, I'm here. Can I get you some water?'

'No, I'm fine really, it was nothing. I'm just a bit emotional lately.'

'Of course you are and you're entitled to be. Your body is still adjusting…' Her voice drifts off into the usual spiel. I sit, looking at her lips move. After a few minutes she checks Shay still has all his body parts and asks a few questions about his routine. Then she hands him back to me. The warmth of the little bundle against my body brings me comfort.

Nurse Elaine removes a file from the leather briefcase at her feet.

'I'm sorry I didn't have your details with me the last time.'

She places the file on her lap and opens it. *Don't tell me she's not finished.* All I want is for her to leave so I can see what's going on out the back. Why are the cops with Pat? She said she was happy with Shay's progress. She can see I'm doing a great job. So, what now? Why doesn't she leave?

'The last time I was here, Laura, you voiced concern over the drugs you were given at the hospital.'

Nurse Elaine leans in closer to me.

'You wanted to know if they could make you hallucinate.'

Sweet Jesus, and people say our health system isn't efficient.

'Oh, don't worry about that, I didn't know what I was talking about, I was just a bit…'

Bonkers. That's what I was. I remember it now, trying to figure out if I could have imagined the card.

The nurse is still leaning forward, looking at me.

'Tired, I was very tired.'

'And do you still imagine things?'

Shifting on the seat, knowing now how crazy I must have sounded, I shake my head. 'God, no.'

'Okay.' She lowers her head to glance through the file. I'm sorry I ever opened my mouth to her the first time she called.

'Do you think, Laura, you could have a touch of post-natal depression?'

My eyes shift from Shay to the wall directly in front of me. I don't blame her asking that question. On her first visit I told her I might be hallucinating and now, this time, I burst into tears before she even has a chance to sit down. How do I explain to her everything's dandy when she's not here?

'No, I'm fine. Honestly. I'm feeling great, actually.' I smile at her. But this woman doesn't want to take no for an answer.

'Are you certain, Laura? Because there are things...'

'No. I'm sure, I'm fine, no depression or anything like that. In fact, I've never been happier.'

Looking back at the file, Elaine turns the page as if searching for something to contradict me with. I'm rocking Shay gently from side to side, eager to find out what is going on with the cops, when she speaks.

'And after the birth of your first baby, Laura, did you suffer from any postnatal depression?'

Chapter Thirty-Two

I wonder how long he's been standing there. Did he hear?

Conor is in the hallway when I finally get the nurse to leave. She insists on calling again next week and I have to agree or she will never go.

'Everything okay?' Conor says, putting his arms out to take Shay from me.

'Yes,' I say, looking closely at his eyes for any sign that he might have been listening. When he leans forward and kisses my head, I'm reassured.

'Well. Are we doing a good job?' He jokes to the nurse.

'Indeed you are,' she says.

Nurse Elaine pulls her jacket closed and walks to the door. I rush after her and open it before she gets there. She hands me a piece of paper with a mobile number on it.

'I'll see you next week but if you need me in the meantime Laura, do call.'

I stop just short of pushing her out the door. Conor is looming in the background, imitating Shay's gurgling noises.

'Will do. Thanks.'

Breathing a sigh of relief when the door eventually closes, I glance through the side window, making sure she gets into her car and leaves.

'The cops didn't stay long.' Conor says.

It's then I notice their car is gone.

'No, they didn't. Did you see my text telling you they were here to talk to Pat?' I move past Conor into the kitchen. He follows me.

'I was halfway home when I saw it, thought I'd continue, take the opportunity to see my little boy.' He kisses Shay. 'And my beautiful wife, of course.'

'I wonder what they wanted with Pat. Do you think he knows something?'

'Pat? Huh. No, they're probably just ticking a box.'

Conor places Shay into his baby bouncer and goes to the fridge. His tall body hovers in search of something to eat. He looks so nice, so sexy in his dark suit. I don't want to lose this man.

'Why were you scared, Laura?'

'What?'

With a slice of ham in his hand, he turns and looks at me before shoving it into his mouth in one go.

'When the police came. You were scared.'

'I… I don't know. I guess anyone would get scared if they saw the cops at their door. They don't usually call with good news.'

Conor laughs. He turns back to the fridge and takes another slice of ham in his hand.

'Well I don't want you to worry, Laura, you sounded extremely panicked on the phone. You have nothing to worry about.' Shoving the meat in his mouth, he walks over and holds my face in his hands. When he's swallowed the mouthful, Conor pulls me close to him and kisses me. The heat of his body against mine makes me feel safe. For a brief moment, I relax, forget about the cops, the card, the nurse, the words I heard over the baby monitor. But it doesn't last long. When he pulls away, I feel my strength leave with him.

Chapter Thirty-Three

And so it begins. The circus. Or what would definitely pass for one. Conor invited Maggie to help me arrange the christening because, as he sees it, she's very good at that sort of thing.

Apparently Father Cormac was delighted to be doing the ceremony this Sunday.

What a week it's turning out to be for him. A funeral and a christening. He even thanked Conor, believing the decision was made to boost the morale of the village, not to facilitate Noel.

The phone call to Amanda didn't get the same reception. She thought it was a mad idea and seemed a bit taken aback that I hadn't put up a better fight. She expressed disappointment at not being able to go on a shopping trip for the outfits we were going to look lovely in. She hummed and hawed about her availability, saying she had plans for Sunday. But eventually she caved in and became excited.

–

'Lots to do, lots to do.' Maggie walks into the kitchen with an old notebook in her hand, her hair and makeup put on hold due to the immediacy of the visit. I notice her age is more pronounced in the greyness of her skin, the wrinkles on her forehead, around her eyes. Her dry hair is tied up in a bun, revealing grey strands that she usually manages to conceal. Maggie's energy level doesn't seem to be suffering though. She's talking non-stop.

Shay lies on my lap. This little person, unaware of the celebration being arranged in his honour. Leaning forward, I take a deep breath, inhaling his smell, it's like airborne Xanax, relaxing me while the other woman in the room goes on and on and on.

Balloons, like we didn't have enough of them last week. The cake, which has already been ordered from someone Maggie knows and believes to be the best cake-maker in the whole world. The music, some local DJ who caters for all ages, according to Maggie. 'We'll just have it airing in the background, not too loud.'

I notice her use of the word 'we,' and smile to myself.

The food will be supplied by the same company who catered for Seamus's funeral four years earlier. The best caterers around, they do all the big events. Suddenly Maggie has my interest. Not that I had intended questioning her about Seamus's death, but the opportunity has presented itself. I'm going in.

'That must have been a very big crowd,' I say, my eyes still focused on little Shay.

'Oh, they came from everywhere. I couldn't believe the amount of people. The church was bursting at the seams and even the church grounds were full. Seamus was a very popular man.'

'It must have been a terrible shock for you, losing your husband so suddenly.' I lift my gaze to look at Maggie and notice her abandon the notes she's been scrawling in her diary to look out the window.

Silence. Maggie is staring into the distance, her lips pursed, her eyes drooping with sadness. I wasn't trying to ignite her grief, but clearly, I have.

'You must miss him,' I say.

Shay has fallen asleep in my arms.

'Every moment of every day,' Maggie says.

Turning her head, she looks at me placing Shay into the crib. 'But life goes on, Laura. You don't notice it at first, going through the motions, relying on the clock to tell you what to do. Time to eat, time to sleep, time to wash.' She moves from the stool and comes over to the crib. 'But now I have you, little man.' Bending over the crib, Maggie kisses Shay on the forehead.

I don't know whether to continue pushing her. I want to ask her who was there when he died but I decide not to. I didn't expect to stir such emotion. Maggie had given me the impression that she was in full control of everything, that her life was wonderful. But evidently it's not. Her heart is broken. She just does a good job at hiding it.

'I haven't gone near the place since it happened,' Maggie says, dragging me back on board my mission. If she wants to talk, I'm all ears.

'It was so horrific. And then having to wait for the inquest.' She walks back over to the island, a slight hint of anger in her voice.

'Did it take long… the inquest?'

'The best part of a year… thankfully it reported accidental death. A worry buried.'

The stool scrapes the floor when Maggie pulls on it, forcing both of us to clench our teeth.

'You'll have to do something about that, Laura, get Conor to put grips on the legs. I think I have some at home.'

She pulls the notebook on the counter closer to her, pushing on her glasses before glancing through the list.

'Now all we've left to do is invite people,' she says.

Not wanting to question her any more on the details of her husband's death, I listen to her list all the people 'we' have to invite. The fact that I don't know most of them doesn't seem to faze her and there is no objection on my part.

Suddenly, I shiver. The person who sent the card is probably on that list. They will come to my party, eat my food, drink my drink. They will laugh with all the other guests. I won't be able to tell who it is. I'll have to smile and be polite and all the time they'll be sniggering in the pit of their belly because they'll know.

–

Maggie eventually leaves, but not before mentioning that I probably want to get started on Conor's dinner. I know that's how she sees me: the wife, the one who must obey, *'til death do us part* and all that. It's probably how it was for her, a servant to her man, until death did part them. I hope she doesn't cause me any problems when I tell her I'm planning to go back to work part-time. I never thought I'd want to but it's becoming clear I'll need some sort of stimulation if I'm to survive here.

When the door is closed, I rest my back against the solid wood and take a breath. Trying to appear nonchalant and not ask a hundred questions was hard.

I think of Conor, how he lives with the reality of his father's death and never mentions it to me. Not even a slip of the tongue when he was drunk. Conor must have it locked up somewhere safe in his mind. And if he can do that, what else is locked in that safe?

Chapter Thirty-Four

There's a robin walking along the ledge outside the window, his red breast illuminated by the ray of sunshine catching his feathers. Stirring the pepper sauce in the pot, I smile. That never happened when I lived in the city. No feathered friend ever visited me there. The only sign of birds near my window on the third floor of Royal Ashton Apartments was the constant blobs of bird shit that were cleaned off by the maintenance crew on a not too regular basis.

Licking the spoon before placing it down beside the pot, I wipe my hands on a sheet of kitchen roll and walk over to Shay.

'Hi baby, wait 'til you see who came to visit you.' His body feels stronger when I lift him, his flopping arms and legs replaced now with eager movements. Nurse Elaine would be so happy with me.

'Do you want to see the birdy?' I say. Shay knows something exciting is going to happen. His eyes are wide, eager; his tongue jots in and out through his blood-red lips. Poor kid is probably expecting a bottle but it's too early.

'Not yet Shay, first we're going to meet a robin.'

Huddling him close to my chest, I take Shay over to the kitchen window. The robin is still picking at something on the ledge.

'Look, Shay, that's a robin.' His eyes won't move their focus from me, so I tilt him slightly, but he doesn't look at the robin; he shifts his eyes sideways, continuing to search me out.

'Not to worry baby, there'll be loads of robins for you to see.'

I'm about to move away from the window when I notice Conor at the end of the garden. He's talking to Pat. That's strange; Conor's home early today. Why didn't he come directly into the house first?

Both men are standing at the edge of the forest, Pat, hands in pockets, kicking the ground below his feet. His head is bent, looking at his shoes instead of Conor. Conor seems slightly agitated, his hand extended, pointing. He's quite a distance from me but I can still tell he's not happy. Conor is arguing with Pat. I don't like this.

A part of me wants to go down and find out what's going on, but Shay is lolling off to sleep in my arms. Gently I rock him from side to side, one eye on his dozing face the other on the two men at the back of the garden.

Beep beep. Shit, the sauce is spilling out over the edge of the pot activating the hob alarm. Rushing to stop it, I pull the handle to the side and switch the ring off.

The smallest job is taking all my efforts and I'm failing, my strength divided between the reality of what I see and what I fear. How long can I go on pushing my worries to the back of my mind? Hoping they will just go away, facing up to nothing. My biggest fear is that I'll fail Shay. He'll be boiling over someday in need of my attention and I won't be there to pull the handle.

After placing Shay in the crib, I tuck the blanket around his warm body. 'Don't worry little boy, Mammy is not going to let you down.'

In the background, I hear Conor walking into the room. He drops his briefcase in the usual spot and walks over to me. The anger etched on his face reduces immediately when he looks into the crib.

'How's my little boy?' he says, bending over to kiss his cheek.

'Great.'

'And you?' Conor kisses me on the forehead.

'I'm fine. What happened with Pat?'

'What do you mean?' he says, stepping away and removing his jacket.

'Why were you arguing with him?'

'I wasn't arguing. We were just talking.'

What will I do? Conor thinks he can just fob me off. Tell me nothing. Until now, I thought he was trying to protect me by not sharing what was going on with Detective Fintan Ryan or the details of his father's death and today, the argument with Pat. Now, I'm not so sure.

'I saw you through the window, Conor. That wasn't just talking, your face is still red, I want to know what's going on.'

Conor needs to know he can tell me anything, that I'm not going to judge him, I just want to know what's going on. If Pat did something, I need to know. He lives in my back garden. He lives in Shay's back garden.

Throwing his jacket on the back of the high stool before grabbing a bottle of water, Conor moves to the island counter that stands between us. The bottle cap rolls to the floor when he puts it on the counter. Conor pours water down his throat. I'm watching him, waiting for him to speak.

'He's a fucking idiot, that man.'

Wow, that's new, Conor cursing! What has Pat done? Whatever it is, he's clearly upset Conor. I've never heard him give out about Pat before, ever. In fact he had a notebook of nice things to say about him when he broke the news to me that Pat lived out the back.

'Why, what happened?' Taming the excitement exploding inside me, I casually walk to the cooker to continue destroying the dinner.

Conor picks up the three letters on the counter that arrived earlier. Bills mostly – no more threatening cards, I hope. He drops them back down without opening them. Resting both hands on the counter he leans forward, anger shaping his face.

'You're not going to believe what that fool told the detective from Dublin.'

'What?' My heart leaps when I hear the word detective.

'He told them he saw me leaving the house in the middle of the night, the night Vicky Murphy was killed.'

Rendered silent, I drop the scourer that I was using to remove the burnt sauce from the hob and slowly turn around.

'Why would he say that, Conor?'

'I don't know.'

'And did you leave the house?' Searching my thoughts for an explanation, I feel my breathing picking up speed. 'Did the brewery alarm go off that night?'

Conor is rubbing his hand through his hair, staring at the countertop before looking up at me.

'Yes... but he shouldn't have said anything to that detective. Now they're going to drag me into this shit.'

'But you didn't do anything, Conor, don't worry...' but my words dissolve in my mouth. Conor left the house the night Vicky Murphy was killed. I never heard him.

My heart is thumping like a bass drum at a New Orleans funeral but I must appear calm on the outside. With my hand across the back of his neck, I lean against his body, closer to his face.

'It will be alright, Conor. What did they say?'

Conor shrugs from under my embrace and straightens himself. He looks bothered, lifting the letters in his hand before throwing them back down on the counter.

'What did who say?'

'The investigators, when they spoke to you.'

'They didn't speak to me yet.'

'Well, how do you know that Pat told them then?'

He looks at me, mouth closed, eyes fixed on mine. He's deciding whether to tell me or not.

'Who told you, Conor?'

'I got a call, someone giving me the heads-up.'

'Who?' I can guess who, but I want him to tell me.

'Ah look, it doesn't matter, it'll probably come to nothing.'

'Who was it, Conor?'

Shoulders slumped, he takes his jacket from the back of the chair and walks towards the door.

'Fintan called me.'

'Fintan?'

'Ye, he just wanted to warn me. He's a good man, Fintan.'

'Can he do that?'

'Probably not supposed to… but we go back a long way and I'm glad he did. At least now I'm prepared.'

—

When Conor leaves the room, I lift two cuts of steak from the plate by the hob and slap them on the hot griddle.

Their sizzle is now the only sound in the room. My hands are shaking. Conor left the house to fix the alarm that night. The night before Shay was born. Why didn't I hear the phone beep? And Pat, if he told the cops he saw Conor leave during the night, does he believe Conor had something to do with Vicky's death? Could Pat have sent the card? My mind is scrambled. My stomach sick. My husband has no alibi.

Chapter Thirty-Five

With my hand firmly gripping the wheel, I cross the Call bridge and watch the clear blue sky lead the way to the city. Nothing much was said last night. Conor admitted he left the house to fix the alarm, but with all the excitement around Shay's early entrance into the world, he hadn't even thought about it until Fintan rang to tell him what Pat said. I spent the whole night with my heart hovering close to my mouth. What does this mean? Surely the cops will believe him, the alarm going off is probably traceable. So why is he so worried?

I wanted to tell Conor I knew the circumstances around his father's death, but it wasn't the right time, not with what had happened with Pat. He did ask how I'd got on with his mother, and if everything was in place for Sunday, but I could see a lot of the spark had gone out of him. I told him she was doing a great job and seemed to have everything in hand. I was hoping he'd suggest we cancel it, but no, the show must go on, and with Maggie directing it, I'm sure it will.

Which is why I'm going to Dublin. Having handed over all control of the party, I'm claiming the christening gown. Maggie doesn't know yet. She'll probably arrive with some yellow dress, bragging about the intricate lace-work, handmade by virgins at sunrise a thousand years ago on the side of a mountain, and worn by generations of the

Caldwell family. Well, she can keep it. I'm putting Shay in something I want.

The traffic builds the closer I get to Dublin. Shay sleeps in his car seat by my side, the hood on his blue jumpsuit cloaking his tiny face. I picked it specially to complement his eyes. It's his first time meeting my old work colleagues and I want him to impress.

In the distance, the familiarity of a world that used to be mine slowly appears. I see the Ha'penny Bridge, its timber gangway a monument to the rare old times, and the Millennium Bridge, a more modern affair, reflective of the progress we've made. Or have we? People still seem eager to get to the other side.

Nostalgia loosens my smile the closer I get. I miss this place: the buildings, the crowds, the choices. Ballycall is too low-rise; the church is the tallest building. The forest surrounding the village means you can't see the place until you're actually in it. Like it was built to be hidden from the rest of the world. I wonder, was that planned? Did some old farmer decide hundreds of years ago that he didn't want his neighbour looking in at him? Don't let your right hand know what your left hand is doing. It wouldn't surprise me. Even now there's a sense of secrecy about the place.

The car park isn't too jammed so I find a space where I can comfortably take Shay out of the car and put him in his buggy without breaking my neck.

Out on the street, my steps are slow. I want to enjoy this walk to my old office, take note of everything I pass. There's a new doughnut shop open on the corner, rows of colourful, tempting treats arranged in the window.

Beyond that, an array of cafes and restaurants that I regularly passed on my way to work, my eyes glued to the footpath or the phone in my hand. I should have visited more of them, instead of always going to the same place – Luigiani's – ordering the same food and expecting the same result. It's too easy to appreciate what you had, after the fact.

The smell of spicy food wafting out from one of the restaurants makes me want to go inside and eat straight away. Maybe Amanda and I could go there for lunch?

With more pace in my rhythm, I arrive outside Imanage a little bit earlier than I expected. Pushing my backside into the door, I open it, dragging the buggy in with me.

The foyer is empty except for a young girl sitting behind a large multicoloured reception area to my left. I don't recognise her – she must be new. I'm disappointed there's no one here to greet me and my baby. I wasn't expecting a band to be playing but a familiar face would have been nice.

'Hi,' I say, watching the young girl lift her head from whatever she's doing.

'Hello, welcome to Imanage. How can I help you?'

'Er yes, I'm Laura, I used to work here. Where you're sitting actually.' I pause for her to comment but she forces a smile and nods.

'Can you buzz Amanda Wright for me please?' I say.

The girl lifts the phone and waits... No answer.

'Oh, well, can I just pop through? They're expecting me.'

I'm pretty sure she's just about to tell me I can't, when I hear the heavy voice of Pete Gunner.

'Laura,' he says, walking straight over. 'How are you? Great to see you again.'

Pete congratulates me on the birth of Shay. He tells me how well I'm looking and invites me to accompany him into the main office area. Unlocking the safety clip on the buggy, I push it through the door that Pete is holding open.

'How are things, Laura? Are you happy with the move? Amanda tells me you're loving it.'

'Yes, it's great, takes a bit of getting used to, but so far so good.'

The diamond on my finger reflects in the large glass-mirrored wall. I see expensive clothes, a Gucci bag hanging from a state-of-the-art buggy, the fairytale ending they all must see. I manage to hold my smile in place while the show goes on. These people are expecting my happy-ever-after to have gone to plan. But there's a cloud, a big dark cloud hanging over my happy world that only I can see. I push the buggy further down the corridor and admit to myself what I've known for a while now. There's rain on the way.

—

Inside the main office, everyone is excited to see us. The space feels familiar. A hug from the past. Same faces, same desks, same pictures on the wall. I hardly noticed the pictures when I worked here.

A small posse has gathered around the buggy, smiling at Shay and telling me how great I look. I thank them for their compliments. Beaming with pride, I show off my little boy. It feels strange to be the centre of attention. That never happened when I worked here. In fact I felt different from everyone else, a fake. I was someone who got the job because her sister was good friends with the boss. At first,

I kept myself well hidden, scurrying like a mouse hoping to become invisible. If it wasn't for Amanda taking me to lunch with her or to the after-work drinking sessions on a Friday, I'm not sure anyone would have noticed me.

But that was then and this is now. And now I feel proud of myself. It surges through me, fuelled by every query and compliment coming my way. Everyone wants to know about my life, what it's like to be a mother, to be married to someone so handsome and rich. I try to act humble, telling them I miss their comradeship, the gossip, going to lunch, the nights out. But they laugh, offering to swap places if I miss them that much.

After a while, having satisfied everyone's addiction to smelling a new baby, I ask where Amanda is. Rose informs me she's holding a course in the blue room which is due to finish in about twenty minutes. Not wanting to overstay my welcome, I tell Rose I'll wait out in the foyer and she walks out with me. Rose is the oldest member of the staff here and one of the nicest. When I first started at Imanage, Rose kept her eye on me. Amanda was great at including me in the fun stuff but Rose was the one I turned to when I needed help with the work. The first day I arrived here, she told me my shyness was a welcome trait around the place, that everyone else was too full of confidence.

'So, you're enjoying it all so far,' Rose says.

'Yes, it takes a bit of getting used to, but so far so good.'

'Good... good.' Rose nods but I can hear a hint of hesitation in her voice.

'What?' I say, turning to look at her.

Rose lifts her head to look at me. 'Nothing. It's probably nothing,' she says.

'What's probably nothing?'

'I wasn't planning on saying anything, but now that you're here...'

The joy I have just filled my cup with slowly seeps out. I know this is not going to be good news; Rose wouldn't sound so guarded if it was. She's almost whispering and there's no one else here except the young girl behind the desk twenty feet away, deafened with headphones.

'Tell me, Rose.' Rocking the buggy forwards and backwards, I sit down on the big green sofa that stretches the length of the window. Rose sits beside me, giving one last glance around to make sure the coast is clear before opening her mouth.

'I'm sure it's nothing important but a couple of weeks back, a young girl came in here asking questions about you. She was about your age. Red hair – pointy chin. I couldn't tell if her hair was long or short because she had a woollen hat on. One of those trendy ones everyone's wearing now.'

I want Rose to get to the point quickly but, having worked with her, I know that's a mammoth request. Rose has always taken the long route, describing the scenery on the way.

'If I remember rightly, she was wearing small gold earrings, nice ones.' Rose rubs her ear. I let out a long sigh which seems to do the trick because she ceases describing the mysterious girl's jewellery and continues with the relevant details.

'She asked me how long you had worked here. At first I thought it must be something to do with the baby about to be born. Maybe the local paper from...' Rose leans forward expecting me to finish.

'Ballycall.'

'Yes, Ballycall. So, I answered her… but then I got a bit suspicious when she asked if I knew if you had ever been in trouble with the law.'

Blood rushes to my head. 'Did she say who she was?'

'She introduced herself at the start but it didn't register with me… anyway, I told her I knew nothing and she'd be better off talking to Amanda. Amanda wasn't here so I gave the girl her number.'

'Could her name have been Vicky?' I ask, my head light, my hand gripping the handle of the buggy like it's about to roll down a slope. It has to have been Vicky Murphy, but why? Did somebody send her?

'I suppose it could have been Vicky, but honestly I don't remember,' she says.

'Don't worry about it, Rose. I'm sure Amanda will be able to tell me.' I try to look unbothered while my insides twist into knots. Turning my attention to Shay, I swallow hard.

'She never rang Amanda,' Rose mutters, brushing down her skirt before joining me to look at Shay. 'I asked Amanda about a week later, but she said she didn't get a call from anyone asking about you.'

Rose puts her hand on my arm. 'I just wanted you to know, Laura, in case you heard from someone that she was in here. I wouldn't like you to think…'

'No… sure, don't worry Rose, and thanks for telling me.'

Shay opens his eyes, pulling our attention his way.

'Hello, little man,' Rose says, smiling into the buggy.

I'm smiling too, but I don't know how.

Chapter Thirty-Six

Amanda arrives in the lobby full of energy and smiles —
a stark contrast to how I'm feeling. Rose's words have
put a stop to my enthusiasm and now I have to fake it.
I do intend telling Amanda what Rose said and asking if
someone did contact her, but first I just want to get out
of this building into the open air.

Amanda hurries over to Shay, pushing her long shiny
hair behind her ear before bending over to kiss him.

'Hi, Shay. How is my little boy?' He's not her little boy.
Shay is mine but I let it go and attempt to act as happy as
she is.

'He really is a little beauty, Laura.' Amanda continues
to look into the buggy. Eventually she turns her attention
to me.

'Love the hair,' she says. 'Was Georgina on duty again?'

'No, I did it myself.' The comfort of small talk no
longer satisfies me. I unlock the buggy and suggest we
leave.

'Can we go?'

'Yeah, what's the hurry? Is everything okay, Laura?'

'Yes, I just need to move… this place is so stuffy.'

It's not stuffy at all. In fact, there's almost an echo.
Amanda doesn't say anything as she pushes the door open
for us to leave.

Outside, I stand still, hands gripping the handle as I take a deep breath. Noticing my anxiety, Amanda becomes concerned.

'What is it, Laura? Did someone upset you?'

'No, it's just...' I'm hesitant, why am I hesitant? I should be able to ask Amanda straight out if someone contacted her about me. But if she says yes, that means she hid it from me and I'm not sure I can handle any more disappointment. If she says no, then I'm left wondering what the hell Vicky Murphy wanted to know about me. Why was she so interested in my past?

'I'm fine, it's just... coming back here, seeing everyone... I don't know why but it freaked me out a bit.'

'Here, let me take him.' Amanda pushes into my space and takes the buggy from me. Walking alongside her I feel strange; something is missing. I'd rather be pushing the buggy myself but I don't say that. Instead I keep my eye on her every move while watching the path ahead for obstacles.

'Well, are you going to tell me?' she says, carefully manoeuvring the buggy through the growing crowd. It's lunchtime in the city, all the suits have to be fed.

'I'm fine now, I got a bit overwhelmed back there.'

Amanda takes her eye off the buggy to glance at me. 'Are you sure?'

'Yes, positive, now where are we going for lunch?'

'You pick.'

–

Luigiani's is just as I remembered it: bright with wooden tables, hand-painted murals and the smell of garlic, tomatoes and freshly baked bread. Vanni is behind the counter when we enter. When he sees us come through the door he shouts out loud: 'Amanda, Laura... welcome.' He remembered my name, I can't believe it.

From the back of the shop, Anna the waitress rushes to seat us, commenting on the new customer in the buggy. 'A beautiful boy,' she says. 'Congratulations.' She thinks the baby belongs to Amanda because she's pushing the buggy.

'No.' Amanda says. 'This is Laura's baby.' And she laughs as she adds, 'Don't jinx me.'

'Oh, Laura's baby! Congratulations, Laura.' Anna pats me on the shoulder before leading us down to a table that has room for the buggy. Shay is asleep, but I know that won't last much longer. He's due a bottle soon but with a bit of luck I'll get to eat my pasta first.

When we've given our order Amanda leans over the table, placing both her arms on top.

'Okay, what is it?' she says. 'I know something's happened so there's no point in you trying to hide it.' She could always read me. Ever since we were kids, Amanda knew if something was upsetting me, exciting me or scaring me. It's like she could read my mind.

'It's nothing really, just something Rose said.'

Her eyes stare at me without blinking. She is not letting this go.

'She said someone was asking questions about me.'

Amanda sits back. 'Who?'

'She didn't know her name; she came in and asked about my past.'

'Why? What did Rose tell her?'

Amanda seems surprised and confused. But then, unlike her, I could never read her mind.

'Nothing much; she said she gave her your number.'

Straightening her back into the chair, Amanda prepares her defence. 'No one rang me asking about you. When is this supposed to have happened?'

'A few weeks back, so it doesn't really matter now.'

'Why are you so bothered by it then? If you think it was nothing.'

'She described a girl, I think it might have been Vicky Murphy?'

'Fuck... are you serious?'

'Yeah, well, it could have been, especially as we know she was studying investigative journalism.'

'But...' Amanda leans forward again, her face animated by the possibilities. 'Jesus, Laura, why would she be asking about you?' She pauses briefly, squinting her eyes in concentration. 'Unless she was using you as an exercise. For her classes, like. Some project they were given. You might have been the only person she knew who came from Dublin...'

'Bit of a scoop, that,' I say, putting an end to Amanda's attempt at easing my worry.

Amanda shuts up, she knows that would be too much of a coincidence. Vicky Murphy was looking into my past. But why? Did someone hire her? How much did she find out? And who did she tell before she was killed? I thought it was over, that I'd finally buried my past, kept it hidden from my new perfect life. But I was wrong. The soil has been disturbed, someone is trying to dig it up.

Chapter Thirty-Seven

'What about this one?'

We're in a small shop specialising in christening gowns and communion dresses and Amanda is holding up a tiny white satin suit. The sun, shining through the shopfront, is bouncing off it, making it look like an angel in her hand.

'No, I want a gown.'

This christening gown will be worn by all the children Conor intends for us to have, so a shiny satin suit is not going to do it. What if our next child is a girl? I hope it is but not for a while yet. Not for a long time. I hope Conor isn't disappointed when I tell him I want to wait at least five years before having another baby. He was so animated when he spoke about having many children. Conor said he hated being an only child. It put him under a lot of pressure to perform all the time. Be the best at this. Be the best at that. The Super Trouper was always shining on him. There was no one else on the stage.

Unlike me, who was always in the shadows. Amanda was the one lit up. The one who attracted all the attention. Even when we were kids, my mother called out her name first. I know it's a small thing but it did annoy me, especially as I was the oldest. 'Amanda, Laura, dinner's ready. Amanda, Laura, did you do your homework?' There were even times when she left my name out altogether, like she'd forgotten it or something. But it suited me not to be in the spotlight.

'What about this one?' Amanda laughs, holding up a big puffy white satin gown with layers and layers of tulle below the skirt.

'Hah, can you imagine Maggie's face if I arrive home with that?'

Amanda is still laughing and trying to figure out how someone would get a baby into the massive christening gown, but I'm not laughing. Rose's revelation won't let me. What was Vicky Murphy doing asking about me? I was wrong coming to Dublin today thinking it would take my mind off what Pat had told the cops about Conor. I should have known things would get worse. They always do.

I'm about to give up. None of these gowns are what I'm looking for anyway. In my head, I have a picture of what I want: Shay's face glowing in a simple lace gown with little puckered arms, no bows, no diamonds, just lace. I realise I'm searching for my own christening gown. The one in the photos of Mam holding me on her lap, the white lace gown cascading down her side. Amanda is still searching through the rails when I say: 'I wonder if Mam would give me my gown?'

The words float across to where Amanda is standing still, her hand frozen to the rail. She doesn't turn to look at me. Her head lowers for a moment then she moves back to look at the gowns.

'That's not going to happen Laura, keep looking,' she says.

My sadness is disturbed by a voice behind me.

'Can I help you?' I turn to see an old man standing there. Thin as a famine victim, his trousers are kept off the floor by a pair of checkered braces. Around his neck, a much-used measuring tape hangs. When he speaks his voice is gentle, probably from years of dealing with the indecisive.

'I can't find what I'm looking for,' I say.

Amanda walks around from where she's standing on the far side of the display cabinet, in case she's missing anything.

'I was hoping to get something simple, beautiful... something made of lace.'

The man is nodding, urging me to continue.

'Maybe with a tiny sleeve... or not, I could get a cardigan.'

He's still nodding, what more information does he need? Pointing at the display in front of me I say, 'These are all lovely but I wanted something... maybe a bit more old-style, not so blingy.'

'I think I might have what you're looking for,' he says.

The man disappears behind a curtain that divides the storeroom from the rest of us.

Amanda looks at her watch. 'I hope he finds what you're looking for soon, Laura, I've to head back to work. I've a presentation at two thirty.'

'You go on, I'm okay here,' I say, but deep down I'm disappointed. I was hoping Amanda would spend the afternoon with me, take some time off work. But that's not going to happen.

'Are you sure? I can wait another few minutes.'

'No, go on.'

Amanda hugs me, telling me she hopes I get what I'm looking for and to drive home safely, she'll ring me later. She will ring me later. I know that much but she won't mention the fact that Vicky Murphy was asking about me. It's how she operates. Worry doesn't have a room in Amanda's head. Unlike me, she is able to forget anything she wants. It's always been that way. Forget and move on. Don't let reality get in the way of a good time.

'Something like this?' Walking towards me, the man holds out a beautiful simple lace gown. There are no frills, no sparkles, no bows. A tiny ribbon of silk edges the neck and arms. It's exactly what I'm looking for. I'm giddy with delight.

I look around to see if I can catch Amanda before she leaves, but it's too late. She's gone.

'It's perfect,' I say, a wave of happiness surging through my body. Taking the gown from the man's hands, I inspect every swirl of thread.

'Look,' I say, holding it over Shay who's staring up at me from the comfort of his buggy. 'Look what Mammy got you! You're going to look so precious, little man.'

For the second time today, I'm excited. When I woke up this morning I couldn't wait to get to Imanage. To see my old colleagues. To show off Shay and have lunch with Amanda. I was looking forward to my trip down memory lane.

My conversation with Rose had put a hasty end to my indulgent glee but now it's back. With the bag holding the gown safely tucked into the end of the buggy, I make my way back to the car park, happy my visit to the city was not a total disaster.

I may not have gotten myself a new outfit for the christening, but I got Shay's and that's the important thing. And I'm grateful for that. Grateful for everything I have in my new world. I never dreamt I could be this lucky... after what happened. I'm going to enjoy every moment while it lasts because if someone does discover what happened, my new world will quickly disappear.

Shay is safely strapped into his seat and I'm about to strap on my own seat belt when I remember. *Maggie*. The picture jumps into my mind out of nowhere. It's like I'm not meant to have a moment's peace. *The graveyard. Maggie handing an envelope to Vicky Murphy.*

Chapter Thirty-Eight

The drive home is a mixture of satisfaction and confusion. If Vicky Murphy is the girl who called in to Imanage asking about me, did Maggie send her? But why? Something would have had to trigger that sort of action. But what? Nobody in Ballycall knows about my past. Not even Conor. Unless she wanted to find out why my mother wasn't showing her face around the place.

The first time I met Maggie, I told her I didn't speak to my mother. She didn't question me as to why, and when I told her she wouldn't be coming to the wedding, she just ran a pencil through the seat allocated for her on the seating chart and said nothing else about it. Which surprised me. Why didn't she ask me why I didn't talk to my mother? If she had asked me I would have told her the same thing I told Conor. We fell out over some inheritance my father had left me. I know it was a lie; I'm not proud of it. Especially because it makes my mother look like the bad person. But I could not tell the truth.

The evening shadows drift in and out of the car as I drive through the village of Ballycall. Arriving at the gates of our house, I feel my anxiety levels rise. I'm almost expecting to see a cop car parked outside. The driveway is empty. Taking a deep breath, I tell myself to relax. Don't always be expecting the worst. Lifting my son out of the car, I go into the house.

'Well, what did you think of your trip to Dublin, Shay?' I find myself talking to Shay a lot. Does that make me a bit mad or sad? Or is it just what mammies do? He seems to like it. His whole body wiggles with the attention.

'You were the best boy today, Shay. Mammy loves you sooooo much.'

I lean over and kiss his face, inhaling his addictive scent. I can't wait for him to answer me. To tell me he loves me. I wonder what his first word will be. Mamma? Dadda? I'll be happy with either just so long as it's not Nana.

Speaking of Nana, I feel like she has a camera on me. I've just about settled Shay into his crib when my phone beeps. She'll be wanting to know where I was and why. Well she can wait. First things first.

The photo of Vicky Murphy is in the drawer where I left it. With my phone hovering above it, I take the best shot I can and forward it to Rose.

Is this the girl who was asking about me?

Now I have to wait. Rose won't have finished work yet and she's one of those people who sticks to the rules. *No personal mobile use during working hours.* I was one of them too. Afraid to step outside the rules. Afraid of getting burnt... again.

Taking the christening gown from the bag, I allow myself a moment of happiness. This is going to look beautiful on Shay. Really holy. My mother would have loved it.

I don't think about my mother too much because it hurts. Forgiving should have come naturally to her. She'd spent so much time in the church where forgiveness was a big part of their gig. *Forgive thine enemy. Forgive thy neighbour. Forgive those who hurt you. Forgive, forgive, forgive...* I never remember there being a clause attached that says, *except daughters. Do not forgive them.*

The door opens. In walks Conor with his suit jacket open. His tie hangs loosely over his shirt. He walks directly over to the crib and finds Shay fast asleep.

'Well, how did it go?' he says.

'Great, everyone thought he was beautiful.'

'And did you get the...' Conor looks at the gown in my hand. 'Is that it?' He moves closer, scanning the tiny garment. 'Is that not for a girl?'

'No, it's a christening gown. They're not gender-specific, Conor.'

His lack of excitement disappoints me. I didn't expect him to jump around with joy, but I thought he'd at least pretend to care.

'Well, sure, what would I know? As long as you're happy with it. I'm going to jump in the shower.' He walks towards the door. 'Mammy's going to put you in a dress, Shay.'

I sense the humour in his voice. It puts me at ease.

-

The phone beeps just as Conor arrives back in the room. Shay is now sitting on my lap sucking on his bottle. I can't very well disturb him and rush to my phone.

Dressed in jeans and a t-shirt, Conor hovers over the open fridge door.

'Sorry there's no dinner ready, I'm not long home and I've already eaten. Do you want me to make you something or see if there's a pizza in the freezer?' I say.

My eyes are fixed on my phone out of reach. I'm expecting the worst: that Rose will confirm it was Vicky Murphy who was asking about me. If she does, I'm going to confront Maggie. I have to know if it was her and if so, why.

Conor unwraps a frozen pizza and places it in the oven as per the instructions he reads out loud to himself. He struggles with the settings, so I tell him to hold Shay, I'll do it. He kisses my forehead while lifting Shay out of my arms and I head straight for the phone, unlocking it with my thumbprint and putting the oven on at the same time.

It's Rose.

> Yes, that's her.

My heart sinks. A shiver of fear runs through my body. Vicky Murphy *was* investigating me.

Chapter Thirty-Nine

Like it isn't bad enough my husband is eating a frozen pizza for dinner after a hard day at the office, his mother arrives to witness it. With a bag in each hand, she strolls past me into the kitchen, babbling on about someone who wouldn't be able to attend the christening. I can fully understand that at such short notice but, seemingly, Maggie has plans to remember this someone in the future.

By the time I close the front door and arrive in the kitchen behind Maggie, she has already formed an expression of disappointment.

'Is that what you're having for dinner?' She chuckles to imply that this is a light-hearted comment. But I know better.

'I was in Dublin today,' I say, walking straight over to the bouncer where I talk to Shay.

'Mammy's going to teach you to be a great cook, not like poor Daddy.' The words leave my mouth before I have a chance to stop them and there's a brief silence as Maggie adjusts to the new atmosphere. Conor tries to defuse it, saying the pizza wasn't that bad.

'Dublin,' she says. 'What had you there?'

'I brought Shay up to meet my old colleagues at Imanage. They thought he was beautiful.' Lifting Shay in my arms I say, 'Say hello to Nana.'

Maggie walks over to say hello to her grandson and immediately the battle is put on hold.

'Well of course they did,' she says, cooing into Shay's face.

With the last slice of pizza in his hand, Conor tells Maggie about the christening gown I purchased. I didn't want him to. I was hoping to break that news to her later but Conor makes it sound like a good thing. Maybe Maggie won't have a problem with it.

Wrong.

'But I thought you were going to use your own christening gown, Conor. The one that your father picked out for you. I have it here with me.'

I turn away from them, taking longer than necessary to tuck Shay into the crib. I'm leaving this one to Conor.

Maggie searches through one of the bags she carried in, and removes a parcel wrapped in tissue. 'I even had it cleaned. Look.'

I take a peek to the left and watch her holding up the gown to Conor. I can't see it – she has her back to me – but I can see Conor. He looks trapped. What will he do?

He sighs, putting the last slice of pizza back on the plate. 'I don't know. Does it really matter?' he says. His hand brushes through his hair, his face reddens. Conor is under enough stress at the moment. I should not be adding to it.

'Of course it matters,' Maggie says, with no sympathy for her indecisive son. As she turns to hold out the gown for me to see, I glance at Conor and my heart tugs at his helpless expression. *This is for you, Conor.*

'It's beautiful, Maggie.' I say. 'We would love to put Shay in Conor's gown, especially as his grandad chose it.'

I know the chances of any man picking out a christening gown thirty years ago is slim to none. But the gown is actually beautiful. And Conor looks relieved.

I wink at him and he winks back, filling my heart with a reminder that we are one, together on this journey. We have each other's back. I know if I'd put up a fight with Maggie, Conor would have sided with me. I have no doubt about that. But not all games are won by lifting trophies. By appearing weaker, I made us stronger. And Maggie doesn't even realise she lost that one.

–

After Maggie has updated us about all the wonderful things she has in motion for the big day, Conor makes his excuses and heads to his office down the hall. This is my chance.

'Will you have a quick cuppa before you go?' I say.

Maggie looks at her watch and hums as if she's doing me a favour. She's one of those people who like to give the impression their life is full, that they never have a spare minute. Always something going on.

'Okay,' she says.

When the tea is poured, I sit opposite Maggie and watch her excited face. Is it possible this woman is capable of hiring someone to check me out? If so, maybe it has nothing to do with wanting to know about my mother. Conor has money, a lot of it. Maybe she wanted to make sure the business was safe, that I wasn't some gold-digger in it for a short while, screwing her husband for all he's worth in the divorce court. It's possible, and I can't exactly say I blame her – after all, she didn't know me. But I want to hear her admit it and I want to know what she found out.

'Maggie,' I say, two hands cradling my cup. 'I wanted to ask you something.'

'Sure, ask away.' Maggie perks up, her old eyes widening in anticipation.

'You know I was in Dublin today.'

Maggie nods.

'Well, I heard something, something that disturbed me.'

'What?' Maggie slowly sips her tea, her eyes focused on me.

'Vicky Murphy.'

I let the name hang in the air to see if I can detect a reaction. Nothing. Maggie is still eager to listen.

'Apparently, she called in to my old company, Imanage. She was asking about me, a few weeks before the wedding.'

Maggie pulls her head back a bit. 'Vicky Murphy, the dead girl?' she says, looking confused.

'Yes.'

'Why was she asking about you?'

Either Maggie is a great actress or she knows nothing.

'Well that's the thing… I was wondering if you had any idea?'

Maggie huffs, raising her head in the air like a peacock. 'If I have any idea?'

'Yes.' I'm staring at her.

'And why, my dear, would you think I'd know anything about that?'

'Because I saw you one day in the graveyard, handing her an envelope and I thought you must know her well, maybe she told you something.'

Her lips are pursed now, her head nodding.

Now she's sighing, shaking her head from side to side. My heart is in my mouth, I'm trying my best to act nonchalantly, while every nerve in my body is poking me.

'I was a bit surprised when you said you had never spoken to her.' I can't believe I'm finding the courage to confront Maggie like this.

'When.... when did I tell you that?'

'The night you and Helen came in here after Vicky's funeral.'

'Oh, don't mind what I say in front of Helen,' she says, straightening herself on the stool.

'But I thought you and Helen have been friends since you were children?'

'We are and that's how we're still friends; I tell her nothing.' Maggie puts her hand out and surprises me by placing it on top of mine. I think she's trying to end the conversation but I can't stop now.

'So why were you meeting Vicky in the graveyard?' I blurt out.

She lifts the cup to her lips as I squirm on the seat opposite her. Her eyes stare above the rim as she sips a little, then she stops to say, 'Well now, that's not really any of your business.' The air stills between us. I've pushed too far. Maggie is not prepared to divulge the reason for her liaison with Vicky Murphy. Not even to her childhood friend, Helen. But why the secret? What is she hiding?

Chapter Forty

Well, that's not quite how I expected that to go. I spend most of the night lying flat on my back looking up at the darkness, unable to complete a full hour's sleep, worrying that I have opened a can of worms.

Conor is burning toast when I enter the kitchen with Shay in my arms. It was a lot easier to carry him when he was inside me.

'Coffee?' he says.

'Yes please, I didn't sleep a wink.'

'Go back to bed when Shay goes down,' he says, pouring water from the kettle.

'I'll try.'

Tucking Shay into the crib, I yawn.

'Will you be okay?' Conor asks.

'Yeah, sure, I'll be fine.' Pulling my dressing gown tighter, I shuffle across in oversized slippers to the breakfast counter. Outside the window, a great blue sky paints a picture of peace and tranquillity. At the end of the garden, the forest looms. Pat is probably still in bed. But since the argument between him and Conor, I haven't seen him at all. I hope he's not dead back there.

'Have you seen Pat since you had the argument with him?' I say.

Conor crunches on his toast, muttering through a full mouth. 'It wasn't an argument.'

'Well whatever you want to call it… have you seen him since?'

'No, I haven't. But don't let that worry you.' Conor butters a second slice of toast. 'Pat is not a creature of habit.'

'I know but still… I hope he's okay.'

'He'll be okay.'

'Did the police contact you yet?'

'No, they're probably busy trying to catch the real suspect, Laura.'

'I know…'

Squashing the subject, Conor puts his jacket on. 'I hope to be home early this evening. Mam has a list of things she wants me to look at before the christening.'

I hold back a sigh at the thought of another night of Maggie and christening preparations. The sooner Sunday comes and goes, and we can have some alone time again, the better. I love when it's just the two of us – the *three* of us now. It also means I'd better make a decent dinner tonight. No more frozen pizzas or she'll take her son back.

Conor is walking over to the crib when the doorbell rings. I'm lifting a slice of toast to my mouth. I stop. For some reason a sick feeling stirs in my stomach. Who could that be? Is it Fintan again? More bad news? Conor turns to look at me. I can tell he's thinking the same. He walks out of the room without commenting. I follow him and wait at the kitchen door where I can see him. The shapes behind the glass send a shiver through my body. I'm on pause, unable to breathe until he answers that door. Conor turns to look at me.

'Don't panic Laura, it will be okay.'

Why is he saying that? Why does he think I'm going to panic? Conor must know why they're here.

The two men step into the hallway and introduce themselves as Detective Owen Murray and Detective Michael Penny. They're both taller than Conor by a few inches. The older one is wearing a suit but the younger guy is dressed in jeans and a casual jacket. I remember seeing them enter the café the other day. At the time it made me uncomfortable knowing why they were here in Ballycall. But now, I'm absolutely terrified.

'Conor Caldwell?' Michael Penny says.

Conor nods, but it doesn't satisfy them.

'Are you Conor Caldwell?' he says.

They know damn well he is, but they're letting Conor know he might be king of the village but he's no one to them.

'Yes, that's me,' he says before turning to me. 'Laura, go back inside.'

I'm stuck to the spot, unable to move, but I shake myself and nod at him. The three men look at me and wait until I've gone back into the kitchen. Without fully closing the door, I stand inside and put my ear to the gap only to hear Conor ask them to move into his office.

Tears are gathering, stinging my eyes, and I feel like I'm going to throw up. With nothing to be heard at the doorway, I move over to Shay's crib and lean in to kiss him. The warmth of his breath against my face does little to ease the fear firmly gripping me. This is it. The cops are going to arrest my husband. They must have something on him and Conor was pretty eager to make sure I didn't hear what it was. With Shay in my arms now, I walk nervously around the room holding him tighter than is necessary, waiting. At the window I look out at the dull grey world and think of Pat. It's his fault. He's the one who brought this to my door, telling the cops Conor left our house the night Vicky was killed. Why would he do that? He knows Conor. He knows he wouldn't do a thing like that. I open my mouth to release the words *I hate you Pat, look what you've done to us.* But the words don't leave. I stop, a fresh wave of dread washing over me. He does know Conor. He knows Conor a lot better than I do.

About twenty minutes later, the sound of the office door opening startles me. Are they going to take Conor away? Is he handcuffed? I put Shay back into the crib. He starts to cry but I leave him and rush to see Conor closing the front door. The detectives are gone. Conor is still here. Thank God they haven't taken him to the station. Relief washes over me as I go to Conor in the hallway. His face is flushed, worry etched across his brow. I break the icy silence.

'What did they want, Conor?'

He shakes his head and walks past me into the kitchen. Then stops, turns to look at me and says. 'You're not going to believe this Laura.' He runs his hands through his hair and looks at the ground then back to me. 'I'm the last person Vicky Murphy made contact with before she was killed.'

'What?' I can barely hear my own whisper. 'But...'

'Yes, she texted me, asking to see me as soon as possible, saying it was important.'

'And did you answer her?'

'I didn't notice it Laura.'

'But did you see it afterwards, the next day, did you not notice her name on your phone?'

'It didn't come up under her name, it was just her number and no, I didn't notice it. My phone was jammed with messages of congratulations.' He moves over to the island brushing his hand over the top. 'They went through my phone and found the message. They could see it hadn't been opened until they opened it but they've taken my phone with them.'

'What does this mean, Conor? Are you a suspect now?' I say.

Conor shakes his head from side to side, unable to answer me.

Chapter Forty-One

Conor hasn't mentioned anything to his Mam. I know because she's still prancing around like Franck from *Father of the Bride*, and Conor is avoiding her as much as he can. I'm now stewing in worry for my husband. He went into work after the cops visit yesterday, but I don't know how he managed it. I could barely dress myself. And now, I have to put all that aside because in twenty-four hours' time, my house will be filled with over a hundred enthusiastic christening guests.

Noel and Abbie dropped in earlier with a gift for Shay – a silver bracelet with his name and date of birth on it. It's beautiful. Abbie said they wanted to give it to us now so Shay could wear it to the church in the morning. When they left, Conor laughed, saying he didn't think his little boy's first big day out would be in a dress, wearing a bracelet. I found it strange that Conor was able to carry on like nothing had happened, making jokes. But I decided to join him. If this is the way he wanted to play it, I'd act my part as the happy wife. I reminded him not to be so macho and that it was possible Shay might like to wear dresses and bracelets when he's older, so he'd better ease off on the man pressure. Conor reacted by lifting Shay in the air saying, 'Whatever's to be is to be. I'll always love you.'

The house is empty now. Conor has gone with his mother to pick up the cake. Shay is snoozing in his crib.

With the coast clear, I lift the card that accompanied the bracelet Noel and Abbie gave us. *To my Godson on his christening day*. I look at the handwritten message inside. I don't know what I'm expecting. Do I think it might resemble the writing in the other card that I don't even have anymore? I can still see it when I close my eyes. *Your husband is a murderer*.

There's nothing to alarm me about this card. It's got a lovely verse printed on it and the writing is small and neat and not at all threatening. But they're still on my list. It's possible one of them sent the cruel card. I'm still wary of Noel, I think he's hiding something, what with Olive not talking to him and him running away to Oman all of a sudden. And Abbie, well she could have sent the card to divert attention from Noel. Or even just to piss me off for ruining the friendship between the four of them. I wish I knew where that card was now.

Outside, there's still no sign of Pat. I wonder if he will come to the party tomorrow after all the trouble he's caused. I gaze out onto the vast nothingness. The empty field. The still forest. There are no clouds of smoke creeping out through the treetops. If Pat is in his house, he hasn't lit the fire. I glance over and see Shay is still asleep. Will I risk it? Will I go down and face him? Ask him if he sent the card? I will, and I'll tell him about the alarm in the factory going off that night and to stop implying my husband has something to do with Vicky's murder.

The grass gets thicker the further I progress, mangled by weeds and rocks and a lack of care. When Shay is older, I plan to fill this space with loads of outdoor toys – slides, swings, monkey bars, goal posts, a racing track, whatever he wants. The still air will be filled with laughter, joy and energy. Shay will invite his friends here to play and make noise. To fight and make up and bring life to the place.

When I reach the trees, I glance back at the house. If I'm to be honest, from here it looks a bit intrusive. A big white stone building in the middle of a green field. It looks like it fell from the sky. Alien to its surroundings. I continue into the forest on the worn path that leads to Pat's cottage. It's darker in here; the tall trees block the sun from entering. But it's not pitch black. I can see the small cottage in the distance. There are no lights on. It looks empty. But Pat might just be asleep. I don't want to startle him if he is.

The closer I get, the more nervous I become. The cottage has one small window on either side of the front door. To the side of the house is an open shed where Pat chops his logs. An axe leans against a huge log in the middle, surrounded by stacks of smaller logs. I look in but he's not in there. Moving to the door of the house, I hold my breath and knock. Knocking again I push on the door, but it's locked.

Mindful that Shay could wake up any minute I peek in the window to my right. There are no curtains, no need, it's very private here. In the middle of the room a square wooden table stands with one chair. Not two. That makes me sad. There's a plate on the table with a crust of bread on it and a mug beside it. Pat's nowhere in the picture. I scurry past the door over to the second window and see an empty bed. Where could he be? The bed is small with a sheet and a couple of blankets on top. Above the bed hangs a cross. The wardrobe, if you could call it that, is a small bockety press with clothes spilling out of it. I think of all I have, just a short stroll away, and I feel guilty. This isn't right. Pat should have a few nice things. When all this is over and if it turns out Pat has nothing to do with it, I'm going to fix his house up for him. Get him some comforts.

The only other place he could be, if he is in the house, is the bathroom, which I can't see from here. I'm not going around the back of the house because the terrain looks pretty rough, with unkempt shrubs, overgrown and tangled. I knock once more on the door, but again, no answer. Time to get back to my little boy.

Chapter Forty-Two

Georgina is holding court with a grey-haired lady when I walk into the salon. She puts her finger up to quieten the lady and says, 'Speak of the devil, hello Laura.' Returning her attention to the lady, she says, 'This is her now, I'll introduce you.'

Walking over to where they're standing, I put my hand out.

'Eilish Ryan,' Georgina says, indicating the lady before pointing to me, 'Laura Caldwell.'

Eilish nods and is about to speak when she's interrupted by Georgina.

'Can you believe it, Eilish is actually going to the christening tomorrow and she's never even been introduced to you.'

'Yes, I—' begins Eilish.

'She's seen you around, but has never spoken to you.'

If Georgina doesn't give her a chance she's not going to be able to speak to me now either. So, I take my attention off Georgina and shake Eilish's hand. 'Don't worry about that, Eilish, you won't be the only one I don't know at the party tomorrow, but you're very welcome and I hope you enjoy yourself.'

Eilish smiles. 'Oh thank you, Laura. I'm looking forward to it.'

The salon is full; every basin, every station full of women getting their hair done for the big christening. I understand now why Georgina is so nice to me; she's making a fortune.

When I finally get to the basin, Georgina herself decides to wash my hair, guiding my head gently into the sink.

'That was Fintan Ryan's wife. The local sergeant,' she says. 'Eilish Ryan... lovely woman... two sons, both up in Dublin, neither joined the guards... which disappointed Fintan.'

My head is hovering over the sink now, the water gushing through my hair, providing the backing track to the local gossip.

'The eldest fella is a bit strange but the younger fella is a lovely chap.'

I'd hoped to come here for a break. To clear my mind of all this unsavoury business with cards and Vicky Murphy. Conor had said he hadn't a clue why she had sent that text. She had never contacted him before outside of the pub. She wasn't even a name in his phone contacts. Vicky must have known she was in danger and hoped Conor could help her. But that's not how the detectives will see it. Vicky is dead. Conor is the last person she contacted. My stomach continues to twist.

When Georgina finishes filling me in on the history of the Ryan brothers, she wraps a towel around my head and brings me over to a basin.

'She wasn't well you know... Eilish,' she says in a low voice, leaning in to my ear to whisper: 'her nerves were very bad.'

A drop of water rolls down my face as I nod at the mirror, pretending I'm interested.

'In and out of the hospital for years.' Georgina pulls away from whispering and says, 'If it wasn't for Caldwell Brewery. Well. God only knows.'

Now I am interested.

'They were so good,' she says, bending back into the whisper again: 'By all accounts they paid for everything.'

I watch myself thinking in the mirror. So, Detective Fintan Ryan owes Conor big time. Is that why he told Conor about what Pat had said to the detectives from Dublin? Has Conor got Fintan Ryan in his pocket? And if so, what else is Fintan willing to do to cover for Conor?

The longer I'm in the salon, the more women arrive, all thanking me for their invitations. I nod and smile because I don't know who they are, and I wasn't the one who invited them. I hope I don't come across as rude but I'm uncomfortable with all the attention, it makes me nervous. It reminds me of that dreadful day when all those strangers were firing questions at me. Questions I couldn't answer.

Eventually the salon quietens, and I'm wondering whether there will be any young people at the christening. I do hope Conor made a contribution to the guest list. I mentioned it to my colleagues at Imanage but I don't expect any of them to take up the offer. It's a bit far to come for a party. Bridge or no bridge.

Back at the house, cars and vans hog the driveway. O'Rourke Flowers, Barry's Party balloons, Ballycall Party Supplies, the list goes on. Maggie has managed to spread our custom across most of the small businesses associated with the village.

I push my way past two young lads that I recognise from the club. They're carrying kegs. Caldwell Beer, of course.

I hope that's not the only choice of alcohol. If I'm gonna make it through the day, I'll need something stronger.

Inside the house, Maggie is directing everyone where to put things. Her hands are flailing through the air as she tells some young girl how to hang lights across the back wall. Why she wants lights, I don't know, the party should be well over by the time it gets dark. But I leave her to it and go up to the bedroom where Conor is taking care of Shay.

'You look lovely,' he says when I open the door. He is sitting on the bed with Shay lying across his knees.

'He likes this,' Conor says, lifting his knees in the air a few inches and smiling. Shay is not reacting at all. He's too young. I don't want to disappoint Conor, so I just say, 'Ahhhh.'

'How's the show unfolding downstairs?' he says.

'I think it's a bit much for a christening party myself but sure we gave her the reins. We can't interfere now.'

Holding Shay against his chest Conor stands. 'I guess we should be grateful she's organising the party. I wouldn't have the patience for that sort of stuff, especially now.'

'Oh, don't get me wrong, Conor, I'm very grateful. I could never pull that off. I'm glad she's running the show.'

I don't want Conor to get the wrong impression. I'm not ungrateful. It's just I never wanted all this fuss and certainly not so soon after having the baby. Maybe if it was in three months' time like we had agreed, before Noel's great escape scuppered the plan, I'd be happy with all the fuss. But now, and with everything going on, I'd be just as happy with a cake and a bottle of wine. A handful of people and an early night.

'I know it all happened very quickly, Laura,' Conor says, pulling the handle on the door, 'but it will be all over by tomorrow night and we'll be able to get back to normal.'

Conor closes the door behind him leaving the word 'normal' hanging in the air. A shiver runs down my spine.

Chapter Forty-Three

Amanda is the first through the door, bright and early like she promised. She's wearing jeans and a t-shirt, her oyster pink dress dangling in plastic covering over her arm. Amanda plants a kiss on my face before dropping everything onto a chair and heading over to the crib.

'How's my favourite godson?' she asks. I'm about to say something about him being her only godson, but I stop.

'What time is the church?' She turns her head to look at me.

'Eleven thirty, but we've to be there about a quarter past.'

'Grand, I'll head up and get changed in a little while.'

When I first moved into the house, Amanda claimed one of the bedrooms as her own. She even has some clothes and cosmetic stuff housed in it. Sometimes, when I get lonely, I go into the room to remind myself that Amanda is not far away if I need her. But I haven't gone in for a while. Shay has completely filled that hole.

The little man knew something was going down when he woke at six this morning. He cried for almost an hour. No amount of rocking or bottles would stop him. Eventually I placed him in the buggy and pushed him down the garden. I tried to get a peek through the forest to see if there was any life coming from Pat's cottage but I couldn't see the cottage from where I was, and the ground was too rough to continue with the buggy. I haven't seen Pat since Conor argued with him and it worries me. Even though I hate that he mentioned Conor to the detectives, I hope nothing bad has happened to him.

I had planned to tell Amanda about the text Vicky sent to Conor when she got here, but I'm too busy to get into that conversation and probably now is not the right time.

'You go and get ready,' she says. 'I'll wait here.'

Conor is stepping out from the en suite when I enter the room, his long lean body wrapped in a towel, his hair combed back off his forehead. He smiles and it lifts my heart, the way he seems so happy to see me. I hope it lasts.

'I'm going to have a shower. Amanda is with Shay.'

'Great,' he says, walking over and grabbing me by the waist, pulling me against his body. The gentle smell of his aftershave makes me take a deep breath and when he kisses my lips, part of me melts. Conor pulls his face away. 'Laura, everything is going to be okay.'

I want to cry, to scream, to ask him what the hell is going on. Why is this happening to us? But I don't. I place my hand on his face and smile. 'I hope so,' I say. He looks deep into my eyes. 'I promise it will,' he says, placing his hand on top of mine. 'Let's enjoy today.'

Conor is wearing a brand-new suit in a light, silvery grey which he ordered especially for Shay's big day. His shirt is also new, light blue, though he called it by some fancy name for light blue when he showed it to me. He has worn the shoes once before, on the day of our wedding.

My dress is not so new. I've worn it before to a wedding – when Alice from Imanage got married. It was the first time Conor met most of my colleagues. They were all very impressed with the man I'd managed to nab and I might have imagined it, but I felt I was treated differently by them after that. They seemed to have more respect for me, asking my opinion, inviting me for coffee and not just as a tagalong. I also think it's the night I got pregnant.

My dress is a nude brocade and – most importantly – it fits me which I'm delighted about. I thought getting rid of the baby weight would be harder. It's moving quicker than I thought. I suppose having your husband accused of murder will do that to a girl. With my hair done and my makeup on I'll be fine. Thankfully, I have my Louboutins. If I lose confidence in my look, I'll just flash the red.

Conor's shoes are sitting on the floor by the bed when I step out of the en suite, bringing me back to our wedding day. The day I became Mrs Laura Caldwell. It seems like such a long time ago. The church, the aisle, the panic, was he actually going to go through with it? It was only seven months ago but so much has happened since. Mrs Laura Caldwell has learned a lot. How big an influence her husband is in this not-so-quaint village. How money is no medicine for a tortured mind and that first impressions don't always last.

–

When the battle to look beautiful is won, we arrive at the church. Shay is like an angel in my arms as we walk to the entrance where Abbie and Noel are standing waiting. I'm nervous. Fr Cormac notices and his kind words soon relax me. After prayers and procedures, he invites the christening party to the altar. I feel like I'm on stage with all the people staring at us. Amanda looks like a movie star at my side. Noel also looks like a movie star beside Conor, only one from a different kind of movie. One with gangsters in it.

The priest lifts the jug of water which he's blessed and now I get nervous again. I hate this bit. It seems so cruel. With great enthusiasm he pours the water over Shay's tiny little skull. Up to now Shay has been playing ball, not a whimper out of him. But now he's crying. I want to stop the priest, tell him that's enough, he's christened. But Fr Cormac has other ideas and doesn't want to waste any of his precious holy water, so he keeps going until the jug is empty. Shay is now screaming.

Eventually, after a little rocking and soothing, my baby stops crying. A few more prayers and then it's time to go. Conor thanks the priest with a thickly-wedged envelope. When I see him hand it to the priest discreetly, I picture Maggie in the shadow of the same spire, handing an envelope to Vicky.

Outside the church, the sun is breaking through the clouded sky. I cradle my little boy close to me and whisper in his ear that I'm sorry. The poor sweetheart is still sniffling, probably wondering what's next, is it safe?

'You're safe now, baby,' I say, carrying him to the car.

Noel and Abbie stand waiting to travel back to the house with us. When we pull out of the church grounds Noel jokes about his newly-crowned responsibilities, how he'll be keeping his eye on us, making sure Shay grows up a fine Catholic.

I laugh along but I'm still wary of Noel, his confidence, his arrogance. I wonder whether Olive will ignore him again. If she does, I might just spark a conversation with her about it. I want to find out what it is she doesn't like about him. If it's something to do with Vicky Murphy. It could be important. Maybe that's why Vicky wanted to speak to Conor. If Noel was having an affair with Vicky, maybe it got messy. Noel is Conor's best friend and

Vicky knew that. I need to get Olive to open up about what she knows.

'Okay, let the fun begin,' Conor says, opening the door of the car when we arrive back at the house. Noel takes Shay's car seat and I flinch, inspecting his every move, making sure he does it correctly. Abbie notices me watching him. When Noel has the car seat safely in his grip, Abbie links my arm like we're best mates.

'You look lovely, Laura,' she says.

'Thanks, you look lovely too.' She doesn't; she looks absolutely fabulous. Abbie is wearing a green pleated skirt and a satin mauve top which clings to her perfectly toned shape. Her hair is a bundle of black shiny curls falling down the back of her head, held in place by a stone-encrusted hair grip. I thought I looked good until I saw her.

Amanda pulls up behind us in her car. She won't be drinking today; she has to drive back to Dublin tonight. She told me she would be taking the role of godmother very seriously and would be looking after Shay while I attended to the guests and enjoyed a drink. At first I didn't like the idea, I wanted my amigo by my side, but realising there was no one else I could trust to take care of Shay – Maggie would be too busy – I agreed.

Chapter Forty-Four

The party is in full swing, groups of people standing, sitting, enjoying the canapés and sipping the drink. It's all a bit tame but I imagine when Conor's friends from the club arrive it will become a more boisterous affair. Conor said they wouldn't be here until about three o'clock because there was a match on.

I haven't had a chance to speak to Conor since arriving back at the house but every now and then he looks over from whoever is hogging his company and smiles. It helps me, re-energises my batteries to keep going. Maggie is bossing some young waitress around as she prepares the buffet, which she says is not to be served until three o'clock. She has the whole thing mapped out and timed. If things go to plan, everyone should be gone by seven. I hope she's right. I'm enjoying myself as best I can under the strain of thinking somebody here may have sent the card but I can't wait to sit down with Conor on my own, my Louboutins cast aside, Shay in bed asleep and a glass of red in my hand.

The crowd seem to be enjoying themselves, all dressed up like they're at a family wedding. Fintan Ryan and his wife Eilish are sitting talking to two other couples at one of Maggie's hired tables. It's unlikely to be Fintan or Eilish who sent the card. Especially now that I know Conor paid for the smile Eilish is currently sending my way. I wave back at her before scanning the room for familiar faces. There aren't many.

Olive and Deirdre are outside the back door where an overflow has gathered. The sun is being kind which is just as well. Maggie has invited a lot more people than she let on. But I'm happy to stand here, nodding and smiling, playing the part of the lucky wife in my big castle with close to one hundred people. It's a far cry from my flat in the city. Ten people in that tiny space and it was jam-packed. And yet, there are times I miss it. Like Friday, when the detectives called. Seeing them in my hallway made me wish I was back in Dublin.

With a drink in my hand, I walk out to the two women. Besides Amanda, who is upstairs feeding Shay, and Conor, who I haven't caught a glimpse of in a while, Olive and Deirdre are the only other people I have anything in common with. Abbie is always stuck to Noel, hanging off his arm like she doesn't trust him.

'Hi,' I say, arriving at their side. Deirdre clicks her glass against mine.

'Great party, how did you manage to organise all of this so quickly?'

'How do you think?' I say, before swallowing down a great big gulp of wine. I haven't allowed myself too much up to now. I felt it was important to keep my composure while saying the first hellos to all these nice people.

'Maggie,' the two women say together, causing the three of us to break into laughter. We chat for a bit, everyone admiring everyone else's attire before moving on to talk about the beautiful church ceremony.

'Shay didn't find it all that beautiful,' I say. The girls laugh again. I join in but my attention is drawn to the lack of activity in the forest at the end of the garden. Still no sign of Pat. I wonder if he will show his face.

Maggie is calling everyone's attention to the buffet which has now opened. A young girl behind the table of delicious-looking food stands ready to dish it out and a queue is beginning to form. I take the opportunity to check in on Amanda who must be bored stiff upstairs. Conor is coming back from the loo as I exit the door.

'Everything okay?' he says.

'Yes, great, your mam is playing a blinder...'

Conor moves towards the crowd who have gathered for the food and I continue upstairs to where Amanda is lying on the bed, reading her phone. She puts her finger to her lips when I enter. 'He's asleep,' she whispers.

'Great, come on down, the food is being served.'

Amanda pulls herself off the bed and slips into her shoes.

'Will he be okay?' she says.

'Yes, gosh, he can sleep on his own, you know.'

'But what if he wakes up?'

I point at the monitor beside the cot and pull her by the arm onto the landing. I want her to come downstairs and be with me so I don't feel like a complete outsider at my own party.

–

The younger crowd are arriving when we get downstairs. I notice Amanda's charm jump up a notch as we welcome them in the door. My attention is focused on their demeanour; does anyone look nervous to meet me? Could one of these people have sent the card? It turns out the seven of them – three couples and one guy – are full of beans, all chat and excited to be here and thanking me for the invitation. I've only met one of the couples before, Bruce and Fiona, and they hand me a present before making their way into the kitchen.

Everyone is eating, except me. I picked at a few canapés earlier and now I'm not hungry. I'm anxious, someone in this room may have sent the card. I take a second glass of wine and go over to where Amanda is sitting with Olive and Deirdre who have moved inside, leaving the outdoors to Conor's mates. Noel and Abbie are standing outside with them. I wonder if that's why Olive moved. Pushing in beside Amanda, I ask if the food is nice and they all agree it's gorgeous.

'Are you not having any?' Olive says to me.

'Not yet, I'll wait for a while.'

I want to mention Noel and I'm wondering how to bring him into the conversation when he walks in through the big glass open door. He glances down at me, smiling, then looks at who I'm with. The smile disappears and he walks on. Olive has seen him but returns her focus to the plate balancing on her lap.

'Did you hear Noel is moving away?' I say.

Olive stops cutting the meat on her plate, but she doesn't look up at me.

'Is he? Where to?' Deirdre says, before filling her mouth with a forkful of ham.

'Somewhere in the Middle East; he could be there for up to a year or more, which is why we had to bring forward the christening. Conor insisted Noel be the godfather.'

Olive continues to cut the food on her plate but says nothing.

'Is his wife going with him?' Amanda says.

'You can be sure she is,' Deirdre says. 'The guy is hardly allowed to go to the toilet on his own, she's always hanging out of him.'

'I wouldn't let that fella off on his own either,' Amanda chuckles.

Olive immediately turns her head to Amanda. 'Why?' she says, lifting her glass.

'I wouldn't trust him as far as I'd throw him.'

'But you don't know him,' Olive says.

Amanda looks over at me, slowly lifting her glass to her mouth.

'She was just joking, Olive,' I say. 'It's just because he's a good-looking man.' I can see Amanda in the corner of my eye trying her best not to laugh.

'Well, people should be careful what they say, even in jest.'

Deirdre is chewing in silence, looking at her plate and no one else. Olive tilts her head back and downs a large gulp of wine. Amanda's comment seems to have bothered her. But why? One minute she's refusing to shake Noel's hand, the next she's sticking up for him. I'm about to mention Noel again in the hope that Olive might say something more about him when a hand lands on my shoulder. It's Maggie.

'Time to cut the cake,' she says, bending over close to my ear.

'What do you mean... cut the cake?' What is Maggie talking about? This isn't a wedding, there's no ritual for cutting a cake at a christening. Is there?

'Conor has gone to get Shay,' she says, hovering, waiting for me to move. I stand up like an obedient child. Shay is asleep. The poor baby has had enough thrown at him for one day, first, getting drowned by the priest, then all the photos we had to stand for.

'He's asleep,' I say, but before I have time to protest any further Conor walks in through the door with Shay in his arms. He's even managed to put his gown back on. Conor probably knew I'd object to wakening him. Putting on a fake smile, I walk over to Conor with the intention of venting my anger. There are times I feel he does whatever his mother wants. It's like she has him under a spell. Or could it be guilt?

When I arrive at Conor's side, I see that Shay's eyes are open and he looks content so I say nothing. Seeing Shay relaxes me.

'So, what do we have to do now?' I say in a low voice, my finger gliding over the warmth of Shay's skin.

'I'm sure we'll be told soon enough,' Conor says. Maggie is all smiles, hooshing people out of the way as she pushes a trolley with the cake through the crowd. More photos. We smile. I'm standing by the cake when I lift my head to view the crowd. In the distance I see Olive whispering something in Noel's ear. Noel's expression hardens. His narrowed eyes follow Olive as she walks away from him.

Chapter Forty-Five

Photo after photo after photo. Maggie made the two of us pose with nearly everyone in the room. It was worse than my wedding day, and this time I had the added burden of scrutinizing each person wondering if they sent the card. But everyone was as nice as could be and I'm still no closer to figuring out who it was. Eventually, Amanda took Shay back upstairs to where he's now sleeping. I hope. I'll owe Amanda big-time for this. She's been great.

In the corner of the room, I spy Olive and Deirdre having a drink, so I slither out from talking to Helen and a group of Maggie's peers, and go over to sit with them. It's too late to go back to the subject of Noel; it might look suspicious after what I had seen.

Grabbing a glass of red wine from the counter, I walk over and ask Olive and Deirdre if they're ready for another drink. Both nod that they're fine. Olive says she'll only have one more or she won't be able to drive home. I'm amazed she thinks she can with the amount she's had already. You wouldn't get away with it in the city but down here the rules seem to bend depending on the occasion. She's not the only one with a car parked outside.

Conor has organised a minibus to collect people later and drop them home, but the mere suggestion seems alien to some people. And with Detective Fintan leading the way – the man must be on his fifth pint by now – I guess they all feel safe. Let's hope the detectives from Dublin aren't planning on making a visit to the village today.

'I know I shouldn't say it, especially when I work there... but I find it hard to drink the beer.' Deirdre is speaking softly so I lean in closer.

'All beer?' I say.

'Well, not all beer, just the Callbrew.'

'Oh. I prefer a glass of wine myself but I used to drink beer when I was younger.'

'So did I,' Deirdre says, a slight slur creeping into her words. 'And I liked it, but after the accident I just can't bring myself to swallow it. It reminds me of—'

'Ah, stop,' Olive interrupts. 'Don't be so stupid.'

'I know but...' Deirdre crosses her arms over her chest and shivers briefly. 'It's just a bit creepy. I was there that day, said goodbye to the man before he ended up—'

'Stop it Deirdre, for God's sake,' Olive says.

Deirdre giggles and looks at me. 'Sorry,' she says.

'You don't have to say sorry to me, I never even met him.'

Olive excuses herself to go to the bathroom, asking Deirdre if she wants one more drink before they go. It's almost six o'clock now and people are beginning to leave. I'm really enjoying myself now, the wine has warmed my attitude, and I'd love for people to hang on a bit longer. Hopefully some of the younger ones will.

When Olive steps away, I ask Deirdre if she knows Pat who lives out back.

'Yes,' she says. 'Where is he, by the way?' She glances around the room, swaying slightly.

'I don't know. I haven't seen him in a couple of days.'

'Maybe he's gone loolah again,' she says, her words very slurred now. Deirdre has clearly enjoyed more wine than she's used to.

'Why? When did he go loolah before?' I say.

'Ah, when Seamus died he went missing for weeks. We had the cops searching for him. He arrived back out of the blue and told no one where he'd been. It took a long time for him to speak to Conor though.'

'Why?' My heart stops. I have the feeling I'm going to hear something I don't want to.

'Well...' Deirdre seems to be struggling getting the words in order and Maggie is moving in our direction, I have to be quick.

'Why, Deirdre?'

She leans in closer to me and whispers: 'Pat always blamed Conor for Seamus's death.'

I'm trying to act cool but my hand is shaking.

'Why would he blame Conor?'

Maggie is only a few feet away now.

'Conor was there that day, he was the one who closed the latch on the vat.' Her words are completely slurred but they cut through me like a sharp knife.

Chapter Forty-Six

My head is spinning. Maggie is talking to me but I haven't a clue what she's saying. All I can see are her lips moving. Conor killed his father. It was an accident. But Conor killed his father. Now it makes sense. The secrecy around the accident. The comment Maggie made about a weight being lifted when the coroner's report came through. And Conor's reaction to the rumours that surrounded Vicky's death.

There must have been rumours circling after Seamus's accident too. Maybe Pat started them, thinking Conor did it on purpose to inherit the business. How wrong he was. Conor never wanted the business. He felt he had been saddled with it. He told me himself. Conor wanted to study astronomy. He only stayed in the brewery because he couldn't leave his mother after what had happened.

'Are you going to say goodbye to Fr Cormac?' Maggie's voice breaks through the whirlwind going round in my head.

'What?'

'Laura, Fr Cormac is leaving.'

'Oh.' I put my glass down on a nearby table and walk with Maggie to the hall where Fr Cormac is talking to Conor. Where I get the strength from, I do not know. I manage to say goodbye and thank Fr Cormac for the lovely service. Maggie is adding to my appreciation speech when I look at Conor. He's looking at me, noticing the change I guess, seeing the white face, the startled eyes. When the priest has left, Maggie passes us both and walks back into the crowd.

'Laura, are you okay?' Conor says, leaning in and taking my arm.

I say nothing. I find myself staring at him. I don't know what to say. I realise I barely know this man. Every day I seem to learn something new about him. And now, he has this big secret that he never told me about.

'It's probably the drink,' he says, watering down his comment with something about my system not being used to a lot of alcohol anymore.

I want to tell him that I know. That there's no need to hide it from me. That I have a secret too. I want to tell him it's okay, accidents happen, but Conor is leading me up the stairs, suggesting I lie down for a little while. I think I will.

Up in the bedroom, Amanda tells me Shay has just been fed and should be okay for another few hours. He's asleep. She hugs me and tells me she's going downstairs to say her goodbyes. I want to tell her what just happened, but my head is spinning and I don't know where to begin. Plus, the bed looks so inviting.

'You've had too much to drink,' she says, telling me to lie down. I do as I'm told. Amanda takes my shoes off and pulls a throw over me.

I lie still. Numb from drink… from shock… from life. I close my eyes.

Chapter Forty-Seven

What time is it? The sky is dark above my head when I wake up. For a moment I can't remember where I am. My head is thumping. Shay? I jump out of the bed and rush over to the cot. Shay is asleep. His tiny lips slightly open. I'm leaning in to feel the warmth of his breath against my face, when the noise from downstairs disturbs the peace.

Laughter and drunk voices. I think it's coming from the hallway. People must be leaving. Shit, how long have I been asleep? I've missed my own party. What will people think? What will Maggie think?

I switch on the light and look at the monster staring back at me in the mirror. Good Jesus, what did I drink? I pull a makeup wipe from the packet on the dressing table and try to remove the black rings around my eyes. My hair looks like it fell victim to a cyclone. What the hell happened? I'm never drinking that much again. And then it crashes into me. The memory, my conversation with Deirdre. The accident.

When I hear the loud cheery voices disappear down the driveway, I step out of the bedroom and listen. It would appear there is no one else left. I can't hear anyone, only Conor clinking a few glasses. Is he cleaning up? Why is he not pissed like me?

The carpet feels soft below my bare feet. I slowly step down the stairs to where Conor is gathering some rubbish off the floor. My head is thumping and my mouth is dry. Will he give out?

He hasn't seen me yet. I watch him closely. Poor Conor, what a nightmare he's gone through with his father's death and yet he still manages to be upbeat and helpful to everyone. I want to hug him, tell him that I know what happened but as I make my way towards him he turns and sees me. He jumps.

'For fuck's sake, Laura, you scared the life out of me.'

'Sorry. I just needed some water.'

Conor is holding his chest.

'What time is it?' I say, looking to the big brass clock that hangs on the wall by the door. 'Eleven thirty... Gosh, that went on longer than expected, how long did your mother stay?'

'She waited until nine but you didn't resurface, and when I went to get you, you were out cold. Then she left with Helen... you can ring her in the morning, it's too late now.'

My hand is holding a glass under the filtered water tap. 'Why does she want me to ring her?' I say.

'Ah, just ring her and say sorry, explain you haven't had much drink lately and...'

I turn around to look at Conor. Is he joking? He continues to fill the black bag he's dragging across the floor. There are paper plates full of half-eaten christening cake, plastic glasses that were only there as a back-up in case we ran out of real glasses and empty bottles among the debris. The wood that covers most of the floor area looks sticky, not to mention the grey stone below my feet. It's multi-coloured now. Totally unrecognisable. I'm guessing the party moved up a gear when Maggie and her cronies left.

'Say sorry for what?'

'She was a bit annoyed you left the party and went upstairs without saying goodbye to anyone, you know the way she gets.'

The pounding in my head is getting worse. I swallow water then pull open the drawer where I keep the paracetamol.

'Are you serious?' I say. 'I have to apologise?'

'If it was up to me, Laura, then no, but just to keep the peace.'

There seems to be a lot of effort put into keeping the peace around here. I can't believe he wants me to apologise. Pushing two pills into my mouth, I swallow the remainder of the water.

'Maybe you're the one who should say sorry.'

Conor lets go of the bag and straightens up to look at me. 'What for?' He looks confused. 'What's wrong, Laura? What the hell did I do?'

'It wasn't just the drink that made me stagger, Conor.' I can hear the anger in my own voice and I don't like it but I can't stop. 'I know about you.'

He moves a few steps closer to me. I put my hands in the air to ward him off.

'What are you talking about?'

'The accident... I know it was you who was working the day of the accident, the day your dad died.'

'Laura,' he says.

'You could have told me, instead of me having to hear it from Deirdre. Can you imagine how shocked I was?'

'Laura, I was going to tell you it's just... well, there was always something. I could never find the right moment.'

'Not to mention how foolish I felt that I didn't already know?' I didn't actually feel foolish at the time. I do now though.

'Laura, I'm sorry, I should have told you.'

Tears are falling down my face now. This is not how I wanted to tell Conor. I wanted to hold him, comfort him, tell him it's okay. But he annoyed me, telling me to apologise to Maggie.

'Yes, you should have Conor, and I shouldn't have to say sorry to Maggie for falling asleep. I know I had drink taken but it didn't hit me until I heard what Deirdre had to say.'

Conor turns his back to me and walks away. He lifts the black bag in his hand and continues to collect the plastic cups. Why isn't he consoling me, holding me close and apologising again?

'I guess you're right,' he says, the tone of his voice deeper. 'I should have told you... and you should have told me.'

'What?' I hear a whisper leave my mouth. 'Told you what?'

'I'm not the only one carrying a big secret, am I?' he says. Suddenly I'm transported to a feeling I haven't felt in a long time. I want the world to stop. The room to disappear. It's like I'm here but I'm not here. In my head I hear her voice. It's going round and round. 'You stupid girl Laura. You stupid, evil, girl.'

Chapter Forty-Eight

The following moments are spent with me trying to catch my breath. Conor rushes over to me. What does he know? How much does he know? How does he know? He's trying to console me; he puts his arm around me, afraid I'm going to collapse.

'Come over here, Laura, sit down, it's okay, sit down.' Conor leads me to the nearest chair where I fall into the seat. He kneels down in front of me and puts his hands on my shoulders. 'Take a deep breath, Laura, I'll get you some water.'

He jumps to his feet and hurries to the tap. The filtered water tap. I don't deserve a filtered water tap.

–

I couldn't believe my luck. Number One Shandon Close and it was all mine. A small, two-bedroomed, red-brick house. Only a short walk to the city. The kitchen was small but it didn't matter. Nothing mattered. I was the luckiest girl in the world.

Earlier that year when I turned twenty-one I received my inheritance which had been held in a trust fund since my father died fifteen years earlier. Amanda still had two years to go before she would get hers but she decided to move in with me. Mam stupidly thought it was a good idea.

Within two weeks the place had been transformed into a party den. The neighbours weren't too happy. Each time they complained, I promised them it was the last of it. But it went on and on and then I got pregnant.

I remember doing the test, Amanda waiting outside the toilet, her fingers crossed, my fingers crossed, both of us praying that it wasn't positive. It was, and the worst thing about it was that I couldn't remember the name of the father. He was just someone I brought back to the house one night after a crazy session in town.

Mam was okay when I told her. I think she thought it might settle me down at last. And it did. I was a very good mother-to-be. I ate well, I didn't drink and I turned up to all the appointments at the hospital. Mam came with me every time. Amanda had started a new job that year at Imanage and things were going from good to better for her.

When the baby arrived, everyone was so happy. Jamie, named after my dad, was tiny. I'd never seen anything so small and frail. The first few weeks were tiring. A complete change in my life.

I was taking maternity leave from the nursing home where I worked and had no intention of going back. I liked the job, the old people were lovely to work with, but the hours were far too awkward to facilitate raising a child, especially as a single mum. I planned to get myself a nice nine-to-five job and put Jamie in a crèche, or maybe my mam would take him for a while.

I never got the chance to ask her. Jamie was only six weeks old when it happened. My whole body wants to fall like dust to the ground when I think about it. His tiny head, the dark tuft of hair sticking up on top of his twisted head. His tiny body dressed in a white Baby-Gro. Lying still at the foot of the stairs.

–

'Laura, Laura.' Conor's voice drags me back into the room. I shake my head and look around. The light in the kitchen is too bright, it's hurting my head. Squeezing my eyes shut, I tell him to switch it off, switch off the light.

'What?'

'It's hurting me.'

Conor is confused but he hurries to the light switch by the door and lowers the glare. It's darker now but I can still see his worried face.

He's standing in front of me, his hand pushing back his hair. He doesn't know what to do with me. He kneels back down by my side.

'Laura, I think it would be better if you go back to bed. We can talk tomorrow – I'll take the day off and we can talk. You look like you're going to collapse.'

I consider the offer but it won't work. I need to tell him now.

'Conor, sit down.' I move a tiny bit to the left and pat the cushion on the sofa. 'I'm okay, Conor. I'm not going to faint.'

A glass of wine sits on the coffee table in front of me. My head would love it but my stomach turns at the sight of it.

'Will you make me a coffee?'

Conor jumps back up from the sofa and walks over to the coffee machine.

'Instant will do fine,' I say, craving the boost. I want to ask him how he found out and why he never confronted me, but not yet. Firstly, I should be the one answering the questions.

Conor arrives back at my side holding two mugs of coffee. I take a sip, then another, and another, nervous but determined to get this over with.

My husband sits, waiting for me to talk to him, to tell him why I kept this secret. I'm hoping for the coffee to perk me up, to give me the strength I need. I turn to look him in the eyes. His troubled eyes.

'Conor, I'm sorry I never told you. I should have told you at the start that I'd a baby.'

He doesn't say anything but his gaze moves from my face to the mug which he lifts to his lips. His quivering lips.

'But the baby died and I... to be honest, I never wanted to think about it again... I found it hard to go there. Remembering took me to a dark place, a very dark place that could take forever to crawl out of. I was so happy with you that... I didn't want to go down there again. I'm sorry. I should have... I know.'

He's still looking at his mug. Why isn't he saying anything?

'And then I got pregnant with Shay and things just seemed to move forward and I didn't want to turn them back...' Placing my hand on his leg, I squeeze it slightly. 'How did you find out?'

'I saw it in your file,' he mutters in a low voice.

'Nurse Elaine's file?'

'No, at the hospital, on the first visit. The nurse took you into a room to weigh you or something and she left the file on the chair. I read it, hoping to find out a bit more about the process. See if there was anything I could be helping you with. I thought it was a mistake. I took the file to the girl who was sitting at the reception desk in front of me and I asked her about something else written in there. Then I casually questioned the date of the first baby, pretending I thought the date was recorded wrong. She confirmed it. Laura Cummins had given birth to a baby boy on the nineteenth of April, six years earlier. So that's how I found out, Laura. At the hospital, on our first visit.'

Conor sounds like he's about to start crying.

'But why didn't you ask me about it?' I say. I'm trying to make eye contact with him but he's looking the other way.

'I don't know.' His voice sounds confused. 'I guess I knew it must have been hard for you to talk about, since you hadn't told me yourself. I presumed you gave the child up for adoption. And I know what it feels like, being unable to share pain. Knowing no one else could truly understand what it feels like. How could they? It's not their pain. I never told you about the accident in the brewery, how I was the one who caused my father's death because knowing about it spoils everything. It darkens the room no matter how bright. I didn't want that for us. You were the only person in my life who didn't know about this darkness so it couldn't win when I was with you. It was like it never happened and I wanted to keep it that way. So I understood why you said nothing about your baby.'

Moving closer to him, I put my arm around his shoulder and kiss his cheek. 'I'm sorry,' I whisper in his ear. Conor moves his face close to mine and for a minute we linger, faces touching, saying nothing. I'm full and empty at the same time. Tears are flowing down my face.

A few minutes pass. Conor lifts his face, looks into my eyes and with both hands on either side of my head, he wipes my tears away with his thumbs. I am beyond lucky to love this man.

He takes his hands away from my face and pulls my body close to his on the sofa. With his arms wrapped around me, I snuggle close to him. I refuse to believe this man could have had anything to do with Vicky's death. The stale smell of beer hangs in the air. My eyes shift to the window, to the dark sky pierced by one lonely star.

'I'm sorry I'm making this all about me. It must have been awful for you, Laura, to lose your baby, I know how much you adore Shay. How wonderful a mother you are to him.'

My heart quickens. The calm I was feeling slips away. *Please don't ask, Conor.* But he does.

'How did the baby die?

Chapter Forty-Nine

Shay looks as happy as I am that the christening is over. He's lying in my arms, fed, changed and safe. My head is still a bit fuzzy but all in all, I'd say I dodged a bullet. I expected the hangover to be a lot worse.

It was after three when Conor and I came to bed. We talked for a long time. If Shay hadn't cried for his bottle, we would probably still be there. He told me how he walked onto the floor of the brewery that Friday evening listening to the Red Hot Chilli Peppers on his headphones. He noticed the lid on the beer vat open. Cursing the attendant for forgetting to close it, he wasn't aware his father was inside fixing a valve. Conor went up the steel ladder attached to the vat and closed the lid. He locked the big steel handle. He still has nightmares of his father banging on the inside of the drum while 'Under the Bridge' was blasting in Conor's ears. It took a lot of therapy and forgiveness to get him to where he is today.

The sadness he expressed when telling me about his father's accident almost broke my heart. The harrowing expression in his eyes, the pain oozing from every word he said, had me in tears. And then it was my turn. I told him about the accident with baby Jamie. It wasn't the whole truth. It's impossible to tell the whole truth.

The clatter of the cleaners downstairs travels up to the room. Conor had arranged for them to come first thing this morning to get the place back into shape, so I wouldn't have to do it. At the time, I'd thought it was a bit over the top but now I'm glad. I don't think I could have faced cleaning up the mess.

'Hi Shay,' I whisper softly. 'What would you like to do today? Sit and relax with Mammy, watch a bit of Netflix?'

Lifting Shay in my arms, I go to the window and watch the clouds gather in the sky. We were lucky yesterday. It never rained and it stayed warm enough for us to utilise the garden. The younger crowd, who had gathered on the decking, were able to stay out there for most of the day. I'm disappointed I didn't get to enjoy their company, anchor a few friendships. The opportunity doesn't arrive very often for me.

My phone rings. It's Conor. He left for work about an hour ago saying he'd be home early today. He didn't think he'd last too long in work after the late night but he did have a few things to do.

'Hi,' I say, lifting the phone to my ear.

'How are you?'

'I'm fine, Shay's eyes are following me… do you know it's your daddy on the phone?'

'Is he okay?'

'Yes, he's great.'

Conor doesn't normally ring this early. Is he afraid? Does he think I can't take care of Shay, that he'll have to keep checking in on me?

'Is everything okay?' I say.

'Yes, I was just wondering if you rang Mam yet?'

'Oh.' So that's it. Conor isn't worried about my mothering skills, it's my bridge-building skills he's checking up on.

'I was going to wait until the cleaners left, but if you want me to do it now...'

'Whatever, no big deal, give me a ring when you've spoken to her.'

When he hangs up I start to feel nervous. When someone says something isn't a big deal, it usually is. Did I really upset her that much? I know I need to thank her, she really did do a fabulous job and I did promise Conor last night that I'd tell her I was sorry for leaving the party early. Keep the peace.

'Shay let's get this over with,' I say, lying him down in the middle of the bed where his eyes investigate the glass ceiling above him. I dial Maggie's number.. She answers straight away.

'Well, good morning,' she says, her voice full of energy.

'Hi Maggie, how are you?'

'I'm great. It was a great day, everyone said so.'

'I know and I want to thank you for making Shay's day so special.'

'You're very welcome, Laura, I'm glad you liked every-thing. Helen said it was one of the nicest events she's been to in years...' Maggie carries on telling me how everyone loved the day. Maybe she's forgotten all about my early exit. Conor might have been overreacting, asking me to apologise.

'And yourself,' she says. 'Did you enjoy yourself?'

'I did Maggie. I'm sorry I fell asleep without saying goodbye but I only planned on lying down for a few minutes.'

'Oh, don't worry about that. Sure, you're only after giving birth to a baby, Laura. You did great to last as long as you did. You should rest today. How is little Shay?'

This doesn't sound like a woman who's annoyed with me. Was Conor exaggerating her comment or did Maggie mute her anger when she received all the praise for putting on such a great event? Whichever it is, I'm off the hook.

'He's great. Are you coming over later to see all the lovely presents we got?'

'I'd love to Laura, thank you. I'll be over around lunchtime.'

—

After I hang up the phone, I lie beside Shay on the bed and place my hand on his tummy. Gently, I roll him from side to side. I think of Jamie, how I never really took time like this with him. I loved him but I was young and stupid; I thought I was missing out on something better.

Since talking to Conor last night, I feel like a heavy load has been lifted from me. At least now I can mention Jamie, acknowledge that he existed. Another man may not have reacted the way Conor did, with kindness, sympathy and hugs. *You're a very special man, Conor Caldwell. I wish I could tell you what really happened.*

I wonder what Amanda will say when she finds out Conor knows about Jamie, that he's known for some time. It was Amanda who convinced me never to mention the baby to him. There was no need for him to know. What difference would it make? she said.

But it did make a difference. It made a difference to me when I looked Conor in the eye and told him I loved him. It made a difference when we both walked down the aisle side-by-side, waving and smiling, the question niggling at the back of my head: would he still want me if he knew the truth? Now it's out there – some of it – and he still wants me.

'Things are looking up, Shay,' I say, sitting up to grab my phone.

Maggie still loves me

I text Conor adding a laughing emoji.

She's calling in at lunchtime xx

I'm lifting Shay in my arms when the phone beeps. Glancing down to where it's lying on the bed, I see a big red heart. All is good.

Even the sun is showing its support. I can see it breaking through the clouds when I look out the window.

'We'll go for a big walk today, Shay. Mammy will take you down to the village and listen to all the nice people saying what a great party it was.'

A few minutes later, I hear the bang of the front door closing. The cleaners have finally left. The house is mine again. With Shay in my arms, I go downstairs and place him in his crib. The house looks spotless. The only sign that a party has taken place is the heap of presents on the kitchen table. And cards. There are lots of cards. My heart sinks when I look at them.

Chapter Fifty

The presents are wrapped to within one inch of winning a competition. Bows, ribbons, bouncing stars, engraved bunnies, whites, silvers, blues. I'm surprised to see such a variety considering there is only one shop in the village that sells the stuff. Molly's Books and Cards.

Pulling the smallest and prettiest one from the pile, I tug carefully on the ribbon. The box inside the wrapping paper holds a small silver hairbrush with Shay's name engraved on it. Immediately, I take it to the crib and run the soft brushes across Shay's solo patch of black hair. Already, I notice a change in him. He's beginning to look like his daddy.

Happy with my little boy's first hairdo, I go back to open the card. I'll have to remember who gave what because Maggie is going to ask me. The card is sitting on the table. A blue envelope with a bunch of little balloons printed on the corner. My mind flashes back to the dreadful card I opened the night I came back from the hospital. I'm not expecting any of them to say Conor killed Vicky but what if one does? What if this is not over? My eyes begin to blur at the sight of all the possible danger wrapped in pretty envelopes. I don't want to open them. I'll wait until Maggie gets here. But that would be worse. What if she opened a card that accused Conor of being a murderer? Christ. If someone was bad enough to send the card the first time round they could easily do it again. Maybe hoping for more of a reaction this time. My mind flashes to all the faces that filled this room yesterday. Smiling, drinking my drink, eating my food. Was it one of them? And Olive, I'd love to know what she said to Noel to knock him off his pedestal. He became very quiet after that. No longer peacocking his godfather role.

My hands shake as I rip through every envelope until each card is opened. Thankfully, there are no more accusations, only congratulations. I feel my heartbeat return to normal and place the cards standing up on the table.

A wave of tiredness washes over me. It's hard work being a nervous wreck, so I lie down on the sofa and close my eyes. The sound of the birds' song travels in through the open window. It's a beautiful sound, a peaceful sound. There are a lot of birds' nests in the forest at the end of the garden, so we're never without this treat.

In the city, the only time I heard a bird sing was early in the morning, very early before any buses or cars or commuters showed up to provide the soundtrack to the day. Now, I can hear them all day long and it relaxes me.

After about twenty minutes, Shay decides I've rested for long enough. His soft cry breaks through the calm. Dragging my head off the cushion, I go to him and pick him up. Shay wants food. I put the bottle in the heater and switch it on.

Outside, I notice the sun has retreated behind the clouds. I also notice smoke drifting above the forest trees. Pat is back.

Chapter Fifty-One

Maggie arrives at the house with an enthusiasm that I've often wished for. She walks past me with her head held high. Even with all the spraying and mopping that went on earlier, I can still get a faint smell of stale beer in the air.

'Well, I'm glad that's over,' she sighs, dropping her handbag on the counter.

'I can't thank you enough, Maggie. I'd never have been able to do it at such short notice.' With the kettle in my hand, I walk to the tap.

'The cleaners did a good job,' she says, glancing around the room while taking her place on a stool at the counter.

'Coffee or tea?' I say.

'Tea would be lovely and if you have any of the cake left...'

The white box sits open on the countertop. The remains of the christening cake, which looks like it was cut with bare hands, are inside.

'I do.' I cut Maggie a slice of cake and think to myself that the cake would be a great excuse to go and see Pat. I need to talk to that man.

'I'll drop a piece down to Pat while you're here,' I say.

'Oh, where was Pat yesterday? I'm only noticing his absence now,' Maggie says.

'He was away for a few days.'

'Away? Pat? Where would he have to go?'

Resting the plate on the counter beside the teacup I leave the question hanging in the air.

'I thought he only left that cottage to go to the pub,' Maggie says, before putting a piece of cake in her mouth.

'Does he never go away for a break?' I say.

Maggie hurries to swallow the cake so she can elaborate. 'No, it's Mass on a Sunday and the pub every day of the week.' She breaks another piece off the slice and lifts it, but before she puts it in her mouth, I ask: 'Did Vicky ever mention Pat to you?'

'Me?' Maggie straightens her head and looks at me. 'Why would she say anything to me?'

'Oh I just thought she might have mentioned him when you met her in the graveyard that day.' With my back to Maggie, I clench my teeth. She's not going to like me mentioning that again, but I need to shake every tree if I'm to find out what's going on. Maggie doesn't take the bait. Silence.

Wrapping a slice of cake in tinfoil, I place it on the counter, letting the silence linger. After a few minutes Maggie coughs, then immediately begins to talk about the party again like I'd never mentioned Vicky Murphy. She moves over to look at the presents, continuing to talk non-stop so I don't get the opportunity to return the conversation to where I left off.

Eventually she asks me some questions, wanting to know who gave what gifts. Especially which ones were from her closest friends. Thankfully I have it all written down and ready for her. Maggie is impressed. She nods her approval, taking the list from my hands. This is my opportunity to go down to Pat.

I wasn't sure if I was going to see Pat again. Which worried me because I want to tell him he made a mistake. Conor left the house to switch the alarm off in the brewery. Conor will be so happy with me for clearing it up with Pat.

'Do you mind hanging on here while I drop this down to Pat?' I say, lifting the foil-wrapped piece of cake in my hand.

'No, not at all, you fire away. I'll keep my eye on Shay.' Maggie walks over to the crib and looks in at her grandson.

'Are you sure you don't mind? I'll only be a minute.'

'I'm not in any hurry, Laura, I could stand and watch this little man all day.'

—

The silence is creepy when I get to the forest, the only sounds are the birds and the crunch of leaves below my feet. I imagine Shay having a lot of fun here when he's older. Hiding from his mammy. Making a treehouse with his daddy. Playing hide and seek with his pals who will always want to come and play with him because he'll have all the best toys and will know how to share them. I'll make sure of that. Just because his daddy owns the brewery does not mean he will be treated any differently from other kids.

The forest smells thick and damp. I make my way to the little cottage, where a dim light flickers from one of the windows. Smoke is coming from the chimney. Stepping into the clearing is like stepping back in time. Or onto a movie set where someone from the eighteenth century is baking bread and shooting at visitors.

There's no bell or door knocker so I wrap my knuckle against the ageing wood and wait. Pat has never had any visitors that I've seen, apart from the detectives. It's probably how he wants it. Otherwise, why would he live here? He had the option of moving into the town when Conor rebuilt the old house.

The sound of footsteps slowly approaches from behind the door, followed by a creak as the door pulls open. My heart is beating faster because I don't know how Pat will welcome me. Lifting his hand to his cap he pulls on it gently and nods. The smell of burning logs wafts out from the open doorway. Pat says nothing, waiting for me to talk.

'I brought you some cake,' I say, holding out the parcel.

Pat looks at it.

'It's from the christening party yesterday. Little Shay was christened. I thought you might have called in but you didn't, so here.'

I push the cake closer to him. Pat leans back, before slowly raising his hand to take it. He looks at the parcel like it is a bomb in his hand. Has no one ever given him anything before?

'It's just some cake,' I say.

Pat nods, then moves to go back inside. If he closes the door, I won't get a chance to say what I came here to say.

'Pat.'

He turns his attention back to me.

'I was wondering if we could have a chat. I think you might have made a mistake.'

Baggy skin droops over his piercing eyes, which are now fixed on me. I can feel my heart racing. Why am I nervous? He's just an old man. What harm can he do? Pat remains silent, waiting for me to elaborate.

'With Conor... you told the detective he left the house the night Vicky Murphy was killed.'

Pat keeps his stare on me.

'Conor did leave the house that night. The alarm in the brewery went off and he had to go to switch it off. It's faulty, it has happened a few times.'

I jerk backwards when Pat lifts his hand suddenly to scratch his forehead. He smiles. It's not a 'happy to see you' smile. It's more a sarcastic 'you've gotta be kidding me' grin. Why won't he say anything?

Wrapping my arms across my chest, I shuffle from one foot to the other. Is he never going to speak?

I've almost given up hope when I hear Pat clear his throat with a raspy cough. His head bends forward but he remains standing in the same position.

'Thanks for the cake,' he says before turning to go back into the house.

What do I do? I can't give up that easily.

'Pat, please. You misread the situation. Conor had nothing to do with Vicky's death, he's not capable of that.'

He turns to me, his eyes a little less intense. Pat thinks I don't know about the accident in the brewery. How he thought it wasn't an accident.

'If it's because of the accident, Conor didn't do it on purpose, Pat.'

He shrugs, disdain evident in his expression.

'That was just an accident.'

I'm pleading with Pat when he says, 'Is that what they told you?'

'Yes. That's what everyone says, including the coroner.'

'Did they tell you about the argument?'

'No... what argument?'

'The day of the so-called "accident". Conor and Seamus?'

I feel like I'm shrinking in front of him. 'There was an argument? The day of the accident? But...'

Deirdre never mentioned this to me. I'm shocked to hear it but what has it to do with the night Vicky Murphy died? Pat clearly believes that Seamus's accident was something to do with the argument. Is that why he told the detectives about Conor leaving the house? Has he been waiting in the woods for his revenge? Does he not know the coroner reported Seamus's death to be an accident? That no one else ever thought it was anything but an accident? Maggie told me.

'Pat. Seamus's death was an accident. A horrible accident.' He's about to close the door. 'Conor barely even knew Vicky, he had no reason to kill her Pat.' I can hear the desperation in my voice. I need Pat to believe me.

'Conor had a very big motive for killing Vicky Murphy,' he says. Then he closes the door.

Chapter Fifty-Two

I stand for a minute, trying to keep my balance. I feel like the ground has been torn from underneath me. What did he mean? Conor had a motive. What motive? I'm barely able to catch my breath. I contemplate whether to knock again but decide against it. Slowly I move away from the door.

Walking back to the house, I see Maggie looking out the window. I have to act cool, like nothing happened. I wave and she waves back. When I get inside, she asks how Pat is and where he has been. I tell her we didn't get into that; we just talked about the weather and he took the cake.

'Oh well, I'll leave you to it,' she says, putting her coat on. 'I've to meet Helen in the coffee shop at three.'

Maggie looks at her watch. Always in a hurry. I want to tell her to take it easy, not to always be running and racing. But I don't. Instead I thank her again for the great party and tell her I'll see her soon.

I collapse onto the sofa. My head drooped in my hands. What the hell is going on? Does Pat really think Conor had a motive or is he just exacting his revenge? I never noticed how much he hated Conor before. But then I wasn't paying attention. I didn't know about Seamus's accident. Conor killed Pat's best friend. But Vicky Murphy? Does he really think Conor killed her or is he just putting two and two together? He saw Conor leaving the house. He thinks Conor killed his dad which makes him capable of murder. It's quite a stretch. But Pat has no life, sitting on his own in that dull, dark cottage, day in day out. Nothing to do but dream up my nightmare.

A dull dead pain throbs in my head. I'm massaging my temples when suddenly I realise that Pat must have sent the card. Pat must really believe Conor killed Vicky. I have to get to Conor. I need to warn him before Pat does any more damage.

Grabbing a little grey jumpsuit from the pile of clothes on the countertop, I walk over to where Shay is stirring in his crib. His beautiful blue eyes are open wide. Excited to see me, he kicks his legs in anticipation.

'Okay Shay, we're going to visit Daddy at work.'

—

The car rumbles through the stone yard and out the gate. The sun is low and strong. Pulling the visor down, I attempt to block the rays from shining in Shay's eyes. My hand grips the wheel as I make my way through the village and down the back road to the Caldwell Brewery.

I should have said no to Conor when he asked if I was okay with Pat living on the land at the back of the house. But I was so thrilled to be moving into that house I would have allowed Fossett's Circus to set up out back.

Conor told me Pat had lived there all his life and had never been a bother. So who was I to come along and evict him? Of course, Conor didn't tell me his mother hated Pat living there. Did he even know? Maybe Maggie was once like me, tight-lipped with her opinions. Maybe she felt privileged to be part of the Caldwell empire. After all, Maggie herself was shoved up the class ladder when she married Seamus. Taking control of her own reins may only have happened when Seamus died.

I swerve down the bockety road and arrive at the entrance of the brewery. Arthur, the security man, comes out to greet me.

I roll down the window to talk to him. The smell of stale beer oozes from his breath.

'How are you, Laura? I heard you had a right old shindig yesterday.'

His face is red, sweat gathered below his security cap. Arthur looks like he might have enjoyed his own shindig yesterday.

'Yes, it was a great day.'

Arthur looks over at Shay.

'So you're one of us now, little man,' he says.

'Indeed he is.'

'You'll be wanting me to lift the barrier.'

'Thanks Arthur.'

Inside the door, the sweet sickening smell of cooking beer hits me in the face. My stomach lurches. This is not the place to come after a night of too much drink.

I take a deep breath and proceed down the corridor to Conor's office, knocking before opening the door. It's empty. Conor is not here. When I knock on Olive's door, I hear a voice invite me in. It's Deirdre.

'Well hello, what a lovely surprise.'

'Sorry for interrupting, Deirdre, I was looking for Conor.'

Deirdre's eyes are red. She smiles through a mask of makeup and perseverance. She stands up and walks over to take the car seat from me.

'Hello, little man,' she says, putting the car seat onto the desk. 'Did you enjoy your party? You do know it's your fault we're all just hanging in here today.' Deirdre's head turns from Shay to me.

'Actually Olive didn't make it in at all,' she says.

'Oh.'

'Yes. She was getting sick half the night. No stamina, that one.'

'I didn't think she had that much to drink.'

'You didn't see her leaving.' Deirdre laughed.

'But didn't she drive home?'

'Don't go there.' Deirdre sighs, then says, 'Well, what can I do for you?'

'Nothing really, I just came in to see Conor but his office is empty. Is he down on the factory floor?'

'Conor was called out. Do you want me to give him a buzz, let him know you're here?' Deirdre sits back down at her desk and lifts the phone.

'No, I was just passing by.' I don't want Deirdre to sense the urgency.

There's an empty Lucozade bottle beside a large bottle of water sitting on the desk. I smile to myself when I see it. Memories.

'Would you like a cup of tea?' Deirdre asks, but I can tell she's just being polite. The last thing she needs now is to entertain me.

'No Deirdre, thanks, I'll head on.' I can see the relief on her face. I wonder if she remembers telling me about the accident in the brewery yesterday. I'm about to open the door when I feel opportunity tapping me on the shoulder.

Turning back around, I say, 'Deirdre, can I ask you something?'

'Yes,' she says, looking a little dubious.

'Yesterday you were telling me about the day of the accident.'

Deirdre nods. Keeping her eyes on me, she takes an obvious breath. 'I can barely remember... but go ahead.'

'Was there an argument between Conor and Seamus that day?'

She huffs a laugh. 'Was there what? There was an argument between those two at least once a week, nothing different that day.'

'Oh, I was under the impression they got on well.'

'They did, they got on very well but they were always arguing. Always the same thing too. Seamus wanted Conor to take over the business. Conor wanted to leave to study something to do with the stars or the sky, I don't know.'

'So that day was...'

'That day was no different, Laura. No different at all, other than Seamus had a fatal accident.'

I nod and pull on the handle of the door.

'Do you mind not mentioning that I asked you about it?'

'About what?' she says, smiling at me before pulling her keyboard closer.

Chapter Fifty-Three

With Shay safely strapped into the car, I turn the key in the ignition and head for home. Knowing Conor and his dad often argued weakens Pat's case. The man sure does entertain his imagination.

Seeing Deirdre struggle through the day with a hangover reminded me of Mondays at Imanage. The Lucozade. The bacon sandwiches. The clock moving at a slower pace than any other day of the week. I struggled to get through every Monday after putting in a mad weekend of partying and drinking until the early hours.

A surge of melancholy washes over me. Do I miss it? I'd certainly love to go back for one more weekend. The freedom was wonderful. Doing what I wanted, when I wanted, with whom I wanted. No one to answer to. Until it all went wrong.

As if reading my mind, Shay lets out a little whimper, reminding me how happy I should be.

'I wouldn't switch you for the world, little man.' I turn to look at him and feel a surge of warmth rush through my body.

Arthur is at the gate when I pull up. He waves at me like we're best friends now. That's one thing I like about this place. Once you meet someone, they never forget you. There's always a hello or a wave the next time you see them.

That doesn't happen in the city. There were times I spent a whole night with people and the next day they ignored me. Just like that, no explanation. It was like I'd spent a night on some alternative planet and woke up the next day on earth.

'You off now?' Arthur says, punching the code into the keyboard to release the barrier. I roll down my window to hear him better.

'Oops,' he says, when the barrier won't release. 'I'll give it another go, there seems to be a problem with it.'

'It must be as bad as the alarm,' I laugh, trying to make light of the situation.

'The alarm?' he says, punching the code in again.

'Yes. Isn't there a problem with the alarm?'

Arthur stands back and looks at the keypad.

'Never had a problem with the alarm,' he says, focused on the keypad.

Suddenly I'm on high alert again.

'Does it not go off in the middle of the night? I thought I heard one of the girls say it did once or twice.'

'Don't know what they're talking about. Maybe their home alarm goes off or something. Not this one.'

Arthur lifts his hand and grips his chin, staring at the keypad like he is doing a crossword.

'So the factory alarm never went off in the middle of the night?'

'Not in my time here. I'd know, I'm in charge of it. It never gave me any hassle, not like this load of shite.'

He lifts his foot and kicks the metal stand below the keypad, then turns to walk away.

'Hang on, Laura. Sorry about this, love, I'll have to release it from the operations desk.'

Arthur disappears into the small security shed. I'm barely able to move. When the barrier eventually lifts I drive through like a robot. This is unbelievable. Conor has been lying to me. Oh my God. What will I do? Where was he going all those nights he left the bed supposedly to fix the alarm? What was he hiding? Could he have been meeting Vicky Murphy?

It's becoming hard to breathe. Pulling the car over to the side of the road, I step out into the air. I lean over the door and take deep breath after deep breath. Shay is still sleeping. He doesn't know I just found out his daddy is a liar. A big liar.

Why would he say he was going to fix an alarm that wasn't broken? What was he hiding? Did he kill Vicky Murphy? The card carves it's message on my mind. *Your husband is a murderer.* Oh sweet Jesus, what will I do? I can't go back to that house. I should have known this was all too good to be true. That just like me, this world I've infiltrated is also fake.

Chapter Fifty-Four

There's only one place I can go. Dublin. I'm going to Amanda's. I've tried to ring her three times but the phone keeps going to voicemail. She must be facilitating one of those stupid motivational sessions. *Pick up, Amanda. Pick up.* I toss the phone in through the window of the car and wipe my tears from my face.

Shay lies asleep, unaware his life has just changed dramatically. His little hands are holding one another and there's a smile on his sleeping face.

I get back into the car and drive. I get as far as the bridge, the big fucking Call bridge, when I realise I have no supplies for Shay. I'll have to go back. My heart is drilling a hole in my chest. I swerve around and speed towards the house. If Conor's car is there I don't know what I'll do. I cannot go in. I can't face him yet. I need to speak to Amanda.

With my head almost hitting the window, I lean forward to see if Conor's car is in the driveway. It's not. One blessing at least.

I park the car, leaving the car door open and hurry into the house. I grab nappies, clothes, bottles, formula, creams and push it all into one of the baby bags we were given as a christening present. Only yesterday. Jesus is this happening?

Rushing up to my bedroom, I open the drawer of my bedside locker and grab my credit cards and phone charger. Then I run down the stairs out the door and into the car. Shay is still asleep.

The evening shadows are following me as I drive down the road. Every inch of me is shaking but I have to do this. I need space to think. Conor has been lying to me all along.

The phone beeps on the seat beside me. I glance over and see it's Conor. *Deep breaths Laura, keep going.* It rings out. He must be calling me to say he's on his way home. Or else he's already home and wondering where the hell I am.

When I reach the city I feel better. Less agitated. Lights shape the bridges and buildings that would otherwise be blurred by the darkening skies. The phone has rung three times. It's Conor. I'm not answering. Not until I'm calm and settled in Amanda's apartment. Then I'll call. I have to. He'll be worried about Shay. His son. The one I kidnapped. Oh Jesus, could I be arrested? No, he's my son too. I haven't kidnapped him. I'm saving him.

My mind is stretching out of proportion. I need to relax. Focus. Just because he lied about the alarm does not mean he killed Vicky Murphy. There could be some other explanation. But what about what Pat said about the motive? And why did Vicky Murphy send Conor a text? *I need to speak to you asap.* Conor told the police he never saw the text and I believed him but what if he did see it? Is that why he left the house? Did he go to meet her? My mind is going around in circles trying to make sense of it all.

When I get to Amanda's apartment, I ring her phone again but there's still no answer. Surely she must have seen my calls by now. I remember there's a key in the next door neighbour's apartment. Amanda leaves it there in case she loses her own. Rachel answers immediately.

'Hi, Laura. Long time no see. Oh, and look is this the little...' She smiles. She can't remember.

'Boy, it's a boy... Shay.'

'Oh, he's lovely.' Rachel bends down to Shay in the car seat.

I can't do this. Not now. Can she not see my distressed face, my stinging red eyes?

'I just need the key, Rachel.'

'Of course, yes, sorry.' Rachel goes back inside and comes out with the key.

'Thanks,' I say, walking away.

'Laura... If you need anything give me a shout.'

I smile back at her. Then turn the key in Amanda's door.

Chapter Fifty-Five

The room feels like a hug when I step inside. The large glass window looking out over the city. The yellow suede sofa that Amanda took weeks to decide upon, it was so out there. The green leather recliner in the corner. The white glass table on the multicoloured rug. It all looks so modern. So young. So not Ballycall.

I take Shay out of the car seat. He's been cooped up in it for hours now. Resting him on the sofa, I flop down beside him. I can smell he needs to be changed but I need a minute to calm myself. To take a deep breath. To not jump out the big glass window.

Shay's little legs kick and I cry again. Conor always says he is going to be a great footballer. He can tell already by the strength of his kick. I close my eyes and see Conor laughing, rolling Shay, trying to get him to kick Conor's hands. What have I done?

The phone beeps again. I stand up to get it and throw it back onto the table as soon as I see it's Maggie. Surely he hasn't been in touch with her already? I've only been gone a couple of hours. I wish Amanda would hurry home. I need someone to talk to.

I change Shay's nappy and prepare a bottle for him. The poor baby must be starving. But he hasn't cried yet. I wonder if he senses something. Does he know not to cry when mammy is crying enough for both of us?

Shay has just about finished his bottle when the phone rings again. I let it ring out and wait until Shay has finished before checking it. It's Amanda. I ring her back.

'Hi, what's the big news? I've four missed calls from you.'

When I hear her voice I burst into tears.

'Laura, what's up? What's wrong?'

I struggle to get my voice to work but eventually I squeeze some words out.

'I don't know what to do Amanda. I'm here in your apartment. With Shay.'

There's silence for a minute and I can hear people calling Amanda in the background.

'Laura, you'll be okay. Stay where you are. I'll be there as soon as I can.'

'Okay.' I cry again.

'Laura, I have to finish off what I'm doing. There's a crowd here from England. I'll just take them to the restaurant and leave. I'll be with you in a jiffy. Don't do anything. Do you hear me, Laura?'

I mumble a yes and hang up the phone.

I need to find somewhere for Shay to sleep. I don't want to leave him in the car seat all night. I look around the room but I can't see anything that would do the job. I go to the bathroom where Amanda has a display of wicker baskets with towels and slippers and tissues and things. The one holding the towels looks like it might work. The basket is quite rough and I'll have to cover it with some-thing soft. Shay is used to sleeping in soft blankets, blue and yellow stars floating on the mobile above his head. I wonder if he'll notice the noise here in the city. Panic rises inside me as I unload the towels from the basket. What am I doing here? Why did I take Shay from the comfort of his home to sleep like the baby Jesus in a strange house in the middle of the city? Again I cry. Again I look at the white clock above the door. Where is she? Where is Amanda? I can't stand this. She must have had to stay for the meal. Just as the thought enters my head, confirmation beeps on my phone.

> Sorry Sis, going to be a little while longer,
> hope you're okay.

I send her a thumbs-up emoji. Then I take the basket into the main room where Shay is sleeping in the car seat.

'Mammy's going to make you your very own manger, Shay,' I say, tears falling down my face. Doubt is flooding my mind. Did I react too hastily? Should I have told Conor what I knew? No. Then he would have just come up with some elaborate story. Yes, I should have given him a chance to explain. Oh, I'm not sure what to think. It would all be so much easier if I hadn't just had a baby. I've heard so much about Conor's past in the last few days I'm completely confused. I always believed Conor was a good man. That he loved me, loved Shay. And now I find out that he lied about leaving the house in the middle of the night. He could have been meeting Vicky Murphy. There are nights she wouldn't have finished up at the bar until two or three in the morning. But even with all this circumstantial evidence that I'm concocting in my head – which is all it is – something is telling me I might be wrong.

The phone rings just as I'm padding the towel baskets with a soft throw from the back of Amanda's sofa. My heart jumps. It's him. It has to be Conor. He must be going ballistic. I reach over and lift the phone. A picture of Conor holding Shay the day he was born flashes on the screen. It was taken at the hospital not long after Shay arrived into this world. It was Conor's first time to hold his son. Conor's face says it all. *I have never been happier.*

I'll have to answer. The longer I leave it, the harder it will be. Not to mention the fact that Maggie will have the army out searching for her grandson. They're probably worrying that we've been in an accident.

My finger shakes as I drag it across the face of the phone.

'Hello.' My voice is a tiny whisper.

'Laura, where are you?'

'I'm at Amanda's.'

'Amanda's? What are you doing there, is she okay?'

'Yes.'

'Is Shay okay? It's very late to be travelling with him.'

I can tell from Conor's voice he hasn't a clue why I'm here and he doesn't sound too happy that I am.

'Laura, you should have told me you were going to Dublin. I've been worried sick and when you didn't answer your phone...' Conor pauses. 'Laura, why are you in Dublin?'

The sound of Conor's voice seems to minimise my fear to a pile of nonsense. I must stay strong.

'Conor, I came to Dublin to get away from your lies.'

'What lies? What are you talking about, Laura?'

'All those nights you told me the alarm was going off, it wasn't, was it? You left to meet her.'

'Jesus, Laura, where is this coming from? Left to meet who?'

'Vicky Murphy.'

'Vicky Murphy?'

'Yes. It makes sense now; you're the one she was having the affair with. That's why you wanted to shut your mother up that night. You couldn't stand her gossiping because you knew you were the gossip.'

'Laura, first of all, relax. You sound like you're going to burst. Is Shay okay? Where is he now?'

'Shay is fine, Conor. He's asleep.'

'Okay Laura, I'm on my way. Stay where you are. I will tell you exactly what is going on and it has nothing to do with Vicky Murphy.' Conor hangs up and I sit on the sofa, phone in hand, heart in mouth. Tears are soaking my face. I grab a tissue out of the fancy glass box sitting on the side table. I switch on the lamp because the room has gone dark and I'm only noticing now. Lifting the phone, I take one last glance at the picture of Conor and Shay on the screen. My body is numb. I don't know what I'm going to hear but I'm pretty sure whatever he's about to tell me, I probably deserve it.

Chapter Fifty-Six

Amanda hasn't arrived home yet. At this stage I'm hoping Conor gets here first, so I text her not to hurry away from her function, that I'm fine now, I'll see her later.

Placing the throw back where it belongs, I walk with the basket to the bathroom and replace the towels. There's a collage of photos on the wall in the small hallway facing the bathroom door. Moving closer, I look at myself as a three-year-old, a seven-year-old, a fifteen-year-old. Amanda is at my side in them all. There's one with my mother. She's holding both our hands. Me in a red coat, Amanda in a blue one. It was taken on O'Connell Street. Mam looks happy in it and so young; I forget how young she was when dad died. It must have been hard for her. Amanda is still in contact with her. I don't ask how much or what's going on anymore. We agreed that was best. Amanda suggested I wouldn't be able to shift the pain if I didn't shift its source. Which was right at the time, but now, since finding happiness, I think about her a lot.

Lifting my hand towards the photo, I caress mam's face with my finger. *I'm sorry Mam.* I don't think I ever said sorry to her at the time. Maybe I did. It's all such a blur now. I don't know.

To my left, Amanda's bedroom door is ajar. I take a deep breath and move away from the photo. Maybe I should put on some makeup before Conor arrives. He doesn't need to see this face. Amanda won't mind if I use hers.

When I eventually find the light switch I go into her room to a small mirrored dressing table against the wall. The room is tiny compared to my bedroom. It could probably fit into my walk-in wardrobe. But it's cosy and full of beautiful things.

I sit down on the little stool at the dressing table and look at the makeup. Foundation, great, I'll have some of that. My face is stinging from the ordeal so I search for some moisturiser which is not on the dresser so I open the drawer. My hand is rummaging around when I realise I'm touching an envelope. I pull the drawer out further and lift the envelope in my hand. I know it's none of my business but curiosity has always been a weakness of mine. Amanda says I'm just pure nosy. She might be right.

There are a few sheets of A4 pages inside which I pull out. It all looks very official. I read the words printed at the top of the page and my heart stops. What the fuck? Why has Amanda got this in her dresser?

The doorbell buzzes. It must be Conor because Amanda has a key. I take the envelope with me and switch off the bedroom light.

The baby bag is sitting in the middle of the table so I shove the envelope into it. I don't want her having that here, anyone could find it. It should be locked away somewhere. With me. Or better still, burnt.

Conor is standing in front of me when I open the door. He's white as a ghost. Immediately he puts his arms around me and hugs me tightly. Tears, more tears. Conor releases his hold on me and puts his hands on my shoulders. He looks at me with worried eyes. 'What must you be thinking?'

I shake my head and turn away from him.

'I'm thinking what I've been led to think.'

He follows me into the room and immediately goes over to where Shay is sleeping. He places his hand gently on Shay's head. I glance over to the bag where I shoved in the envelope and pray Conor finds no reason to go to it. If he sees what's inside, the game is over.

'Well?' I say, crossing my arms, waiting for Conor to speak.

'Laura, come, sit down.' He sits on the sofa and reaches his hand out to me. He's beginning to show the signs of stress. Maybe it's the light in here but it's the first time I've noticed a grey hair on his head. His skin too is beginning to look dry. Unlike the athletic sparkle I've become used to.

'There is something I need to tell you, Laura. I didn't think I'd have to. I thought it was all over. But now I realise you deserve to know the truth. I'm sorry this has caused you so much pain.'

I move over to the sofa and sit beside him, but not too close. I need to hear what's going on before I do that. When I see the anguish in his eyes, my heart prays that there's a good explanation for what's happened. But my head is warning me not to get too comfortable. This man has lied to me.

Chapter Fifty-Seven

It all happened when Conor's father died and he dutifully took over the company. Everything was in good shape. Seamus had left it that way. And it stayed that way for a while until Conor could no longer look at the vat in which his father had been trapped that tragic day.

Disguising it as a bold business move, Conor changed the system to a newer, modern one that could produce twice as much beer in the same amount of time. It cost a lot of money to install the new system. The company borrowed it.

Everything went well at first. Out with the old and in with the new seemed like a good idea. Until it wasn't. The orders never came in to match the amount of beer they were now producing. The bank wanted its money. Things got tough.

Conor says if it wasn't for the entire village relying on the factory in some shape or form for its income, he would have let it go under. His mother was set up for life and he was still young. But he didn't want that to happen. His father wouldn't have let it happen. So when he was approached to sell the excess beer on the black market he jumped at the opportunity. It was only going to be necessary for a year or two. Then he'd be in a position to continue without it. So he went ahead. But like most bad ideas he regretted it the minute he started.

Every Thursday, two trucks would come to the premises late at night and load up. At the end of every month Conor received a load of cash. Olive was the one who cooked the books for him. It worked seamlessly. No one found out except Detective Fintan Ryan who observed it happening one night. Conor convinced him it was a short-term measure to save the factory and therefore the village, so Fintan Ryan agreed to turn a blind eye.

With hard work and a lot of marketing, Conor's orders began to increase to the level that would free him from his involvement with the black market trade. Then the recession hit. There was no way out. He either had to stick to what he'd been doing, or fold. He stuck.

Then the detectives arrived from Dublin to investigate Vicky Murphy's murder. Detective Fintan Ryan thought they might discover what was going on at the factory, and that was, apparently, the argument I heard over the baby monitor. Fintan Ryan ordered Conor to pull the plug on his black market arrangements.

Conor panicked. He felt his new perfect life was under threat. What about little Shay's future? He had it all planned out. And me. How was he going to tell me the money was drying up? But he had to do what Fintan Ryan asked him to. Things would be a lot worse if he was caught. So Conor put an end to it.

–

I can't believe my ears. Conor Caldwell is a bad boy. Jesus Christ, what next? Without saying a word, I get up and walk to the window. I see the city, drawn in lights. The shimmering colours shape the buildings, the traffic, the life. I take a deep breath and sigh. What am I supposed to do with this information?

Conor turns around on the sofa to watch my every move.

'You have to forgive me, Laura, I don't know how I'd exist without you.'

These words are the best words I've ever heard in my whole life. I've never felt so needed. I close my eyes to capture the moment. Then taking a deep breath, I turn to look at him.

'But you lied to me, Conor.'

'I know I did and I promise never to lie to you again.'

My head is hurting. All that worrying and crying takes its toll. I sit back down beside him and notice the hope creeping into his expression. His worried eyes pierce a hole in my heart. How could I have thought for one moment that this man had had an affair with Vicky Murphy? Or even worse, killed her? *He lied to me.* But now that I've heard the story I can understand why.

Chapter Fifty-Eight

There's a mug of tea on the bedside locker. The room is bright. I'm fully clothed and back in my own bed. In the corner of the room the cot sits empty, blankets strewn over the edge. Conor and Shay must be downstairs.

My phone is flashing. Three missed calls from Amanda. Conor must have put it on silent when he brought the tea up last night and found me asleep. I'd say she's itching with curiosity. I'll have to call her and explain all. But not yet. Firstly, I want to see my little boy.

Shay is lying in Conor's arms when I enter the kitchen.

'Is he okay?' I say, reaching over to kiss his tiny head.

'He's perfect. Totally unaware his parents are loopy.' Conor smiles at me. 'And you?'

'I'm grand, just want to jump into the shower before you head to work if that's okay?'

'Take your time Laura, I'm in no rush today.'

—

I'm wrapping a towel around my refreshed body when suddenly I remember the envelope I shoved into the baby bag. The one I found in Amanda's dresser. The one that tells the whole story, not just the highlights.

Feck, I hope Conor doesn't notice it. There have been enough disclosures over the past few days to last a lifetime. No need for another one. Though I should tell him about the card that kicked off this whole tortured way of thinking. Tonight, I'll tell him tonight.

I drop the towel, pull my dressing gown on and rush downstairs. Conor is still engrossed in Shay when I barge into the room with my hair dripping.

The bag is on the counter where I left it last night. It doesn't look like it's been touched.

'I think I put my cream in here,' I say, grabbing the bag and walking back out.

In the bedroom, I take the envelope and look around me. Where can I put it? I'll kill Amanda for holding onto it. She's the one who kept telling me to let go, embrace the future, not to carry the past on my back. And now I find her with this. What was she thinking, keeping it in her apartment?

For now, I'll shove it under the mattress. Later, when Conor's gone to work, I can tear it up into tiny little pieces and dump it.

As one hand attempts to lift the weight of the mattress, the other slides the envelope underneath. But as I do so, I feel something else in the envelope, something lumpy, hard and small.

Releasing my grip on the mattress, I reach inside the envelope and pull out a USB stick which I presume belongs to Amanda. I place the USB on the bedside locker and hide the envelope under the mattress.

I wait until Conor has gone to work and Shay is sleeping before I ring Amanda. I snuggle up on the sofa, pull a throw over my legs and dial her number. I feel lighter today. Yesterday was such a nightmare. It's hard to believe how twisted a mind can get if it's not fed the proper information. I had convinced myself that Conor was the one having the affair with Vicky. Now in the cold light of day it seems so unlikely. Conor loves me. Why would he have an affair?

Of course, I don't blame myself for not figuring out the reason Conor was leaving the house in the middle of the night. It would be impossible to grow that scenario with no seeds. Beer smuggling. I didn't even know it existed. So, like good old-fashioned insecure Laura, I panicked and thought the worst. Amanda will not be surprised. She might be proud of my actions though – taking Shay and running when I thought Conor could be lying about Vicky. Especially with Vicky dead.

The phone rings out, which surprises me. I thought Amanda was eager to hear from me. She must be holding a conference.

Relaxing on the sofa, browsing social media, I hear footsteps slowly dragging across the gravel. It's Pat. I huddle down into the sofa hoping he's not planning to call in here. Suddenly, I'm nervous. What if he does knock? Will I answer? I huddle further into the sofa, attempting to disappear from view. The footsteps fade past the house. Pat must be going down to the village. I hope he's not calling to the police station with more demented nonsense.

A few minutes later my phone buzzes. I have a message. Amanda.

> Sorry I missed your call. Finishing up a presentation. Then I'm free so I'll be down, put the kettle on.

Well that's nice. Amanda cares a lot about me. Sometimes I feel I give her nothing back but grief. I'll have to change that. Be more supportive. Ask her what's going on with her life, if there's anything she needs me to do for her.

Shay whines in the corner of the room. He missed his bath yesterday, what with his mammy running away with him. Taking him in my arms, I hold him close to my chest against my heartbeat. It relaxes him.

'Mammy's going to make you an extra special bath today. I have a beautiful new ointment that your uncle Aidan and his very tall wife gave you.'

The pile of gifts is still sitting where I left them on a side table. I haven't put them away yet. I look and find the special bottle of ointment that Aidan's wife went on and on about. 'Just two drops in his bath,' she said, making sure I knew how precious it was. I don't know what its claim to fame is because she rambled on so much I'd zoned out of the conversation.

'Here we go, Shay.' I take the bottle, along with Shay, to the bathroom where I fill the baby bath with lukewarm water and two drops of magic. My hand gently glides the water over Shay's belly. He pouts and puffs with excitement. Shay loves the bath. Maybe he'll be a swimmer instead of the footballer Daddy wants. I don't care as long as he's happy.

When Shay is resting in the middle of the bed, wrapped snuggly in a fluffy towel, I raid his wardrobe for clothes to put him in before he falls asleep. Waking him up is not a good idea. I find what I want to dress my little angel in and holding him close to me, I inhale his freshness. God, he smells like innocence.

I'm about to leave the room when I notice the USB stick on my bedside locker. I grab it and take Shay down to his crib. He'll probably sleep for hours after his bath.

After Shay has dozed off, I plug the USB into my laptop and click on the file. A few files appear on the screen. I click on the first one named 'Photos' and the screen flashes but the file won't open. Clicking on the second file… it opens. I click on one of the folders and see a draft. A newspaper report. Written by Vicky Murphy.

My heart sinks. What is this? And what the hell is Amanda doing with it?

Chapter Fifty-Nine

'What's wrong?' Amanda walks through the door, immediately sensing my fear.

I don't know what to say so I nod at her to follow me and walk her to the laptop on the table. I point. It's all I can do. Point.

'What's that you're showing me?' she says, pulling a stool closer and sitting in front of the screen. 'Am I supposed to know what it is?' She squints her eyes because Amanda refuses to wear glasses. She thinks they age her so she'd rather go blind.

'Do you know what this is?' I say, zooming in on Vicky Murphy's name.

Amanda takes a deep breath and leans back.

'Where did you get this?' she says.

I'm not sure what to make of her reaction. She genuinely seems like she doesn't know what she's looking at. Her eyes are glued to me and there's trepidation in her voice. 'C'mon tell me, where did you get it?' She leans back in to read the screen and attempts to open a file.

'You don't know, do you?'

'Is it Conor's?'

'No, it's not Conor's.' Why did she pick him? Does she think that's why I ran to Dublin yesterday? 'Amanda, are you for real?'

She turns her attention to me and looks confused.

'I found this in your apartment yesterday,' I say.

'What?' Amanda jumps off the stool.

'Yes. In the envelope with my court case report.'

Her head drops back. Amanda looks at the ceiling. 'Oh,' she says. I can almost hear the penny dropping. Then she brings her gaze back to me. I'm shaking and praying and staring at her.

'Okay. I was hoping I wouldn't have to tell you this, but here goes.'

Vicky Murphy did ring Imanage. Rose did give her Amanda's name and number and Vicky Murphy did make contact with Amanda. It happened a few weeks ago. Amanda said she knew immediately something was up. The conversation started out with Vicky saying she was trying to track me down because I was an old friend of hers from school. Of course, what Vicky didn't know was that she was talking to my only old friend. Someone who knew everyone I'd ever known. If there had been a Vicky Murphy in my life before now, Amanda would have at least heard of her. So she was suspicious from the start.

Amanda didn't know what to do. She decided to play along, fill her in on my life up to now, leaving out my darkest hour. But Vicky was persistent. Amanda says she would have made a really good investigative journalist.

Anyhow, when she asked Amanda had I had any other kids the alarm bells rang even louder in Amanda's head so she called Vicky out. Asked her what she was really doing. Vicky came up with another story. Said she was doing a piece for the Ballycall newsletter to celebrate the Caldwell grandchild being born. It was to be printed when the baby arrived...

Only someone who didn't know Amanda would believe she'd fall for it. Amanda played along. She agreed to meet Vicky and give her some photos of me when I was a baby to enhance the piece. They agreed for Amanda to call in to Vicky when she was in Ballycall.

Amanda was in Ballycall the next week as it turned out, just in time. She went to Vicky's apartment after visiting me.

Having manipulated her way inside the apartment, she confronted Vicky.

Vicky tried to keep the charade going but when Amanda demanded to know why she asked about whether I had another baby, Vicky caved. She admitted she had found a story on the internet that she believed could have been about me.

Threats flew around the room. Amanda told her she held the power to destroy her chances of ever being hired by a Dublin newspaper. Vicky said she had evidence that would destroy me. After an angry exchange, Amanda promised Vicky that if she gave her the evidence and withdrew from investigating me, she would use her contacts to get Vicky a job as a journalist.

Amanda didn't have any contacts. What she did have was the ability to win a battle. The war never entered her mind. How she planned to follow up on her promise she didn't know but she would come up with something. She'd ask Pete Gunner, her boss at Imanage, if it came to it. He knew every overweight cigar-smoker in the city.

So that's how she ended up with the court report in her apartment. Vicky gave it to her, said she'd withdraw her investigation and would say nothing to Conor. Amanda made her delete the file on her computer and swiped the USB from it when she wasn't looking. She was afraid Vicky had already made a copy. Amanda was good at covering angles. Even jagged ones.

–

'Did you ever hear from her again?' I say.

'Just the once a few days later. I told her things were in motion. Then – well, we all know what happened then.'

'Why didn't you tell me?'

'Ah,' Amanda stands up and walks over to the crib. 'There was no need to worry you Laura, it was sorted. *Fait accompli.*'

My head is buzzing. I can't believe this went on behind my back. Amanda, once again saving my ass. But she should have told me. She lied to me when I asked her if Vicky Murphy had contacted her and she's the one person I thought would never lie to me.

'How is my little godson?' she says, immediately changing the subject like she was just discussing the weather.

'But…' I'm in shock. Staring her out. Stuck to the floor.

'But nothing, Laura. It's over. Now, how is my godson?'

The USB is burning a hole in my thoughts.

'We'll have to give it to the police, Amanda.'

'What?' she says, reaching into the crib to lift Shay.

'The USB.'

'What? Are you mad? Where will we say we got it?'

'I don't know but it could hold information, evidence.'

I'm thinking of what Pat told the police. How he practically accused Conor. Christ, my head is going to burst.

'I don't know. We'll tell them something. I'll say I found it somewhere.'

Holding the little bundle against her chest, Amanda rocks Shay gently from side to side.

'Mammy is losing her marbles,' she says to Shay.

'I'm not, Amanda, it could be vital. Someone sent that card. Pat is trying to nail this on Conor. If there's anything here that could help…'

'Okay… Okay… Relax, Laura… I'll tell you what,' she takes her eyes off Shay for a moment to look at me, 'let's see what's in the files and then we'll decide.' She lifts Shay away from her into the air. 'But first, this guy needs changing.'

Chapter Sixty

Shay lies on the changing mat. Happy. He's decided his hands taste nice and is now trying to put them in his mouth. I brush a piece of fluff off one of his toes before putting his feet back into the Baby-Gro. Then I lift him in my arms and take him to where Amanda is heating his bottle. I wonder what he'd think of all this. So much has happened in the first few weeks of his life. Thank God he doesn't understand. He'd probably want to crawl back into my womb if he did.

'I think it's warm enough,' Amanda says, handing me the bottle. She sighs then sits on the stool by the counter. I'm only noticing now that she's getting some lines on that beautiful face of hers. It doesn't surprise me. One week in my life and even the bald would go grey. She's like my guardian angel. Imagine doing all that for me and not being able to tell me. Amanda knows I would have freaked out if she'd told me. I'm not like her. I panic. Or at least I did.

'Anyway, you never told me what happened yesterday,' she says.

Two cups of coffee and a salad wrap later, Amanda knows all about Conor's dance with the dark side. Amanda says she didn't think he had it in him but is glad to hear it has come to an end. 'Illegal is illegal,' she says. 'No matter how nice the guy or noble the cause.'

The room has darkened while we've been talking. Amanda turns her attention to the laptop on the countertop. She opens the USB. The file named 'photos' still won't open but some of the others do. There's a piece Vicky had written about the day the Spar shop opened in the town and the effect it had on some of the smaller shops. There are quotes from different business people for and against it. From what I can gather, the piece appeared on the Ballycall Facebook page and nowhere else.

There are other short pieces in this file, all referring to local interests dated years back. There are also lists of newspapers, local, national and international, all marked as having being contacted. Vicky Murphy did not dream small. The articles are named and dated and say who they were submitted to. I wonder if anyone ever read them.

I lower my head in sadness. This is Vicky Murphy's world – her plans, her efforts to make a better life for herself – and now it's all gone. It feels wrong searching through it.

'Maybe we shouldn't be doing this, Amanda.'

Amanda looks at me. 'But I thought you wanted to give it to the cops – which would be an even bigger violation of her privacy.'

'I know, I...' My thoughts are jumping around in my head. 'I don't know what to do.'

Amanda jumps off the stool.

'Wait. Think about it. See if you can open the other file. Maybe there's something in the photos. Try it on Conor's computer.' She closes down the lid on my stone-age laptop. 'This thing is way out of date,' she says, sliding off the stool.

I nod at her, my head heavy with sadness. Vicky Murphy had beautiful dreams, evident from all the pieces she wrote, the places she wanted to work and see. But she never got to fulfil any of those dreams. Someone brutally murdered her.

Chapter Sixty-One

Amanda wasn't long gone when Conor arrived home. We had a lovely dinner and shared a bottle of wine which was a welcome change from yesterday's drama. I had planned on telling Conor about the card but everything was so nice and peaceful I wanted to keep it that way.

He's fast asleep now at my side, his handsome face shadowed by the full moon hovering above our heads. Shay sleeps in his cot.

Careful not to disturb either of them, I slip out from under the duvet. I grab my dressing gown and quietly leave the room. Sleep has abandoned me. It's just not happening tonight. The worry of what else could be on the USB keeps rolling around in my head.

Amanda doesn't want me to give it to the cops because she doesn't want to be associated with this whole situation. And I don't blame her. Amanda has goals. Dreams. She plans to be sitting in big chairs on high floors in the years to come. Having any kind of dalliance with the law could jeopardise some of those plans.

I'm not sure I agree with her. I don't think she'd be in any trouble for what happened between her and Vicky. But it's not up to me. It's not my future. And if I can do anything – even something as small as doing nothing – I will. I owe her. So Amanda's name will not be mentioned.

But I can't do nothing. There could be something on the USB that would help the detectives solve the murder. I feel I must do something, since Pat is practically accusing Conor. I'm worried. Those detectives are looking at Conor because of the text Vicky sent him and what Pat told them. I might find something important in those photos, something that would take the heat off Conor. If I do, I'll give it to the detectives. I'll tell them what I'll tell Conor. The USB came through the letterbox.

Taking the USB in my hand, I tiptoe out of the room and down to Conor's computer. Hopefully I can open the folder. Conor has the most up-to-date Mac on the market. Well, at least it was when he bought it.

I remember his face, giddy, like a child in a queue for McDonalds. He kept smiling over at me as Harry from the football team – an IT genius, apparently – rigged it up for him in the side room off the hall. Which Conor now calls his office.

Inside the office I'm immediately greeted by the smell of newness. Conor had it decorated a few months ago and the décor hasn't quite settled in yet.

A big wooden desk sits proudly at the far end of the room. It reminds me of a scene in a movie. *The Godfather*, I think, when they all come in to see the boss. Conor doesn't use it for anything like that. He says he set it up in case he wanted to do some work from home when the baby arrived. But so far, the only thing I've seen him do in here is lead a group of virtual men to war or a team of animated soccer players to World Cup success. The walls are covered in images of the solar system and the ceiling is painted like a sky. Every book on the glass shelf relates to the universe. If they ever need a stand-in to solve the mysteries of the universe, Conor will be ready.

Leaning over the keyboard, my fingers trace the edge of the screen searching for the slot to put the USB in. I'm mindful of the hour and pray that Shay doesn't wake up while I'm doing this. Not that Conor would mind me being in here. He doesn't. I've been in here lots of times. But he might not be happy about my eagerness to probe the contents of this USB in the middle of the night. It doesn't really fit in with his new relaxed 'let it go' mantra.

Eventually, I locate the slot, pull the seat from behind me and sit down. The screen lights up instantly when I hit the power button. It's asking for a password. Shit. I forgot about that. Maybe it's Shay. No. Laura. No. ShayLaura. No. Laurashay. No.

Ah well, worth a try. I'll ask him for the password tomorrow.

Before closing down the computer, I take one last chance to see if it's written on something. It wouldn't surprise me; Conor is so trusting.

I open the drawer closest to me. It's full of computer games and bits and pieces but nothing that looks like a password. The second drawer is much the same but with a few leaflets added. When I open the third and last drawer I find a batch of DVDs: *Star Wars, Game of Thrones, Star Trek*.

I'm about to close the drawer when I notice a key lying in the corner. I take it in my hand. It's not like any of the other bits and bobs in the drawers. It's old. Very old. Old enough to open the door of an old cottage maybe. I wonder, is it?

Footsteps shuffle on the floor above my head. With the key and USB in my dressing gown pocket, I quietly close the door and walk up the stairs. Conor is about to lift Shay when I walk into the room.

'I thought you'd made another attempt to escape,' he whispers, his arms stretched out, ready to take Shay. Is he never going to let me forget that?

'I'll get Shay,' I whisper back. 'You go back to bed. I just needed some water.'

Conor lies down, pulls the duvet around his shoulder and is fast asleep by the time I have the bottle in Shay's mouth.

Chapter Sixty-Two

My eyes are fixed on the forest, on the trail of smoke puffing out from the trees. Pat hasn't left to go to the village yet. I hope he does so I can check if the key I have in my jeans pocket will open the door. If Pat is so sure Conor had a motive, there might be something in that cottage to shine a light on his theory.

It's not every day he makes the trip to the village. Sometimes it's late into the night but Conor will be home then and I can't very well tell Conor that I'm going to break into Pat's cottage. He'll think I've completely gone over the edge. So here's hoping Pat's milk has gone sour or something, and he has to go down to the shop.

Amanda phoned on her way to work asking if I'd found anything else of interest on the USB. I told her I couldn't open it so she suggested emailing it to her and she would get someone at Imanage to have a look at it. She thinks Simon in IT will be able to do it. She also said she had a mad busy day ahead of her at work but she would get to it as soon as possible.

It's been a long time since I had a mad busy day ahead of me. Minding Shay keeps me busy and I love it but it's a different kind of busy. I know what to expect: when he'll eat, sleep and have his bath. Excitement is delivered in the form of a new sound coming from his mouth or a previously undetected movement.

Grey clouds race across the sky. The trees at the end of the garden are blowing from side to side. It's a dark gloomy day and on these days the large open wild spaces are not at all welcoming. I wonder if the weather will keep Pat locked inside or pottering in his wood-shed instead of venturing down to the village. I take one last glance out the window but there's no sign of him.

I wonder what my mam would say if she could see the beautiful life I've carved out for myself. She might even be proud of me. She might be able to forgive me. Amanda has told her all the details of my new beginning but as we agreed, Amanda and I don't talk about her anymore. It was putting Amanda under too much pressure. Telling me she'd told mam about Shay was hard enough for her.

I did try to ring my mother a few months after the trial. I rang her a couple of times. I wanted to hear her voice to tell her how sorry I was and beg her forgiveness. But she never answered. Maybe I should try again. It's been such a long time. But that just makes it harder to make the move.

I know my mother would have accepted the accident if it was just that. Accidents happen. I remember when she came to the hospital. I was crying. She was crying. Jamie was dead. He had fallen down the stairs.

Amanda had gone out that night and Jamie was upstairs. He was fed and changed and sleeping comfortably. I remember checking in on him. The little blue bundle lying in the cot. I decided to have a drink. Just the one. I was bored and lonely and feeling very sorry for myself, that I couldn't go out and enjoy myself like everyone else. Earlier that week I'd had a glass or two of wine with Amanda. I felt fine. Got up in the middle of the night for Jamie's feed, no bother. Sure, I could do it again. Only this time I didn't stop.

When Amanda arrived back she had found us both at the foot of the stairs unconscious and had called the ambulance. She doesn't speak about it. How awful it must have been for her to walk in on that scene: her sister and her nephew both lying on the ground. Only one breathing.

The next day the police had arrived at my hospital bedside. My mother was with me and she had heard them question me about the amount of alcohol in my system at the time of the accident. They mentioned something about gross negligence. I could hear their words cutting a hole in my life. I wanted to kill myself. My little boy was dead. His tiny body lying in a cold mortuary because of me. My selfishness. I had survived the fall, only I knew I hadn't. Any happiness, joy, excitement, any reason to live had vanished when Jamie slipped out of my arms.

I had looked over at my mother. Her face had changed in front of me, her eyes filling with tears that rolled down her pale skin. She listened to the police asking me questions. Her daughter was the reason her grandchild was gone. I remember the last words she ever spoke to me. 'You stupid, evil girl.'

–

My phone beeps. I look out the window. Still no movement from Pat. Lifting my phone, I open the text from Amanda.

> You're not going to believe it. Have a look at the email.

My heart begins to quicken once more. I rush back to the laptop and open the email that has just come in. My fingers wiggle over the keyboard as I wait for the message to download. My stomach is in a knot. What is in that folder? What am I not going to believe?

I click on the message. Then the file attached. The laptop flashes two photographs onto the screen. I freeze. This can't be right. Holy fuck. I did not see that coming.

Chapter Sixty-Three

Frozen to the spot, I sit staring at the image of Noel and Olive wrapped around one another. In one photo, they're kissing. Not like friends. This is a 'please do not disturb' kiss. In the other, she's sitting straddled across his lap. They're sitting on a small grassy hill, a sunny blue sky in the background. He's kissing her neck. My eyes are unable to move away from the image. What the hell is going on? Vicky Murphy must have been doing a bit of Jessica Fletcher on these two. I wonder who asked her to. Abbie?

That must be why Abbie never lets him out of her sight. She's either linking his arm or following him from one room to another. Did she know about the affair? Did she ask Vicky to investigate Noel and take her down a path that would ultimately lead to her murder? And Olive, that must be why she's being so cool with Noel. He's leaving her. Going to Oman with Abbie and ending the relationship. Maybe Olive was the one angry with Vicky for bringing her secret love life to an end.

I wonder what Conor will say. This is unbelievable stuff and I'm here on my own with a new baby and no one to discuss it with. I really should ring Conor and tell him what I've found out. We're going to have to give this to the police now. No question about it. This is bad. Noel and Olive were having an affair and Vicky had proof. I wonder if they knew she had photos of them. Surely, though, if Olive and Vicky were close friends like everyone said they were, Vicky wouldn't have taken those photos? She would have warned Olive that someone was suspicious about her and Noel. Wouldn't she? Maybe she did. I can't wait any longer. I'm ringing Conor.

Conor's phone answers after two rings.

'Hi babe,' he says. He sounds happy.

'Conor... are you busy?'

'Not particularly. Everything okay?'

'Not exactly. Would you be able to come home for a while?'

'Is it Shay? Is he alright?'

'Shay's fine,' I say. 'In fact he's great. He's smiling up at me as we speak.'

He's not. Shay is fast asleep in his cot but I want to reassure Conor.

'What is it, then?'

'I have to show you something.'

'What?'

'I don't want to tell you over the phone, Conor. Can you come home?'

'Okay, give me half an hour. I need to finish something here.'

'See you then.'

I hang up and look at the screen again. Olive is another reason I couldn't tell Conor over the phone. She could have been standing near him. She might have heard, or he might have asked her if it was true before I had a chance to talk to him.

The room darkens. I stick the kettle on and return to the window. It's lashing rain now. Pat probably won't venture out in that. I'll have to wait. The idea of Noel and Olive having an affair is pure madness. But what does it mean? Had either of them anything to do with Vicky's murder? Maybe they found out what Vicky had stored away on the USB. That would be motive enough for Noel. I don't think Olive had anything to lose except her good name.

I never would have thought that of Olive – having an affair with someone's husband. And there I was, feeling sorry for having robbed her man while all the time she was chewing on another bone. A bone that wasn't hers to chew.

'Beware of the quiet ones,' Mam always said. 'They're usually quiet for a reason.'

Like me. I was quiet for years after Jamie's death.

And Noel. What the hell is he at? He has a beautiful wife already. One with loads of money. Why would he be interested in destroying all that? Danger, maybe? Some people love tinkering with it. Testing themselves. Standing at the cliff's edge looking over. Or love. Maybe Noel and Olive are in love. But when? How? So many questions… I wonder what Conor will say.

I don't have long to wait for the answer. I'm just about to lift Shay from the crib when Conor walks into the room.

'Well,' he says. 'What's so important that it couldn't wait until tonight?'

I walk to the laptop and press a key to refresh the screen, then walk over to get Shay's bottle.

Conor sits on a stool and looks at the screen. He sighs and clasps his hands together under his chin.

'Where did you get these?' he says, his voice low. He closes down the laptop and looks at me. He looks deflated.

It must be hard for him – two of his best friends living this lie.

'They were on Vicky Murphy's USB.'

'What are you doing with Vicky Murphy's USB?' I take a deep breath, I can't tell Conor I found it in Amanda's apartment. I promised her.

'Eh… it was put through our letterbox…'

'What? Why would someone send us Vicky Murphy's USB? When did this happen?'

I realise this is the perfect opportunity to mention the card. Shaking the bottle, I walk over to the crib where little Shay waits for me to pick him up. Conor is still looking at the screen. With Shay in my arms, I say, 'This morning… and that's not the only thing that was sent anonymously, there was a card.'

'A card… What card?'

'I should have told you earlier, I know, but I didn't want to spoil the moment. It arrived the day I came home from the hospital. I opened it.' I'm looking at Shay so I don't have to see Conor's face when I tell him. 'I thought it might be someone playing a sick joke so I didn't—'

Conor interrupts me. 'What about the card?'

'Well, it was basically accusing you.'

'Accusing me of what?' He's off the stool now and walking towards me.

'Of killing Vicky Murphy.' I clench my teeth and peep in his direction to see what he's doing. Conor stands with his eyes and mouth wide open, looking at me like I've two heads.

'I know I should have told you, Conor, but I put it away and then when I went to get it to show you, it was gone.'

He's speechless.

'I think it might have been Pat.' I say. But Conor remains silent. Gobsmacked.

'I wanted to tell you but then I didn't have it and so much was going on and I thought you might not believe me—' I'm rambling on when he interrupts.

'What do you mean it's gone? Gone where?'

'I don't know, I put it under a magazine on the counter.' I point to the island in the centre of the room. 'The night I came home from the hospital. But it was gone when I went looking for it the next day.' Conor's eyes are fixed on me. I can tell he can't believe what he's hearing.

'What exactly did it say?'

A hot tear burns down my cheek. My body is shaking. Conor is going to hate me for not telling him about the card. 'It said, *Your husband is a murderer, where was he the night Vicky was killed?*'

Conor looks away from me, hands on hips, eyes on the window. 'Sweet Jesus, what's going on Laura? You should have told me.' He turns, his worried eyes stare at me.

'I wanted to, Conor, but the card was gone, I had no proof, I was afraid you wouldn't believe me.'

'And it wasn't there when you went to look for it?'

'No.'

'Have you any idea who might have taken it?' I shake my head. 'I don't know, maybe…' I want to say Maggie but I'm not sure he'd appreciate me accusing his mam. 'I don't know Conor.'

'Well I do.'

'What?'

'It was my mother.'

'Maggie, but… how do you know?'

288

'Because no one else would. If she opened that card and read it she would have taken it. I know. She would not have let me see it.'

'But why wouldn't she say anything?'

'Mam has been trying to protect me from the rumours since my father died: how some people thought it wasn't an accident. Noel used to tell me how she spent the first few months defending my honour. I told her not to listen to the rumours. That we knew the truth and nothing else mattered.'

'Oh God Conor, I'm so sorry. I...' I go to him and, with my son on my shoulder, I wrap my arms around him. Conor holds us. 'We still don't know who sent it,' I say. He unlocks my grip and looks at me. 'Laura, it's not true, so it doesn't matter who sent the card.'

'But do you not want to know?'

'Why, what difference would it make? I know who my friends are. I know the people who have stuck by me.' Conor walks over to the computer. 'And now one of those friends is in trouble.'

'So what do we do?' I say. But there's no response. Conor is still trying to digest the murky information on the screen in front of him.

'You'll have to show it to the detectives, Conor. Vicky took these photos and now Vicky is dead.'

Conor is silent. I can tell he's listening and not listening at the same time, his mind racing around in circles. Maybe I should leave him alone for a while.

'I'm going upstairs to change this little man,' I say, walking out of the room.

After a few minutes, Conor follows me up to the nursery that Shay will eventually move into. It has been decorated in blues, creams and yellows. There are cuddly toys, bean bags, a rocking horse and a cartoon painting of the brewery with animals looking out the windows on one of the walls. And, of course, the solar system. Conor had it all commissioned specially. Some of the aspects are painted on the ceiling, others hang from strategically placed wires. The sun takes centre stage. The moon hangs to its right. A myriad of planets float across the room, all ready and waiting to entertain Shay when the time comes. When it gets dark the whole thing glows. It's pretty special to see.

'You didn't show those photos to anyone else, did you?' Conor says, standing over me. The smell of his aftershave mingles with baby powder creating a kind of confusing smell.

'No.'

'Good. Well, don't. Wait until I have a word with Noel.'

'But—'

'He's my friend, Laura. He's Shay's godfather. The least I can do is talk to him about it first. Tell him I saw the photos. Get his side of the story before those out-of-town detectives get their hands on them. He's supposed to be leaving for Oman in two days.'

Conor leaves the room and by the time I come downstairs, he's already rung Noel.

'He'll be here shortly,' he says. 'I'll speak to him in the office.'

Damn it. If he speaks to him in there, I'll hear nothing.

'Don't talk to him in there, Conor, that makes it all seem very official. He's your friend. You stay here. I'll bring Shay upstairs. I want to lie down for a while anyway. My head is splitting from all this.'

Conor walks over and hugs me. 'Okay, Laura, thanks.' He looks older all of a sudden, a lifetime of worry showing in one moment.

'It will be okay, Conor,' I say, rubbing my hand against his cheek. The skin is cold beneath my touch. I kiss his lips but they don't react. I hate seeing him like this.

'Will you be okay?' I say.

Conor nods.

I walk over to the crib to get a blanket. Conor is staring out the window with his hands stuck into the pockets of his trousers. I hit the reverse button on the baby monitor.

Chapter Sixty-Four

The buttons on the monitor flash all the way to red.

'What's up, matey?' Noel has arrived.

Conor coughs. Then a brief pause. Then I hear his voice.

'This isn't easy, it's a bit sensitive, actually.'

'Ooh.'

'Jesus… how do I say this?'

'Say what, man? You're beginning to freak me out here. What's going on?'

More silence. Then: 'Where did you get those?'

Conor must be showing Noel the photos on the laptop.

Shay is being rocked from side to side with more vigour than is necessary, so I place him into the centre of the bed and move back over to sit beside the monitor. I'm so nervous I'm afraid to open my mouth in case my heart falls out.

'They were on a USB that was sent to me belonging to Vicky Murphy.'

'Vicky Murphy? Who the hell sent you that?'

'Not the point.'

Typical cheater, trying to move the attention to the messenger. I'm glad Conor didn't fall for it. I'm picturing him glaring at Noel. Waiting for an explanation. The monitor is showing no activity. I'd say Noel doesn't know where to look.

After a couple more minutes of silence the light flashes red again.

'Well I guess you know now. I can't deny it happened. But it's over, Conor. It was only for a short while and both of us regret it. I'm sorry it happened. I'll never be able to forgive myself, I—' Noel is ranting on. I can almost hear a violin in the background.

'Did you know?' Conor interrupts him.

'Did I know what?'

'That Vicky had these photos.'

'No. Christ. No.'

Suddenly Noel seems to register the consequences and says to Conor: 'Shit, Conor, I hope you don't think I had anything to do with what happened to her. I didn't even know she had these. Fuck. What was she doing with them? Did someone...'

Noel stops, mid-sentence. If he's acting, he's good. But then again, he *is* good. He's been having an affair, for Christ's sake. Acting on a regular basis. Lying to everyone around him, including Conor, his best friend; the kind of friend who'd move his child's christening forward just so he could be godfather. Conor must be so upset to find out that Noel has been lying to him. They've been friends since they were both at school together and his loyalty after Seamus's death clearly means a lot to Conor. They holidayed together, supported the same football team and went to the games together. They were each other's best men at their weddings, for God's sake.

Shay whimpers a little, kicking his legs and waving his arms. He must be looking for me. Taking him off the bed, I rock him gently from side to side. The last thing I want is for his cries to drown out the monitor.

'It's okay, Shay. Mammy's here,' I whisper. Then I kiss his warm forehead.

'What would you do with this information, Noel?' Conor is back on.

'I'd... I don't know, I...'

'Would you show it to the police?'

'You can't do that, Conor. Come on. It was just a stupid affair. It's over. No one got hurt.'

Silence.

'Look Conor, please don't show the police. I'm sorry. I can't take it back but I can make up for it for the rest of my life. I'll make it up with Shay and...'

'Don't bring Shay into it, Noel.'

'Sorry, but I promise it's over. You have to forgive me. And I had nothing to do with Vicky Murphy being murdered. You know that! You know me, Conor. You're only going to bring untold grief to Abbie and Olive if you show that to the police, and for what? Nothing. No one will gain from you doing that. Please, Conor.'

Noel sure can beg. I'm barely able to breathe listening to him. I hope Conor doesn't fall for all that crap.

'Just go, Noel. I can't think straight.'

'I really am sorry, Conor. It was bad of me not to tell you but—'

'Just go. I'll call you later.'

There's a bit more said in the hallway but I can only hear mumbles. Then the door closes. Reaching my hand out, I switch off the monitor and lie down on the bed with Shay resting beside me. His eyes stare at me. His little hand stretches out as if trying to touch my face. I take his hand and kiss it, waiting for Conor to come up to the bedroom. When he doesn't arrive after twenty minutes, I decide to go down and see how he is. He must be so confused, not knowing what to do. Should he put his years of friendship ahead of doing the right thing? It must be hard being faced with that decision.

I wiggle off the bed and put Shay in his cot. A blue light appears, flashing in and out of the room.

Chapter Sixty-Five

'Go back upstairs Laura.' Conor orders me out of the hallway.

'No, what's happening? Why are you doing this?' I scream at the detectives, gasping for breath between each word. My eyes fill with tears. The younger detective is putting handcuffs on Conor's wrists. The older guy is reading him his rights.

'Stop it. It wasn't him. He did nothing.' Everything is spinning around me. I grab the handrail to stay standing. 'He did nothing. It was Noel... Noel killed her.'

'Go back upstairs Laura.' Conor's voice is getting more agitated. But does he think I'm just going to stand here and let them take him away?

'I have proof,' I say. I hear the handcuffs clicking closed. The older guy steps in my direction.

'Mrs Caldwell, could you go back upstairs please, this isn't helping.'

'But he didn't kill her.' I hear my voice fading as Conor's voice pierces through the buzzing in my head.

'It will be okay Laura, take care of Shay, I'll be home soon. I'll be back tonight.'

The next thing I know they're gone. I don't know how long I've been standing here in the hallway. But I fear if I let go of this handrail, I might fall and break into tiny pieces. My eyes are fixed on the hall door where my husband was hauled out by two detectives from Dublin.

I think of Shay. Shay! I run up the stairs and check he's okay. He is. I take a few deep breaths, just like I'd been taught to do whenever living seemed impossible. *Breathe in Laura.*

What will I do? What can I do? My tear lands on Shay's rosy-pink cheek. 'It's my fault Shay. This is all my fault.' The words escape my lips like whispers in the night. It's here. Karma has found me.

–

The house is silent. I carefully step down the stairs, Shay gripped tightly to my chest. When I get to the kitchen I switch on the light and wait for someone to call. I thought the phone would be hopping by now but it seems nobody knows yet. I consider ringing Maggie but decide against it for the moment. I don't want her calling over here. I need my sister. Amanda. The phone rings. Leave a message. Always the same.

The laptop sits open on the counter. I tap the keyboard bringing the photos of Olive and Noel back onto the screen. My head feels heavy. I lift my phone and try to call Amanda again but still no answer. My phone rings. It's not Amanda. I don't recognise the number. My head throbs as I answer it. Fear hijacks my body. What am I going to hear now?

'Laura… Laura.' A deep voice says.

'Yes.'

'Laura, this is Detective Fintan Ryan. First of all, are you okay?' The sound of his voice unravels my strength and I begin to cry.

'Laura?'

'Fintan. What's going on?'

'Laura, I don't want you to panic. Conor asked me to ring you to see if you're okay, if you need anything. The detectives are speaking to him now. It could take a while but you're not to worry.'

I almost laugh at this request. 'How can I not worry? They arrested my husband.'

Fintan's voice softens. 'I know it looks bad Laura, but it will get sorted.'

'How, how will it get sorted? He didn't kill Vicky Murphy, Fintan, you know that.'

'I know. I know Laura. Look, hang in there. I'll be back to you as soon as I've any news.'

'Fintan, I need you to call here. Can you come over now? I have something to give you. Something that might help Conor.'

'What is it?'

'I'll show you when you get here, can you come?'

'I'll be there in a few minutes.'

I close down the file and remove the USB.

Chapter Sixty-Six

It's been over an hour since Detective Fintan Ryan left with the USB and I still can't find any peace. Outside the window, I watch the darkness thicken around the forest at the end of the garden. Pat left the cottage earlier, not long after Noel called. I saw him shuffle down the driveway when I was in the bedroom. I doubt he's back yet.

Suddenly I remember I have the key. Should I go down there? Pat said Conor had a motive. But why does he think that? Maybe the answer is in his cottage. But I can't go down there now, it's dark, what about Shay? I'm sorry I didn't ring Maggie earlier. She could have watched Shay while I searched the cottage, I don't have time to wait for her to come over now. I'm tossing plans around in my head. Sitting here adding to the darkness is not helping Conor. I need to do something.

Shay is burped, changed and huddled into a baby sling that someone gave to us as a gift. I never thought I'd use it but I hadn't allowed for this scenario.

With my baby comfortably stuck to me, I walk to the end of the garden holding a torch for guidance. The light from the house is shedding some brightness but the closer I get to the forest, the darker it gets and the more nervous I become. A cold breeze brushes past like a ghost trying to frighten me. I wrap my arms around Shay to protect him. The key, heavy with risk, is in my other hand.

When I get to the door, I look around to make sure we're alone. We are. Nothing but the birds sleeping in the trees and the insects below my feet. My heart is in my mouth as I put the key into the lock and turn it. Bingo.

For a moment I hesitate. What if Pat comes back and finds me here? I don't care. I want answers. I glance behind me to see if he's coming but I doubt I'd see him if he was. Everything is so dark. I step inside. Shining the flash-lamp onto the wall I locate the light-switch and flip it on. I sigh with relief. A part of me is surprised it works.

A damp musty smell hits me in the face. The hallway is tiny, with bare stone walls. There are three doors, all closed. With one hand protecting Shay, I push on the first door.

The bedroom door creaks. My nerves are on edge but I have to keep going. I look around the room to see if I can see anything that might help me. It's a tiny space. Pat must find it strange coming into our house – the big needless spaces. I wonder if he resents Conor ending up in all that luxury while he struggles to put a decent blanket on his bed. It's just a single, steel-framed bed with one hairy blanket on top. A small glass, the base coloured with whiskey debris, sits on top of a pile of books by the bed. A makeshift wardrobe lies against the wall, in which Pat's Sunday suit and shirt hang alongside a jacket and an old worn Ballycall GAA Club jersey. It must have been his own one from days past. Conor told me Pat and his dad started up the club. Judging by the state of the jersey, that was a long, long time ago. The material is thick like wool, heavy with a worn discoloured collar and a hand-stitched crest. I put my hand on the hanger to turn it around and see the number one sewn onto the back. Keeper.

I'm on edge. Conor is probably in an interview room now answering questions he should not be asked. Why does Pat think he killed Vicky? Why does he not believe he left to go to the brewery that night? I wonder what will happen if Conor tells the detectives about the black-market beer. He's going to have to if he's to clear his name of murder. Then a thought flashes into my head. If it's black-market, there's probably no evidence it took place at all. Conor will have no alibi.

I quicken my search leaving the bedroom and pushing open the door to the kitchen. In front of me stands a dresser with lots of drawers. Shit, this could take time. I kiss Shay's head. 'Are you okay little man?' But he doesn't stir. His soft breath landing on my skin comforts me. 'I'll have you home soon baby. We're doing this for Daddy.'

Pulling out drawers and opening presses, my eyes rapidly search through everything in front of me, the continuous reminder of Pat's lonely life. One cup, one plate, one pot, one everything.

Shay is still asleep on my chest. He hasn't even whimpered. Stretching my neck, I look to see if there's anything on top of the kitchen presses. I hear a thud outside and my heart stops. I freeze. I listen but I can't hear anything. My nerves have me sick but I remind myself Conor must be even more nervous.

I'm about to close one of the drawers when I notice a lodgement book. Bank of Ireland. I don't know why but it piques my interest so I take it in my hand and open it. I stare wide-eyed at the name on top of the slip. Pat is lodging money into Erin Murphy's bank. Vicky Murphy's mother.

Chapter Sixty-Seven

I'm exhausted. Every bone in my body is tired from shaking and shivering with fear. I'm sitting by the window waiting for Pat to return. My mind is in overdrive. I need to speak to Pat to find out what is going on. Why is he giving Erin Murphy money every month? I'm sure the detectives will be interested in this information but first I have to find out what it means. I don't want to hand a shovel to the men who are trying to bury my husband.

Is Pat Vicky's father? Hence the need to point fingers. Or did he kill Vicky and is now trying to divert attention from himself? One way or the other, I'm sitting here until he returns and I'm going to make him tell me.

I've heard nothing from Conor, or Fintan yet. But I expect Fintan will contact me before this day ends. Which it's going to in two hours. Shay is asleep upstairs in his cot. The monitor sits on a ledge beside me. I wonder does Maggie know her son has been arrested. Hardly. She would have been over here by now, crying and panicking and making the tension in the air unbearable.

When I couldn't get an answer from Amanda, I sent her a text telling her Conor had been arrested. She hasn't texted me back yet. Amanda is probably having a great night entertaining clients, eating and drinking and laughing. No time to check her phone.

It's all coming back to me now. Those nights before I met Conor. Amanda out having a great time. Me, sitting crying, looking out a window. At least this time, I have Shay. I have a reason to go on, to fight the fight. And I will. If misery has taught me anything, it's not to become friends with it.

The sound of footsteps on the gravel outside quickens my heartbeat. Pat is shuffling down the side of the house. I jump from my stool and run to the back door. His slow struggling body comes into view.

'Pat, can I have a word?'

He stops, lifts his drooping head and looks at me.

'I need to talk to you Pat, it's very important.'

He moves his gaze from me to the forest as if contemplating whether or not to ignore me. But he doesn't. He walks over to me. I stand back and ask him to come into the house. I'm not as nervous as I thought I'd be. I'm too eager to find out what this man knows.

'Maybe you'd like to sit down,' I say, pulling out a chair for Pat.

Pat removes his cap and sits. His silence makes everything so much harder than it should be. I've never heard him volunteer to start a conversation, but then—

'Where did you get that?' He lifts the lodgement book from the table in front of him and stares at me.

'I got it in your cottage Pat. You need to tell me what's going on.' My voice sounds a little harsh.

'When were you in my cottage?' His eyes are drained of life, without colour. Dark strands of hair streak through the grey showing hints of how it used to be.

'I was in your cottage earlier Pat. I'm sick of your allegations. Conor has been arrested because of you. Now tell me. What is going on? Why are you giving money to Vicky's mother? Was Vicky your daughter?'

Pat jerks back in the chair. 'No. No,' he says. 'Not *my* daughter.'

I could feel my heart thumping against my ribs. Blood rushing around my body. 'Whose daughter was she?' I say. Pat turns his head and looks out the window. I fear he might shut up again so I persist. 'Whose daughter Pat?' He turns around. There's a look. I can see it in his eyes. Pat knows if he answers my question, everything is going to change.

'Seamus's. Vicky was Seamus's daughter.'

I'm trying not to act too overwhelmed by this revelation but I'm pretty sure I'm not pulling it off. My mouth won't close. My eyes won't blink. Vicky was Conor's sister. It all makes sense now, why Pat thinks Conor killed Vicky. For the brewery, just like he killed his father. Pat must think Conor knew Vicky was his sister but Conor didn't know. Well, I'm presuming he didn't, but the way things are unfolding I wouldn't be surprised if he did know, if the whole world knew about it. Am I the only fool in this village who believes what they're told? But no. Conor couldn't have known. Could he? And Maggie. Did she know?

'Pat, did Conor know?'

He nods his head.

'But...' I can't think straight, my head is filling with scenarios and suspicions. 'What makes you think Conor knows?'

'Vicky told him the night she was killed.' Pat's voice is very low and hard to hear but to me the words are loud, crashing into my head, smashing my world. Pat must see my stress. He pulls his chair closer to the table and starts to explain that Vicky found out the day she was killed that Seamus was her father. Pat himself told her. Seamus had left instructions in his will for Vicky to be told whenever Erin or Pat deemed it to be the right time. Pat knew Erin would never tell her. She never wanted Vicky to know. Pat had mulled over telling Vicky ever since Conor got married and with Vicky about to become an aunty, Pat had decided it was the right time. Vicky had to know. He was sick of keeping it from her and he was getting older. He didn't want the secret to die with him.

The allowance Pat was getting from the brewery was not for himself like everyone thought, it was for Vicky. Now Pat is convinced Vicky told Conor that day and Conor killed her to keep the brewery for himself. Just like he killed his father.

'But Vicky never got to speak to Conor,' I say. 'She sent him a text to contact her but he never answered it, he was busy at work and then I went into labour. He didn't even see it.'

Pat pushes his chair back and stands. 'Well he is going to say that, isn't he?'

'But what if he's telling the truth Pat? Have you considered that? What if he didn't get to speak to Vicky?' Pat puts his cap on, straightens his back and stands. He has no interest in hearing my opinion.

'Did Maggie know?' I say.

Pat shakes his head. 'No, Maggie never knew Vicky was Seamus's child.' He stops for a moment, staring into space. Is he only now considering all the people this affects? The damage revealing his secret will do. The damage it has already done.

He's about to walk out the door when I remember the card.

'Pat.'

He turns slowly, his eyes sad, his body tired.

'Did you send me a card?' I'm standing staring at him. My legs shaking. My trembling hands clenched tightly.

Pat sighs and turns back to walk out the door. 'Someone had to warn you,' he says, then steps out into the night.

Chapter Sixty-Eight

The lights from the village twinkle in the distance. I'm sitting in my bedroom at the window with Shay in my arms, feeding him his bottle. His eyes are still closed but he's sucking away. I try not to cry with him in my arms. I don't want him feeling my distress, the scent of my sadness seeping into his soul. This is my pain, my punishment, it has nothing to do with him.

There has been no news yet from the station. I rang but got no answer. Fintan needs to know about the card Pat sent me. His mind has become twisted from years of sheltering someone else's secrets. Pat thought he was warning me by sending the card. Did he not know it would scare me, send me down a road tortured with fear and paranoia? Not knowing who I could trust?

I thought Fintan would have called me by now. Maybe Conor is on his way back. Fintan might be driving him home at this very moment. Or is that just me being optimistic? Trying to think positive. Putting all those sessions with the therapist to good use.

But who am I kidding? Everything points to Conor. The text. Leaving the house in the middle of the night. And now the big motive. Vicky was his sister. Vicky was entitled to half of everything.

But still, something doesn't seem right. I don't believe that Conor would kill someone. He never even wanted the brewery. He wanted to go to college, not bottle beer. Ironic that Vicky was the one going to college. I wonder what she thought when she found out she owned half of the beer she was selling behind the bar every night. Ripped off maybe? Excited? Afraid? A tsunami of emotions brought to shore by one strong gust of wind, the truth.

I notice the lights of a car coming down the road. I stand and move closer to the window. Is it them? Is Conor coming home? I remember to smile at Shay before looking out to see the car passing the entrance.

I think of Maggie. What will she think when she hears about Vicky? Her husband was a cheat. Was it just a once off or were there other women? Did Maggie know and decide to live with it, hiding her pain behind lipstick smiles and fancy fur coats? Or is she about to have her heart broken?

The night has never looked so dark and rain is beginning to fall. I burp Shay, change his nappy and put him down to rest. I switch the mobile toy on above his head and leave the room.

The house feels eerie, like it's waiting for something to invade it. Something unwelcome. I go down to the kitchen and take a bottle of red wine from the wine rack. I'm pouring some into the glass when I think of blood. Splattered blood, pools of blood. Jamie. I empty the glass into the sink and switch on the kettle. A thought enters my head. Conor could have killed Vicky. Why am I so convinced he didn't? I've only known him a little over a year. He was able to hide the beer smuggling from me. Maybe he didn't want Vicky to find out about that. There would have been a big audit, a big dividing of the wares, and Conor's little black-market empire would have been discovered. Oh Christ, what if that's true? What if Conor is guilty?

The rain is pelting down now. I make myself a cup of coffee and move over to where the laptop is. Maybe the photos on the USB will divert suspicion from Conor. After all, Noel had a motive too. Vicky's photos could have cost him his home, his wife, his career, leaving him with nothing. I'm glad now that I gave the USB to Fintan.

I check my phone, still nothing. I'm about to call the station again when the front doorbell rings. I rush to open it and find Detective Fintan Ryan standing there. But there's no Conor.

'Can I come in?'

'Yes, yes.' Standing back, I direct Fintan into the kitchen. His jacket is soaked. His face is grey. I've a million questions and yet nothing comes out of my mouth. I wait for him to speak.

'Are you okay?' he says. I nod, staring at his lips, eager for him to say more. 'Conor is okay Laura, he's doing okay, considering.'

'Is he coming home?' I say.

Fintan shakes his head. 'Not yet, they're not finished with him. I just wanted to ask you something.'

'Me?'

'Yes, it's just about the USB you gave me earlier. I was having a look at it down at the station and well...' Fintan wipes the dripping rain from his forehead. 'Where did you get that Laura?'

'What?'

'The USB, where did it come from?'

I feel myself turning red, heat washing in waves over my body. I promised Amanda I wouldn't mention her name.

'Someone put it through the letterbox, I don't know who. Why? Was it helpful?'

'Very.'

I take a deep breath and relax. They're now going to focus on Noel. Conor will be set free. I knew it couldn't have been him.

'When did the USB arrive?'

'Just yesterday.'

'And you've no idea who put it in the letterbox?'

'No, but does it matter? It shows what it shows,' I say, wondering why they care. Surely the photos are enough proof that Noel had a motive without needing to know where it came from.

'Well, it's a bit more complicated than that,' Fintan says. 'The last file Vicky saved onto the USB was dated the day she died. Whoever took it from her computer was the last person to see her alive.'

I freeze. I can see Fintan's lips moving but I can't hear anything. I try to open my mouth but it won't open. Could she have...? No, not Amanda. She wouldn't do a thing like that.

But Amanda said she called to Vicky the week before she was murdered so... So why did she have that USB in her apartment? Unless... Amanda lied to me? Amanda was there the day of the murder. She was the last person to see Vicky Murphy alive. I can't breathe. The space around me blurs as I realise what this means. *Did Amanda kill Vicky?*

'Are you okay, Laura?... Are you ok?' Fintan's words gradually come into focus. I force my eyes to blink. 'I— I'm fine, I just...'

'I know it's a shock Laura, but we need to find out who had the USB if we're going to prove Conor didn't take it from Vicky's apartment.' He looks at his feet then back at me. I can tell he's not falling for the letterbox story.

'So, I'll ask again, Laura. Where did you get the USB?'

Chapter Sixty-Nine

I can feel Fintan's eyes on me. But what do I say? If I tell him the truth, that I found the USB in Amanda's apartment, Amanda will be arrested. She could go to jail and all because of me.

If I don't tell him where I found it, they'll think Conor took it from Vicky's apartment. Conor will be charged. Shay's daddy will spend his son's childhood in prison. Choosing between the two people I love most in this world, my two best friends, is an impossible task.

Amanda is the one person who has always been there for me. When I was arrested for causing Jamie's death, she stood up in court and told the judge how wonderful a mother I was, which helped get my sentence suspended. Amanda never judged me.

As kids, she was always looking out for me. I remember playing skipping on the green in front of the house one day when Sharon Grey pushed into the queue in front of me. I stood back and let her. Amanda dragged her by the hair to the end of the queue and told her if she cut in front of me again, she'd beat her up. Amanda was only six at the time. I was almost nine. She had already sensed how weak I was and gradually became my bodyguard, my life coach, my everything. She wrapped an invisible blanket around me and took me everywhere with her. Even to Imanage, where she got me the job that led to my meeting Conor.

How could I betray her now? She was trying to protect me by going to Vicky's. Trying to keep my new perfect world intact. This is my fault.

But Conor. How could I possibly send Conor to jail? He's Shay's father. I love him. The moment I met Conor was the moment I began to live again. Conor gave me back everything I'd lost: respect, confidence, the ability to get excited about something, anything. He took my dull existence and made it worthwhile. He loves me and I love him.

Conor has suffered enough pain. People don't see it. They just see money and privilege and luxury. They don't see the sorrow gnawing at his soul. And I know for certain that Conor didn't kill Vicky. My husband is *not* a murderer.

–

'Where did you get the USB, Laura?' Fintan sighs. He's tired, waiting for me to answer. Fintan is not aware that if I answer, I'll be sending someone I love to jail. And all because of my secret. I should have told Conor the truth about Jamie in the beginning. If I had, Vicky Murphy would be alive today.

'Laura,' Fintan says. He wants answers. He wants the truth. I lift my head. Tears blur my vision. I wipe my eyes and look straight at him. This the hardest thing I've ever had to do but I must do it. I have no more room for secrets, dragging me down. Keeping me afraid and wrapping me in guilt. I'm a mother now and this time I'm going to be the best mother a little boy could have.

Chapter Seventy

'Careful, Shay.'

Shay is making his first attempt to crawl up the stairs. I'm behind him, hands outstretched, ready to catch him if he falls. In the background the radio blares as I wait eagerly for the news to air. It's been over a year and they're sentencing her today. Manslaughter. Eight long years, the solicitor reckons. I wanted to go to the court to be with her but Amanda didn't want me there.

'Good boy, Shay,' I sing, encouraging his progress.

In the distance, my phone rings but I ignore it. Shay's journey is more important. He giggles each time he reaches the next step. I wish Conor was here to see his little boy climb his first mountain.

We've all been climbing mountains since Amanda was arrested. Seeing her in custody is heartbreaking. Amanda had gone to Vicky's apartment to protect me and I gave the detective her name. At first she wouldn't talk to me, but eventually, after a few visits, she told me what happened.

A few days before she was killed, Vicky contacted Amanda about a piece she was writing, Ballycall's newest arrival, for the *Ballycall Journal*. Amanda became suspicious when she asked if it was my first baby and agreed to meet her with some photos of me as a child, to enhance the story. Amanda confronted Vicky and discovered she had been right. Vicky was going to print the story about my past which she'd dug up on some newspaper archives site. Amanda begged her not to but Vicky wouldn't give in and told her to leave or she'd call the police. Amanda walked towards the door. She could see everything falling apart, I could lose Shay and she wasn't going to let that happen to me, again. She turned around and in one mad moment of uncontrollable anger, she grabbed a knife from the countertop and stabbed Vicky.

Tears rolled down her pale face as she told her story. Her hair was scraped back into a ponytail. Dark rings circled her sunken eyes. The glamorous city girl look was gone. Replaced with a prison tracksuit and a broken heart.

I reached out to touch her hand. 'I'm sorry, Amanda.' My whisper, barely audible through my tears.

'No,' she said, lifting her eyes to look at me. 'I'm sorry.'

–

'Daddy will be home soon, Shay.' I watch my little boy turn his head to look at the door.

'Da Da.'

'Yes, Da Da.' I scoop him in my arms, nuzzle into his belly and carry him back down the narrow stairs of our cosy two-bedroom house.

It's a lot different to Ballycall. The sound of traffic replaces the birdsong and no one lives at the end of our tiny garden.

Pat is still in the cottage apparently, even though the house is up for sale. Maggie keeps us up to date with all the goings-on. At first she wasn't happy when Conor told her he was leaving the brewery to study astronomy. And still, even now, each time she visits she comments on how hard it must be to live in such a small space, having been used to such luxury. I want to answer by saying nowhere is as small as Ballycall, but Conor always winks at me, keeping me quiet and making me smile.

It was hard for Maggie, having to come to terms with the news about Vicky. If she suspected Seamus of being unfaithful, she didn't say. Let bygones be bygones is Maggie's motto, though she still gets the odd dig in about Amanda. The outsider who brought murder to the village. I've learned to let it wash over me. To concentrate on the good things. Conor, Shay, the sun shining.

With Shay in his highchair sucking a carrot stick, I chop the cilantro and put the finishing touches to the couscous.

'Who's this coming?' I say, hearing the front door open.

The carrot stick is dropped. Shay looks at the door. He smiles with arms outstretched when Conor walks in.

Conor is wearing torn jeans, a t-shirt and hasn't shaved today. He's determined to make a claim on his student years. He drops his satchel to the ground and kisses me before taking Shay out of the chair.

Moving away from the village was the best thing that ever happened to Conor. He left behind a past he'd never wanted for a future that is his own. He still sees Noel quite a bit. Abbie dumped Noel when she found out about the photos and Noel and Olive are now together. I'm happy for Olive. She got her man and now she's sitting in Conor's office at the brewery.

'Are you hungry?' I say, placing lamb chops into the sizzling pan. Shay points at the rising steam with excitement in his eyes.

'Starving,' Conor says, a touch of city lingo creeping into his words.

He lifts Shay into the air, piloting him across the room. Lifting a spoon to scrape some yoghurt from a tub, I watch Shay's face light up and hear my phone ringing again.

'Who could that be?' I say.

'Do you want me to get it?' Conor says.

'Yeah, see who it is.'

Conor puts Shay back into the highchair then takes my phone from the table.

'No contact name, just a number,' he says, swiping it open before I have a chance to tell him not to.

'Hello,' he says. 'Yes, she's here, hang on.'

'Who is it?' I mouth silently, to which Conor shrugs his shoulders.

Wiping my hands on some kitchen roll, I take the phone from him.

The voice is low. Nervous. But I recognise it immediately.

'Mam.'

A letter from Jackie

Dear reader,

Sincere thanks for reading my third novel, *Five Little Words*. I'm grateful to you for sharing your precious time with Laura, Conor and the folks of Ballycall.

If you enjoyed it, I would love to hear your thoughts via a review. Knowing what you think of the story is important to me.

This story is not true and all the characters are fictional.

To those of you who have already read my first two books, *Familiar Strangers* and *The Secrets He Kept*, I thank you for your support and reviews.

You are welcome to contact me with any questions or comments at anytime. I'm available on Facebook and Twitter.

Best Wishes

Jackie Walsh

https://twitter.com/JackieWalsh_ie
https://www.facebook.com/jackiewalsh.ie/

Acknowledgements

Many thanks to my publishers at Hera Books, Keshini Naidoo and Lindsey Mooney. Thank you for having faith in me and for your continued hard work and guidance.

To those who have supported my journey so far, in particular, those who read *Familiar Strangers* and *The Secrets He Kept*. Your kind words of support and great reviews are truly appreciated. Every positive word you send my way, pushes me on.

To my writer friends who have encouraged me along the way, Patricia Gibney, Louise Phillips, Niamh Brennan, Grainne Daly. Andrea Carter, Declan Burke, Conor Kostick, Vanessa Fox O'Loughlin and many more. Marie Brennan, thank you for your help and hard work.

To my family and friends, whose support I am extremely grateful for. The girls in Lollipops, who've risen to the challenge of these difficult times. Well done ladies, and thank you.

For the people I meet on the street, Pat, neighbours, friends who stop to tell me they've enjoyed my book. Every word of encouragement cheers me on.

Paul, Layla, continued love.